WHATEVER IT TAKES

WHATEVER IT TAKES

EVERY REASON 2

HEATON WILSON

Matador
9 Priory Business Park,
Wistow Road, Kibworth Beauchamp,
Leicestershire. LE8 0RX
Tel: 0116 279 2299
Email: books@troubador.co.uk
Web: www.troubador.co.uk/matador
Twitter: @matadorbooks

ISBN 978 1 80046 185 7

British Library Cataloguing in Publication Data.
A catalogue record for this book is available from the British Library.

Printed and bound in Great Britain by 4edge Limited
Typeset in 10.5pt Adobe Garamond Pro by Troubador Publishing Ltd, Leicester, UK

Matador is an imprint of Troubador Publishing Ltd

For Lorna – my wife, and the best friend I ever had.

PROLOGUE

He was quick-sipping a latte with the delicate efficiency of a hummingbird. His long fingers fluttered over the keyboard, obeying his brain's instructions: turning thoughts into pixels.

He was too preoccupied to know this would be the end. The internet cafe was fairly crowded, so he thought nothing of the nudge on his arm, or even the brief sting; but by the time Jamie knew something was wrong, it was already far too late.

He was unable to voice the terror as he felt his internal systems shutting down.

When the police came, his fingers were still on the keyboard; his latte still emitting faint waves of warmth; his eyes open, seeing nothing.

ONE

DCI Jane Birchfield leaned down to slurp water from the tap, and groaned as she straightened, arching her back to ease a condition she called 'cheap chair knackered spine syndrome'.

At least she was grateful for the streaks in the mirror. If she positioned herself just right, the bags under her eyes completely vanished.

God, what a day!

It sounded like a Christmas song. Four grieving relatives, three final warnings, two forced entries, and a splitting headache to boot. And she distinctly remembered talking to herself too loudly, along the lines of: 'The next person to send me an email about health and bloody safety…'

She'd forced herself to read the latest missive dutifully, before pressing delete and consigning another pile of data to that great dustbin in the cloud, or wherever these things went these days.

Someone on a tedious IT awareness course said she should think of The Cloud (note the reverential capitals) simply as another network, or a storage unit. Jane immediately pictured one of those depressing pre-fab buildings you see on otherwise empty industrial estates, with excruciatingly contrived names like 'SafaStore'. They attempted to disguise their drabness by painting them in primary colours, then divided them into shed-sized steel spaces: mortuaries for surplus furniture and the detritus of broken marriages.

Jane preferred not to think of it at all. Tech stuff baffled her. But if pushed, she would say The Cloud was actually a verb, with no reverential capitals in sight, as in – *to cloud: to make or become less clear or transparent.*

Anyway, what did that pillock of an IT consultant know about anything? His Powerpoint presentation was mercifully and ironically cut short when his laptop made a sound like several cars crashing, much to the immature amusement of a Premier Inn conference room full of chief supers wearing cheap cologne. And Jane, the only Acting Chief Superintendent. And, of course, the only female.

She was trying to distract herself, but she knew it never worked for long. She leaned on the basin and tried to calm herself with the deep breathing exercises she'd learned at pilates. In through the nose for a count of four, feel your stomach inflating, then your chest, hold for four, breathe out through a straw for four, hold for four… and repeat.

Sadly, it wasn't really helping. No matter how hard she tried to switch off, one single fact kept intruding: she was Acting Chief Super for a reason that had brought her to tears so many times over the last two months. But the man she was standing in for would tell her to snap out of it, and she was on her way to see him now.

So, what would he say? Something on the lines of 'Come on Jane, get a grip'…

She patted her hair into some sort of order, trying yet again to ignore the fact that she looked just like her mother; and the grey was starting to show.

Jane took one more breath, and stepped out onto the antiseptic silence of the hospice corridor.

The reception desk had struck her as eerily similar to the one at the Premier Inn conference. But it was empty now, a member of staff having already signed her in. She walked the few paces to room 20, and leaned against the door. It was heavy, and sighed as it opened, and again as it closed, sealing her in a room that was silent save for the gentle high pitched pulse of the equipment that was keeping Chief Superintendent Charles Aston alive.

The big man looked small now, almost emaciated, and lost in a bed that looked more like a bank of computers on a workbench.

The last time she was here, the nurse told her they had 'stabilised' him.

'He's not feeling any pain now. But he isn't going to get better, I'm afraid.'

Jane had been too direct, she knew that even as the words shot out of her mouth: 'Well, I guess that's why he's in a hospice, isn't it?'

She'd apologised straight away, but the nurse had sat down with her and made her feel like she understood. Her name was Rebeka – 'with a K' – and she was so young.

But no amount of niceness could compensate for the facts. The man who'd given Jane her chance at Ashbridge – the man who'd stood up for her through all the sexist, bigoted, brutal harassment – was now a pale parody of that clumsy, lovable, irritating, smiling, clever, wonderful man, and Jane had just wanted to scream at the injustice of it.

Charles turned his head slightly as the door whispered shut, and, though he was wired to the machines, she could almost sense the life fading from him. Jane wondered why, if technology was so wonderful, it still couldn't conquer cancer. Was it enough to just keep someone alive a while longer, or better to let them go? Were we being cruel to be kind?

'Hello Jane.'

His voice was hoarse. Jane sat next to the bed, placing her hand briefly and carefully on his so as not to compress the tube that was running into it..

'Hello sir.'

'I sound like Darth Vader, don't I?'

'I like Darth Vader. He's my hero. Appeals to my dark side.'

Charles moved his head and his mouth twitched as his eyes gently closed.

Jane sat forward in the seat and tried to catch his attention again.

'Want me to get you anything?'

There was the memory of a smile in his eyes as he turned back to look at her. 'A large whisky and soda, please Jane.'

'Coming right up, boss.'

His ragged breathing rasped into a chuckle. Behind the bed, a control unit like the ultimate hi fi system flashed blue and green numbers.

'Sorry, boss, there's the usual Friday after work queue at the bar, so shall we just stay here and have a chat?'

Charles nodded, though his eyes were beginning to close again, and Jane saw him pressing the trigger in his other hand, the one he'd told her was his good gun because it fired in another shot of morphine.

Jane kept talking. 'Well, today, I've spent most of my time deleting emails and filling in online reports, so a drink at the bar would actually be a pretty good idea.'

She had to move closer to hear his reply; the sentences slowly delivered, compressed between rattling breaths.

'Don't let work take over your life, Jane... Not worth it... Look at me. I was counting the days... retirement, golf, rugby on the box... meals for two offers at Marks and Sparks... Things don't always go according to plan..'

'I know, boss. I know... What was your favourite meal for two then?'

'Oh I didn't care about the food. I just wanted the free bottle of wine... Listen, Jane. You've got to stop worrying about me. You don't need to come every day. Look after yourself. Save your energy. Spend time with that man of yours. And don't worry about the job. I've told 'em you're the right man...'

Jane smiled as he winked. 'Thank you sir—'

'Stop calling me sir. You're the boss now. Now go on – get home, get some rest and don't argue. I'm too tired.'

'And I always win when we argue...'

'Yes, you did. Well, sometimes... Now, go on. Thank you... you know...I know why I'm here...I'm not scared.' He squeezed her hand, gently. 'It is what it is, Jane. OK?'

Every instinct told her to stay, but he was saying goodbye, and she couldn't stop following his orders even now.

The hot tears came, and her voice broke. 'Night, boss.'

His eyes were already closed. Jane closed the door without looking back, choking back the sobs as she walked quickly out to her car, and shouted and cried and hit the steering wheel until her hand hurt.

Allan heard the click of the door, the ring of the mobile phone, then the long stage whisper conversation in the hall, and shook his head.

Eight o'clock. He'd had the dinner in the oven for an hour and it was probably overdone. Now she was finally here, and her bloody phone rings, so guess what...

He summoned a smile as Jane stepped into the kitchen. 'Good day at the office, Ms Birchfield?'

'Hug me Allan.'

'Yes m'lady.'

He kissed her hair as she rested on his chest. It smelled of perfume and misty rain, and his irritation soothed. 'Tough day again?'

'God awful. You?'

'Not bad. Signed up a big store for a few adverts, and the new council leader has agreed to do an interview.'

Jane pushed away. 'Agreed? I shouldn't think he needed much persuading, did he?'

'No, you're right. Phoned him up, used my charm. You know? The same charm that charmed you.'

'Oh, that charm? Yeah right. Well I can't wait to read what he's got to say for himself, and what a great job he's doing for Ashbridge. Not.'

'Don't worry, You'll be gripped. Anyway, come on… I want dinner and you're keeping me from stuffing my face. What time do you call this?'

'I do apologise. You set it up, and I'll get changed.'

'What? You mean you're not going straight out again?'

'Don't be sarky. And don't listen at the door, unless you want to hear me having pointless conversations with mum. You know, whenever I talk to her, it's like neither of us really knows what the other's talking about."

'Ha! Hurry up before I eat all the oven ready chips…'

'Oh lovely. Chips… Cooking doesn't get tougher than this.'

'Was that your attempt at sarcasm?'

'No, I'll save that for when this wonderful dinner is placed before me.'

'Get lost.'

'On my way.'

Jane went upstairs as Allan set about the task of tipping a ready meal from its foil container, and scraping the slightly overdone chips from the baking tray onto plates, consigning to the pedal bin those that had turned to charcoal sticks. But then he heard Jane's mobile again, heard her muffled voice, and then footsteps coming down the stairs, and she hadn't even had time to change.

Allan sat at the kitchen table with a glass of red and two loaded plates. 'Don't tell me…'

'Got to go. Allan, I'm so sorry.'

'What is it this time?'

'Someone found dead at an internet cafe.'

'But you're the Chief Super now, not the DCI, for God's sake!'

'Come on Allan, you know I'm just covering; extra responsibility I'm being paid for. I can't just leave it to Creasey. Anyway, it might be natural causes. In which case, with all due respect to the deceased, I'll be back home in time for some chips. If you save me any…'

'Just go.'

'Allan…'

'No. Go. I don't want a conversation. We'll have that another time.'

'Oh really? I can't wait.'

'You know how I feel, so you can't be surprised. See you later, Jane.'

'Don't wait up.'

'Don't worry. I won't.'

'Oh for… I am trying to hold down a new job, cope with a mother who doesn't know me, the boss I love and respect is dying, and I'm working all the hours God sends – And you… Just grow up, Allan!'

Allan drank the wine in one. 'You'd better go.'

'Allan…'

Allan pushed his chair back and yelled in her face. 'Just go, all right?!'

Jane turned and walked out. He'd never shouted at her. Ever…

She left him standing there. She'd never seen him lose it, never seen or felt the rage that must have been building inside him.

She slammed the front door, leaned back against it for a moment, and stepped out into the semi darkness of the spring evening.

Her phone rang again. The screen glowed green, backlighting three letters… MUM.

Jane rejected the call and got in the car. It was a relief to close the door, and block the outside world, at least for a while. She started up the car, got the sat nav to work out the way to the Pretty Cool Cafe, and drove away at speed.

Forensic Phil was wearing a coffee foam moustache, and grimacing.

'Evening, Jane. God – you look as bad as this tastes—'

'Thanks. Wipe your mouth for Christ's sake and tell me what the hell's going on.'

Phil exchanged a look with George Creasey, whose pock-marked face was as impassive as ever.

'Sorry, boss. This is a weird one. Come and have a butcher's.'

Phil handed her a pair of blue plastic overshoes and white surgical gloves and led her through dark stained wood louvre swing doors into a room, which was basically a narrow corridor with wood effect kitchen worktops down both sides, computer base units underneath, and keyboards and monitors on top, with a tatty looking desk chair in front of each one.

Roughly half way down on the right, a man wearing a green baseball cap, white hoody and grey tracksuit pants, was slumped in his chair, his right hand resting on the keyboard in front of him.

George spoke quietly. 'Name's Jamie Castleton, ma'am. His driving licence is in his wallet. We're checking out his details now.'

Phil kept walking, but Jane stopped and tried to empty her head so she could focus. First impressions count, as Uncle Bill always said, and that meant shovelling all today's crap into the rubbish bin part of her brain. Or maybe it was recycling day, who knew?

Anyway, she noted with gratitude that Creasey had seen the signs, and stood a pace behind, waiting. Phil turned, saw, and stopped too, as Jane took it all in.

The Pretty Cool Cafe was well past its sell by. 'Cool' didn't quite cut it. 'Pretty' didn't either. The coffee machine in the cramped kitchen and payment area they had just come from percolated its aroma everywhere, and it mixed with the acrid warmth of computers, and the sweat of those that had been using them, to create the kind of smell you get on an overcrowded train on a wet day in the rush hour. The phrase smelly static sprang into Jane's mind, for some reason.

The only access to the internet area they now stood in was through the kitchen/reception, which itself had a single door onto the High Street, and a door smothered in local event posters that presumably led to the owner's back office.

Jane counted twelve desk chairs, and noted that all the base stations were still switched on. Not surprisingly, in a dump like this, there was no sign of a closed circuit tv camera.

She frowned as she looked closely at the body. He looked in his early 20s. He wore the street uniform of hoodie and trackie bottoms, but those and his Adidas trainers looked new.

Not a mark anywhere on his clothes, his face slightly pink spotted. He obviously looked after himself and Jane didn't see him as the type of lad you'd expect to be using an internet cafe.

And, of course, he was someone's son.

Jane sighed and turned to DS Creasey, her most senior guy, and the one she trusted to keep an eye on the team while she was acting up for Charles Aston. 'Is this place still open?'

'No boss. It shuts at 6.30. They're open from 9.30, seven days a week.'

'So it's 7.10 now. When did we get the call?'

'6.45, boss. The owner said he'd been clearing in the kitchen and was giving this guy a bit of extra time because he's a regular. It was only when he went over to turf him out that he realised something was wrong.'

'Where is he now?'

'Back room, ma'am. I'm keeping him out of the way till we're ready.'

Jane nodded. 'So we'll have plenty to talk to him about. Was the place busy till then? Full?'

'Apparently, just four people. This young fella, and three others. No names yet. Not sure if the owner… Mr Gonzales… is thick or just unhelpful, but we can get what we need from the machines once forensics have been in. The punters have to do a log in…'

'Right. It looks a bit of a dump, so we need to be very clear about what this guy was doing here. He just doesn't strike me as your usual punter for a place like this. So, Phil…'

'Yes, m'lady—'

'No larking about tonight. Not in the mood, ok?'

'Sorry, Jane. Right. Scene of Crime will be here in a minute. Come with me.' Phil walked to the body. 'As you can see, he's a white male, in his early 20s I'd say, quite thin build but he looks in pretty good nick, apart from a minor skin condition—

George grunted as he hitched his corduroy trousers a little further up his considerable paunch. 'If you can call being dead, good nick.'

'Yes, thank you, George. As you have already noted, boss, he appears to have looked after himself. Not a hint of cigarette smoke, or alcohol, or any other substances for that matter, and his clothes look newish. Pending full forensics, I can only say at this stage that there are no obvious signs of violence, no signs of a struggle anywhere in the room, no blood, nothing in fact to indicate why this apparently healthy young man should be dead. It's fascinating. I can't wait to get him on the slab...'

Jane continued to observe, trying to let Phil's comments soak in, while not being too distracted. Phil and Creasey maintained their respectful silence.

She paced the area, taking in the clutter of cables, pens, CDs in paper envelopes, paper cups, scraps of paper, software manuals holding on for dear life on crowded shelves. It felt just like any busy office, anywhere. Except that High Street shoppers could look in as they walked by. But how the hell did this young lad die here? And why? Surely not natural causes?

'So, we need to establish the cause of death, and the time, urgently. We have to know fast if it's natural causes, an accident, or murder. Why does he seem to be locked in this position? Was it a massive electric shock? A heart attack? What was he doing on this computer that was so absorbing he apparently didn't even know he was dying? I mean, look, his forefinger is still on the full stop key. It's almost as if he'd been arranged in that position...OK. George, after you've established ID, can you concentrate on the computers, obviously starting with his? Get onto it as soon as forensics give the ok because we need to know the full story – what was he doing on that computer tonight? We also need to track down who else was in here in the last few hours, and Phil – you know what to do.'

'Find out how he died? Oh all right then.'

Jane smiled despite herself. 'Thanks Phil. Sorry, both of you, I'm just narky tonight... Anyway, come on... At first glance, it looks like it has to be natural causes. But something is telling me different. So let's check the cables in here so we can rule out any malfunction, or even foul play, from that direction. And keep the owner right here. Sounds from what he says that, for a time, it was just the two of them in here, so he's not going anywhere until we've ruled him out. Once we know a bit more about Jamie, his background, and what he was doing here, we can go from there, ok?'

Creasey was taking notes. 'The owner says everything is stored on a central server, boss. Want me to check that out?'

'Ah yes, everything's in The Cloud, these days.'

Phil wasn't fooled. 'I thought you said no larking about tonight, Jane?'

'You're right, Phil. Let's get down to work.'

TWO

THE CLOCK RADIO CAST a blue sheen over the bedroom.

Irene Castleton was so used to lying there, watching the tiny flat screen tv on the dressing table, waiting, that she only usually began to fret in the early hours if Jamie still wasn't home. Now, it was only just after 7, so why the worry?

She'd gone through his things today without the slightest guilt. Well, he seemed so... Irene searched for the words, her brain fugged by that cheap white wine... so... intense? Yes, that was it. He'd always been a bit distant, even as a boy, hanging back when friends came round for him; abnormally focussed on even the most ordinary television show; but coming to life when Irene had finally won an eBay auction and gave him an HP laptop for Christmas.

Nowadays, he was always out and about, with his laptop in his rucksack, and he must be earning good money. He got the black box out to show her... a new Asus, he'd announced, not that Irene had a clue what he was talking about.

'Asus?'

'Yes Mum. Asus. It's a Zenbook Flip. They're really cool.'

'Zenbook Flip? Sounds like a yoga move. What on earth…?'

He'd laughed at her. He was always laughing at her; never actually talking, giving anything away.

Irene sat up in bed, suddenly tense. She didn't know where the feeling came from. She'd always been a worrier. Why was he always out so late anyway? Everyone else finishes work at 6. But somehow she knew… something's wrong, something's happened. And she did what she always did at times like these.

She poured herself another glass of Lambrusco, from the bottle on the bedside table.

Three miles away, Allan sat in the three up three down terraced house in the old part of Ashbridge that he shared with Jane.

Once upon a time, it was a two up, two down, but now it flaunted itself to the neighbours with a two storey extension at the back that took up most of the yard.

It stood in one of the few streets that had withstood the tsunami of beige brick apartment blocks, including those with white railings that stopped you opening the patio doors four storeys up.

He smiled briefly as he remembered the house hunting, and Jane's scorn: 'Patio doors you can't walk through. Has the world gone totally bananas?'

Allan Gary Askew – known to his friends as Aga – stared at the Baxi Bermuda gas fire, and tried to summon up the maturity to stop sulking, call Jane and make peace, something he'd been churning over since he'd lost it with her.

Three years they'd been together. Yes, they'd fought and each won their share of arguments. True equality. And most of the time they were just happy in each other's company.

The sex was good, though they weren't at it like rabbits like in the early days, and to be honest, it suited both of them. Most nights, the invitation 'let's go to bed' didn't come with inverted commas and a seductive wink.

They'd been very happy, but just lately, the grey clouds had rolled in, enveloping them in longer and longer silences. Maybe they were both just so busy earning a living, they should just accept that this was a phase they needed to go through. Stay together, be companions and supports, then, later on, when they'd earned enough and sweated enough blood for their careers...

And yet... bit by bit, the spark was going, the warmth was fading, and lots of other metaphors of the kind usually Allan edited out of his newspaper copy.

He'd said it to himself so many times as he'd waited for her to come home after another 12 hour day...'if we wait too long, it might be too late.'

Too late...

His mobile blasted out the theme tune to 'Chariots of Fire'. It was Jane. Calling him. Beaten him to it. That wasn't supposed to happen.

'Hello Jane.'

'Allan... I just wanted to say... well... Are you ok?'

'Yeah, course. You?'

'Totally knackered. There was a young guy found dead in an internet cafe. On the case now. Just waiting for Phil to give me something that helps us decide if it's natural causes or not. Then I've got to go and break the news.'

'How old?'

'Early 20s. Jamie Castleton. Look Allan – '

'Let's just call it quits, shall we? I've been a bit sulky, even by my standards. I know you've got a lot on, and things like this are so –' Allan stopped. Some wiring in his brain made a connection. 'Wait. Jamie Castleton?'

'Yes. Do you know him?'

'My God, yes I do! At least, I think so. I know the name, anyway. The Jamie I know is a clever computer guy. I used him to set up our network at the office, set me up with secure data storage. A few months ago. Not seen him since. Did a good job, too. Christ, could it be him?'

'Bloody hell. That's spooky. You'll have to tell me what you know, anything. Got to go. Oh, hang on…I just wanted to say, well, we need to talk, don't we?'

'Yes. I reckon you probably owe me a drink… I'm sure it's your round.'

'I thought a pint of best might come into this at some stage.'

'And the pie of the day.'

'And the pie of the day, ah yes, naturally. Listen, I'll take time out tomorrow. Shall we go out to the pub tomorrow night?'

'It's a date… Jane?'

'Yes?'

'Nothing. Well, just, sorry for earlier, you know? It's just – Well, you know… And I can't believe I know this guy. Kind of puts things into perspective. Just – take care.'

'It does. I will. You too. So…love you.'

'Love you too. Bye.'

Allan threw his phone onto the sofa. That wasn't the way he'd wanted the conversation to go. It was like she'd leeched the anger out of him, or trapped it inside, more like. A few minutes earlier, he'd been yearning to get the good times back, and now he felt cheated because he hadn't been harder on her. What the hell?

He poured another glass of red. Then picked up the phone, opened the calendar, and flicked back through the months till he found Jamie's appointment, and tried to piece the fragments of memory together of when they'd first met…

'Mr Askey?'

'Great start, mate. The name is Askew. You're thinking of Arthur Askey, a famous old comedian.'

'I wasn't thinking of him. I've never heard of him. Sorry.'

'Before your time, obviously. No need to rub it in... Shall we start again? You must be Jamie, right?'

'Yeah, Jamie Castleton. Thanks for giving me the job.'

'Hang on, hang on... I haven't, yet.'

'Maybe not, but I know you will. I'm good. And I'm quick. So, could you explain what exactly you need to do, and I'll come up with a way for you to do it?...'

Jamie's voice was a surreal mix of Liam Gallagher and Paul McCartney, which placed him approximately mid-way between Manchester and Liverpool. That's right, and he had Liam's cocky aggression twinned with Paul's boyish charm. Which was why Allan had started calling him Liam McCartney, much to Jamie's bewilderment.

But Jamie was right. He was good, and he was bloody quick.

Based on just one half hour meeting, he'd sent an email the next day with a spec and a quote, and he'd got the job done two days later, working anti-social hours, too, so there was not a single interruption to normal newspaper business.

He'd seemed so... what was the word?... professional, yes, and likeable.

Jane came back into his head then, and stayed there. Allan thought about finishing off the bottle, but he knew it wouldn't help. His mind was made up. He filled up his wine glass with water, drank it down in one, then switched on the laptop and brought up Google Maps.

Forensic Phil's voice sounded strangely robotic and artificial through the car speakers. And loud.

'So far, Jane, big fat zero, sorry.'

Jane slowed to check the street sign. There it was: Beacon Street. Even now, she didn't totally trust the sat nav. She checked the rear view mirror and took a hasty left.

'So can we rule out foul play, or not?'

'Definitely not at this stage, no. The only superficial indicator of anything at the moment is a tiny pin prick on his upper arm.'

'Where we all get vaccinated.'

'Yes, but it's not exactly in the usual place, and the angle of insertion and slight bruising makes me wonder if the jab was administered from behind. I may be clutching at straws but something feels wrong. So I'm going to take a much, much closer look. Plus, I need to get the blood and tissue test results back. This could be a tough one to crack. I'm going to cut the poor lad open later.'

'How long till I can let his mum identify him?

'Give me a bit of time to do the basics and prepare him for viewing – around 11. But I've got a feeling I might need a bit more time to give you a definite.'

'Is George there?'

'Yes, do you want a word?'

'No, just ask him to email me with anything he's got from the computer checks so far, ok Phil?'

'Will do. Is that straight away, or—'

'No, just sometime before bedtime.'

Phil paused and then dragged out the words. 'Ok. And Jane?'

'Yes Phil, I know… I'll be ok. No need to wait around after you've prepped everything. I'll catch up with you tomorrow. Just make sure someone is around to witness the ID with me later tonight. Eleven should be ok. Maybe George could do it, yeah?'

‘Of course, I’ll sort something. Actually, I could do with a chat sometime soon, if that’s ok.’

‘Sounds ominous. All right, catch up with you soon. Goodnight Phil.’

Jane disconnected, took a right turn and reversed into the only parking space she could see on Jamie’s street – Bakers Avenue.

Leaning back in the car seat, she practised her deep breathing, composing herself for the ordeal ahead, but it didn’t work and within nano-seconds was wondering if Allan was right about her not delegating enough.

She knew George was more than capable of breaking the news to relatives, and had loads of experience of doing it. He could probably run the investigation, too. So why was she here? Was she on a permanent justification trip, feeling she had to make up for being a woman by working twice as hard, because she was the most senior female cop in the region? Or was it that she actually felt more comfortable doing the day to day detective work, and chose to give it more of her time over office work and people management? It was often said, probably by Charles now she thought about it, that we all moan about the time we spend doing things we don’t want to do, when really, we choose to do them because it’s safer, or a habit.

Jane closed her eyes briefly, tried to shut out the meanderings of her mind, then opened them slowly, and looked down the street.

The Castleton’s house was one of a terrace of identical, but quite substantial stone houses. Still terraced, but a cut above the one Jane and Allan had bought on a joint mortgage.

A respectable neighbourhood, her mum would have said, and that was about right.

You could tell by the neatly labelled wheelie bins that this was a house proud street. And the supernaturally clean cars suggested a lot of retired people lived here, which in turn suggested to Jane that she had probably already been spotted by a curtain twitcher.

Locking the car door, Jane walked slowly, looking for number 136. George had established that Jamie lived alone with his mother, and that he was an only child. He was checking on the whereabouts of the father now. So the likelihood was that Mrs Castleton was going to be feeling even more alone and broken, which was why Jane had asked George to get Jag and a Family Liaison Officer to come over some time in the next 15 minutes.

Number 136 was a tall narrow, three storey structure, with a large bay window intruding on an unkempt front garden that earned the label garden simply because weeds were making themselves at home in the gravel.

There were no lights visible from the street, no curtains or blinds drawn either, upstairs or down.

Jane stooped slightly to squint through a clear pane of glass in a multi-coloured panel on the front door. All was in darkness.

Suddenly, Jane tensed as she heard steps coming up behind her. She swung round to see a very tall woman wearing a dark coat and white bobble hat, with a carrier bag, and looking very disgruntled.

'What are you doing snooping around my house?'

Jane heard the clink of bottles. 'Mrs Castleton?'

'Who wants to know?'

'Mrs Castleton, I am with Ashbridge Police. Can we go inside please?'

Mrs Castleton just stared. The words came slowly and sounded almost sinister. 'It's about Jamie, isn't it?'

'Please, let's go inside and I can explain.'

Mrs Castleton brushed past her without another word, then turned and handed Jane the carrier bag while she took door keys out of her pocket. She held the door for Jane, who went into the darkness of the hall, still carrying the bag.

'Go through to the back and put that on the table will you?'

Jane heard her fumbling with the door chain after she'd shut the door, then the light came on, and she led the way into the kitchen.

They sat down, the carrier bag between them on the table.

Jane showed her badge. 'I'm so sorry to have to tell you, Mrs Castleton. Something has happened to Jamie.'

'I knew it. He's been killed, hasn't he?'

THREE

'So can you track back to recover what that lad was up to?'

Paolo Gonzales' enormous frame was a tight fit in the shabby desk chair in his cramped office on the first floor of the Pretty Cool Cafe. The back of his shirt was stained dark with sweat, and no wonder – the warm air heater on the wall was groaning with the effort..

The equally large, and now claustrophobic, Detective Sergeant George Creasey removed his jacket and slung it over the back of his chair, sipping water as Mr Gonzales squinted at a screenful of foreign language.

'What is that you're looking at, Mr Gonzales?'

'Is code, URLs, all that, yes.'

'From the deceased's computer?'

'No, no. From server. Have to find unique address.'

George grunted and looked at his watch. This was taking forever. And he had that thought lurking at the back of his mind: could he even trust that the information he would get would be accurate? What if that lad had been here every night looking at porn or paedophile sites or some other illicit stuff? In that case, the proprietor of this 'respectable business' – as Mr Gonzales described it – would be doing everything he could to remove the evidence… wouldn't he?

George made a note to get one of Phil's IT guys in to take a peek. Mark Manning would know what to do.

Mr Gonzales scratched the dark stubble on his cheek and leaned back.

'Okay, sir. Have tracked down. Will print off screen so you keep.'

'Thank you, Mr Gonzales. Before you do that, do you mind if I take a picture of that on my phone?'

'No, no secret here. Please…'

Mr Gonzales wheeled out of the way, then turned to check the paper tray in the printer, while George fumbled to get the screen image focussed. He took an extra shot, just in case.

'So what are we looking at here?'

'Web site addresses, email messages… browse history, sir.'

'Anything interesting or unusual about it?'

'No sir. Jamie was a good boy. In here a lot. Very quiet, like I said. Some of them make lots of noise and try to do bad things—'

'Like what?'

'Dark web, drug supply, all things. I have controls here to tell me, so I throw them out. Never throw Jamie out. Very good boy.'

'Dark web. I've heard of it, but…'

'Clever. Dangerous place. Need very good computer skill to go there. Many criminals use it. No way to track, see. All anonymous.'

'OK, thanks, we'll need to look into that. But no evidence here that Jamie was going there or trying to go there? No sign of any dodgy activity?'

Mr Gonzales rasped out a laugh. 'Jamie a nice guy, but clever, too. He would know not to try here. So, what can I say?'

'So, tell me, in simple language if you can, what was he doing when he came in this evening?'

Mr Gonzales pressed a couple of keys and the printer sprang into life. 'OK, you want coffee first?'

George tried very hard not to betray his real feelings about the vending machine coffee on offer, having discreetly spat a mouthful into Mr Gonzales' pedal bin about ten minutes ago.

'That's very kind of you, but no thanks. Don't let me stop you, though…'

Jane offered to make tea, but Mrs Castleton was clearly more interested in the wine in her carrier bag, so she waited as she unpacked, then poured herself a tumbler of white wine.

'What made you think that Jamie had been killed, Mrs Castleton?'

Irene stared intently at her wine, took a gulp, and set the glass down on the kitchen table with great precision. She looked up and seemed perfectly in control.

'He's my only child. We've been together a long time. It's like having a twin. You just know.'

'I'm so sorry, Mrs Castleton. But I have to ask lots of questions, especially when a death is suspicious. At the moment, we don't actually know very much, and we are waiting for the results of the examination we have to carry out.'

'When can I see him?'

'I was going to offer to drive you there in—' Jane's phone beeped as a message came through. '—please excuse me.'

The message read: 'Shirley here ma'am. Do you want me to come in now?'

'Sorry, Mrs Castleton. A colleague of mine is outside. Is it alright to let her in?'

Her tone was sharp and bitter. 'Need reinforcements, do you? It's all right. I'll come quietly. Isn't that what they say?'

'No, no. It's someone who is a specialist in supporting people through the shock of bereavement. But she will only be with you for as long as you want her to be. We certainly do not force this on anyone.'

'I see. Yes, let her in. I'll put the kettle on.'

'Thank you, that would be nice.'

Jane walked down the hall, amazed at the cliches that always come out at times like this. Put the kettle on. That'll be nice. I'm so sorry for your loss. Words… or just diversionary tactics? Keep feelings at bay as long as possible?

Shirley French was 22 years old, slightly built, impossibly pretty, and the station's best Family Liaison Officer by a country mile. She was a beat copper in a rough part of town, and when she wasn't surprising young thugs by breaking up street fights, she was quietly and compassionately defusing so many domestics the locals called her The Vicar.

She smiled as Jane opened the door.

'Good evening, ma'am. How is she?'

'Hello Shirley. Good to see you. Quick heads up. The first thing she did was assume her son had been killed, so that's obviously something we need to explore.

'She is calm on the surface, but there's a fair bit of aggression there, so you need to be careful. I'm wondering if she could be a slow fuse waiting to explode, so it could be a long night. Either that, or she really is going to keep it together and send you packing…'

'Thanks ma'am. I'm ready for anything.'

'I know you are, thanks Shirley. I've offered to drive her in later to ID the body, so we'll play by ear whether you come with us or wait here for me to bring her back. I'm still waiting for Jag to join us, so I've got options. I may need to leave you both to it. Who knows? Come in.'

'Yes, ma'am. I saw Jag on my way out, and he was just finishing off a phone call, so I don't suppose he'll be long.'

'Good. OK, let's go.'

Irene had made up a tray by the time they got to the kitchen, and was pouring hot water into a new looking teapot.

'Irene. Let me introduce you to Shirley, who is a liaison officer. She's here to support you as much or as little as you decide between you.'

'Hello, Mrs Castleton. OK if I call you Irene? Why don't you sit down and I'll pour the tea?'

'Yes, right, thank you, Shirley.'

Jane noted that Irene's tumbler was already empty.

'So, Irene, as I was saying, I was going to drive you in later this evening so you can formally identify Jamie. Is that alright? Do you feel up to it?'

'Yes, I'm ok. I've got used to being on my own. I know it's going to hit me bad sooner or later, but just now I feel…'

Shirley put the tray on the table, sat next to Irene and put a hand on her arm. 'A bit numb?'

Irene looked into Shirley's eyes and gave a faint smile. 'Yes dear. Numb's the word.'

Jane waited a moment, wondering if the play on words was deliberate.

'Tell me what Jamie was like, and what he did with his time.'

'He was into computers from a very early age. No idea where he got that from. His dad was a brickie. Didn't see him for dust when he found out I was pregnant, so I brought him up myself.'

'Must have been tough.'

'No, not really. Well, at times, yes. I had a good job. Worked for the council, and they were good about letting me adjust my hours, giving me leave, that sort of thing. It also meant I got a little pension when I got early retirement at 50, so I've managed, just about, and could spend time with Jamie as well as being able to afford some child care when I needed it.'

'When you say he was into computers, do you mean that was his job, or just a hobby?'

'It was his life—' Irene stopped and her hand shook as she reached for the wine bottle. Shirley held her hand for a second, then poured some into her glass as she gently and swiftly moved the conversation on: 'So he earned money from it?'

Jane felt the phone judder in her pocket, and quietly stepped into the hall. Jag was outside. Moving quickly, she let him in, signalled him to hurry and stay quiet, then they both returned.

Irene sipped her wine.

'Yes, he did. Worked for himself. Just put himself about, adverts in the paper, business cards in pubs and shops. I remember him coming home soaked and he said he'd been putting envelopes through doors on the industrial estate. He was a good worker, but—'

Jane waited, and Shirley caught her eye and got the message. Let her talk, in her own time. Shirley poured tea and handed it round, introducing Jag. Irene didn't appear to register the fact that she had another visitor, took another sip and leaned back in her chair.

'He was a lovely boy. Everyone said so. But over the last few months, he seemed to change, got a bit hard-edged, stayed out later, didn't have much to say to me. At first, I just put it down to a good looking lad growing up and thinking, what am I doing living at home… but he was losing his sense of humour, seemed preoccupied – oh I don't know… like he had something weighing on his mind. I couldn't get it out of him, though I tried.'

Jane took a mouthful of tea as she looked at Jag, and he took it as his cue to step in.

DC Jahangir Desai looked annoyingly fresh, as always. Everyone called him Jag, and he was known as the hardest working, friendliest and most ambitious officer in Ashbridge, if not Manchester. Jane rated him highly, and had encouraged him to make the transition from beat officer to detective after his support on the Fiona Worsley murder three years ago.

He wasn't the only black police officer in Ashbridge, but there were those who targeted him, and Jane was certain it was because he was rising through the ranks. There was no shortage of legislation, training and the equality standards that were supposedly there to create a more just society, but, as Jag said: 'The whole of society is institutionally racist, so why should anyone be surprised about it in the police force?'

It was almost as if each pathetic attack made him stronger. Jane – now the most senior ranking woman police officer in Manchester – had lived for years with discrimination of a slightly different but no less offensive and hurtful kind, and took extra pride in seeing him grow into the job.

It had occurred to her more than once that she was looking out for Jag in much the same way that Charles Aston had looked out for her…

Jag spoke softly.

'Hello Mrs Castleton. My name is Jag and I work with Jane and Shirley. Sorry I was late. I was thinking about how close you must have been to Jamie. I wondered if you had any theories. Could he have been worried about money? Getting into debt?'

'I couldn't work it out. It's not as if he gave me any clues. All I could think was that he was having some kind of trouble at work.'

'Where was he working? Who for?'

'I don't even know that. He just went out with his bag in the morning and came back and went up to bed with it at night. Sometimes, he wasn't coming home till very late.'

'How late?'

'Gone midnight, sometimes. I was so worried. I've always liked a glass of wine. My weakness, I suppose. And over the last few months, I've felt so lonely… I know I've drunk more than I should, but – '

Irene stopped, her body suddenly rigid. Shirley caught Jane's eye this time and it was a warning to be ready. Seconds later, Irene began sobbing silently, her shoulders shaking with the intensity of it. Shirley put an arm round her shoulder and held on. Jane gently moved the wine out of the way as Irene slumped forward, her head resting on her hands as the sobs became tears.

'I'm sorry…'

Shirley moved closer to her. 'Shhhhh… it's ok Irene. It's ok…'

Then Irene sat upright, roughly knocking Shirley away, and shouted: 'No it's not ok! Jamie found something out! I know it! That's what got him killed!'

Phil's tea had gone cold, but he sipped it anyway, both elbows on the white melamine worktop he used as a desk in the lab, frowning as he went back over his notes.

A lifetime in forensics, and he still couldn't give Jane a cause of death, and that hurt.

He'd been steeling himself to tell Jane his decision for weeks now, but all that was forgotten tonight as he pressed his fingers to his temples as if that gentle pressure would somehow divert his brain down a different road.

Nothing.

He looked up to make sure no-one was around, then resorted to talking to himself – a habit that he usually followed only at home. He could hear George Creasey moving about in the next room, but he wouldn't come in unless it was an emergency – George was a tough guy, except when it came to bodies being cut open. Phil had tried to coax him through it as he wielded the knives and forceps by explaining it was a labour of love and that every single component of a victim's body was a precious thing to be treated with respect. George had merely grunted and become interested in something in the corridor outside.

Phil grinned to himself. They were a hell of a team at Ashbridge, and Jane was a hell of a boss. Charles Aston had been, too, God bless him. It would be so hard to say goodbye.

But that wasn't going to happen just yet, at least not till he'd cracked this one.

Phil swivelled his desk chair around and started talking into his voice recorder.

'No signs of violence. No sign of self defence. No defects in the vital organs. We've ruled out suffocation, choking, heart failure. The only thing we have is that needle mark. But no evidence of any nasty substances in the blood test… Though the guys at region might find something with their equipment. What could cause a healthy fit young man to apparently just die instantly?'

Phil left the question hanging, then switched the recorder off, and walked over to look at Jamie's carefully reinstated body, the stitches running in a perfectly straight line from throat to groin.

Phil felt the weight of responsibility. He'd always cared for the victims that ended their days lying on his stainless steel bench, every one of them. But this lad was a bit special, and Phil knew he would not rest until he'd uncovered the truth.

He put a hand on his head and whispered.

'What did they do to you, Jamie?'

It was only when he said the words that he realised he'd already made his mind up. This was a murder inquiry.

FOUR

PHIL HADN'T MADE AN announcement officially.

He'd not even confided in Jane yet, but the time had come. She would try to talk him out of it but his mind was fixed. He would tell her that 40 years' service was quite enough, thank you very much; that he was hoping the old expression was wrong, and life actually began at 60.

Phil could only recall one occasion in all that time when he'd got it totally wrong. He'd never forgiven himself either.

His estimate of the time of death had been a critical factor in the arrest and conviction of a woman accused of murdering her own sister. But he'd got it wrong, and she'd won on appeal.

It was a long time ago, but Phil knew he would beat himself up for ever over that one.

That mistake was very much in his mind now, as he wrestled with the problem of Jamie Castleton. The time of death wasn't the issue. But after examining Jamie for over an hour, Phil was still clueless.

And Jane wouldn't like that. She was thoughtful, cared about people, but only up to a point. Phil had spotted the same spark that had convinced Charles Aston to promote her. It was the kind of spark that could light a fire under people who let her down, didn't perform.

And now it was late, he was tired, and Jane was on her way back.

He tidied Jamie up one more time, covered his body with the sheet, and wheeled the trolley over to what he called his fridge filing cabinet. Opening one of the steel doors, he slid Jamie into his assigned space, patted Jamie's chest in the same gesture of unacknowledged reassurance that he gave everyone that took up residence in this cold, stark place, then turned back to his bench to look through his notes again.

Jane pushed the heavy white door open and saw Phil with his head in his hands, elbows planted on the bench. He didn't move when the door hissed shut again, or hear her footsteps on the rubberised floor.

As Jane got closer, she was struck by how much Phil had aged: the grey and thinning hair, the age spots on his hands, the wrinkly flesh round his neck, and she found herself wondering, not for the first time, whether all the people she trusted and cared for and valued were slowly fading from her life.

Then she remembered Jamie, gave herself a reprimand for these non-productive and self indulgent thoughts, and gently cleared her throat.

Phil turned, startled, then smiled and patted the stool next to him.

Jane sat down.

'Before we start,' she said. 'I just want to say… I so wish you weren't leaving, Phil. You've been such a star, and I can't believe there'll ever come a time when we won't be having these conversations. Who's going to solve all our crimes, if you leave?

And who will I be able to rely on, totally? What with you, and… the boss…'

'Hang on, when did I say I was leaving?'

'Come on, Phil. I know you well enough by now. When you told me you wanted to talk to me, my first thought was why you were being so formal. The second thought was the light bulb moment. Or should I call it the dark cloud moment. It's not unexpected, Phil, but don't do this to me now.'

'You know I won't let you down, Jane. I just wanted to get it off my chest early, and to you. You've been so good to me…'

'Purely for selfish reasons.'

'Rubbish! With all due respect, Ma'am'.

As they laughed, Jane fought off the empty feeling: Charles, Mum, Allan, and now, this.

'Ok Phil, let's do this properly when we both have time, and we're about 500 per cent less knackered. Can we focus on Jamie first?'

'Thanks boss. Yes, of course. I've been doing a lot of thinking about him. But, before we get going, can I ask you about Charles?'

Jane sighed and pinched the bridge of her nose. 'I think it's over, and he knows it. Saw him earlier, and, well…'

'Oh God. You two were quite a team. We'll all miss him, but you…'

'Yes. And it makes the idea of you leaving even harder.'

'You're very kind, Jane – sorry, boss… but I've been round the clock a few times, and I just think if I don't leave now –'

'I know. There is a life outside work, so I'm told.'

'There is, and, if it's any consolation, I'm not going anywhere until we've worked out what happened to that poor boy.'

'Ok, and thanks for being up front about it. Still nothing for me?'

'The beginnings of an idea, but nothing more than that. It's one of those situations – you know, that Sherlock Holmes thing – where you have to eliminate everything that you think is possible, and then consider the impossible.'

'Right. So…?'

'So, first things first, I have ruled out natural causes, so I'm pretty sure now that we are looking at murder. But—' Phil paused and scratched the back of his head. 'I've been going back over the notes I made, and so far, there is nothing that says clearly to me – this is the cause of death.'

'Bugger.'

'Can't argue with that, Jane. Bugger is definitely the word…'

'My immediate problem is I need to do the next of kin thing. I can't make my mind up about the mother, so I've put her off doing the ID tonight. Left her with Jag and Shirley for now. She seemed certain it's foul play. So much so that she wouldn't be surprised it was murder. Something about Jamie being up to something, and that's why he was killed.'

'Really? But she didn't elaborate?'

'No, not yet. I've left her with Shirley for a while. They seem to get on, so maybe she'll open up a bit more to her. She's upset, of course, so maybe not thinking straight…'

'Not surprising, poor soul… I'm not going to be able to give her – or you – certainty just yet. Hang on, though, if she thought that straight away, you don't think…?'

'I don't know, but why was that the first thing on her mind? Knowing exactly what happened? I can't help thinking I'd just scream and want to be on my own. But she seems so…'

'What?'

'… fixated? I don't know if that's the right word… Whatever, she knows something. More than she's telling us.'

Phil leaned back on his stool at a precarious angle and stretched. 'Guilty might be the right word… No, surely not! Not his own mother? Oh God… People never stop surprising us, do they, especially when they've just been told they have lost a loved one? I remember, I must have come across as a right uncaring bastard. Just fretting over details, you know, almost businesslike. But two weeks later… well, I was an emotional wreck. If I was in her shoes I'd want certainty, and at the moment I've just got possibly, maybe even probably… and the probably I'm thinking of is not something I've ever come across before.'

'Phil! That's the worst forensic report I've ever heard!' She wriggled to get a more secure position on the stool and leaned in. 'Ok, come on, tell me about the impossibles you are considering.'

'How about a quick brew while I do that?'

'Thank you waiter. One tea. White. Without.'

It was late, but Jane was wired after hearing Phil run through the list of possibilities, or impossibilities, and she couldn't face going straight home to face an inquisition from Allan.

Jag had messaged her to say Irene was being more forthcoming, and would Jane like him to come and collect her. She could have let Jag handle it, but immediately said yes and resisted the temptation to promote him again, or marry him, for his endless selflessness.

Now she was settled into the passenger seat as she enjoyed the traffic free drive, as Jag quietly and smoothly navigated the complex web of major and minor roads that led back to Jamie's mother.

Just for a short time, there were no phone calls, no demands for information or explanation… just the sedative sound of Jag's Peugeot 406, the occasional rustle of an irritated wiper as it cleared the screen of intermittent rain, and…

'We're there, ma'am.'

Jag hid a smile as Jane sat up and tried to pretend she hadn't been dozing. Then she caught his eye and smiled too.

'I didn't fall asleep, did I DC Desai?'

'Certainly not, ma'am. And fortunately, neither did I.'

'You have a glittering career ahead of you, Jag. If I did close my eyes, it was only because I was thinking strategically.'

Jag delivered his trademark high pitched giggle as they stepped out.

Mrs Castleton's mood had altered. Jag briefly filled Jane in as they walked up to the house.

It turns out she had already been through more than enough. She was divorced about 15 years ago on the grounds of her husband's abusive behaviour and adultery. She got the house, husband Alec got five years, and while there was no record of him offending after his release, George was still trying to track him down.

Shirley let them in and announced: 'I've got tea.'

Irene had aged in a very short time, and was now showing the signs of distress that you'd expect of a grieving mother. Jane leaned in a little closer and put a hand on her arm as she sat down again. Irene looked down for a moment, and when she looked at Jane, her eyes were shining with tears.

'Mrs Castleton… Irene…'

'No, no, don't worry about me. I'm all right. Been on my own, really, for a long time. I don't know what I'm going to do…'

Shirley poured the tea with perfect timing, handed Jane a cup and offered one to Mrs Castleton, who took it with both hands as if it was a precious object, something to hold onto. Jane briefly wondered where the wine went, and sensed Shirley's influence.

Irene was obviously using every ounce of will power to act normally, when inside, she was screaming. It happened so often, as if people felt sorry for the police officer who was telling them that their life had just been shattered, trying to make it easier for them. Jane remembered breaking down when she found out about Charles Aston, and marvelled at how much pain people were able to withstand.

But now, Irene was beginning to unravel. Maybe it was the sincerity of Jane's sympathy. Would it have been better to stay detached?

Jag handed Irene a tissue and she dabbed her eyes as the words began to flow.

'He was such a good boy. My husband knocked us both about, but me more than Jamie, and afterwards he'd just come and sit with me and hold my hand...'

Jane gently interrupted, and then cursed herself immediately for her impatience.

'Do you remember, you said he was working on his computers *out there*. What did you mean by that, Irene?'

'That's what he did for a living. Computers. Fixing them for people. Showing them how to do new things, you know.'

Jag chipped in. 'He was in one of those internet cafes in town. Did he often go there?'

Irene sniffed loudly and sipped tea. 'I don't know. He was staying out later than usual, like I said.'

Jane stirred a half teaspoon of sugar into her tea. This time, she needed it. 'This could be important, Mrs Castleton. It will help us a lot. Did he say why or where else he'd been? Did you ask him?'

Irene looked alarmed. 'Why does it help? What do you mean? He's died...'

'The thing is Irene, we still don't know why he died. Our police doctor is working all night, and I'm sorry we can't give you a definitive answer about that yet. But we'll find out. All I meant was, anything you can tell us about Jamie and his lifestyle – his habits – could be helpful for the doctor. It might give us a clue as to why this happened.'

Jane was struggling for the right words and it was showing, but it seemed enough to pacify Irene for the time being.

'When can I see him?'

Jag looked at her across the square yellow formica table. 'We were wondering if you would like me to come and call for you in the morning, and I could drive you in to see him. Would that be ok? About ten? We may have more information by then, but I can't promise that, I'm afraid.'

Irene nodded, and gave a deep, shuddering sigh.

Jane took her hand and spoke softly. 'Earlier, you said you were sure that Jamie had been killed. Because he found something out. Why did you say that, Irene?'

'I don't know. He'd just changed. Preoccupied all the time, you know? He was so clever, and I just could tell he was up to something; doing things with his computer. Then this happens…'

It didn't ring true, somehow, and Jane disguised her frown as one of concern, as she patted Irene's hand. 'That's ok Irene. Get some rest now. Have you got anyone we could call to come and stay with you tonight? A friend, or a relative, or a neighbour?'

Irene shook her head. 'No-one. I'll be fine. I'll see you in the morning.'

Shirley shook her head. 'No Irene, don't worry. I'll stay here with you. I can sit down here while you're upstairs. Just for tonight, yeah?'

Irene stared at her tea.

Jane had so much more to ask, and they would need to go through Jamie's room with a fine tooth comb, but now was not the time and she would message Shirley to make sure no-one went in there overnight. She stood up, walked to the kitchen door and turned.

'Goodnight Irene. Thanks very much, Shirley. Can you drive Irene in, in the morning? I'll arrange for someone to come and keep an eye on the house tomorrow while you're out Irene.'

'I'll show you out.'

'No, please, stay where you are, Irene. We'll see you in the morning.'

Jane smiled at Shirley, mimed 'I'll message you', then led the way down the narrow hall, followed by Jag, and stepped out into the cold air that seemed to rush through her system like a drug. She stopped to breathe it in.

'Excuse me, ma'am. Are you all right?'

Jane nodded, and looked back at Irene's house, its front door paintwork glistening in the misty rain and the weak streetlight. In the distance, she could hear the hum of traffic from the dual carriageway; the main road between Ashbridge and Manchester.

'I'm fine, Jag. Just thinking… if we could open every door in this street, what would we find?'

Jag laughed, and Jane turned to look at him, with a questioning look in her eye.

'Sorry, ma'am. I think you would find my favourite word in the English language.'

'Really. And what might that be?'

'Vestibule, ma'am.'

'Vestibule?'

'Yes, ma'am. I love that word. Vest-i-bule.'

He laughed again and Jane found herself joining in, but she turned to face Irene's house again and the laughter died away.

'Come on Jag, take me back to the station. Then let's go home.'

Jag nodded, but he was still giggling as he unlocked the car, and held the door open for her.

'Phil, go home. It's late.'

'I will in a minute, boss. I'm so close, though.'

'Good. I'm intrigued. But it won't hurt to confirm it in the morning, ok? I've told Irene she can come and see Jamie at 10. Now, come on, get out of here. Oh, and we'll try and fit in that chat you wanted, at some stage.'

'Ok boss. You win. The Horlicks is calling me. But there's no rush for the chat. Something tells me you'll be pretty busy for the foreseeable.'

Jane walked back into her office, switched off the fluorescent ceiling light, flicked on the desk lamp, and sank heavily into her chair, head in hands, gently massaging with her fingers.

On the desk, neat as ever, her A4 diary perfectly positioned at centre stage, with her black fountain pen lined up parallel. At her right hand, a red three tier document tray marked 'IN', 'OUT' and 'SHAKE IT ALL ABOUT'. The silly labels were a gift from Charles Aston when she'd been promoted – by him – to the position of DCI. She'd laughed when he marched into her office and ordered her to stick them on her multi-storey tray.

'You will find, Jane, that most of your paperwork will end up under the 'shake it all about' category. That's where most of my stuff lives. The kind of memos, letters, and sticky notes that seem important at the time, but never quite escape onto your desk because something new appears. And that's fine, just as long as none of my orders end up in there, is that clear, Detective Chief Inspector?'

'Clearly understood, sir.'

'Good. Well, carry on, DCI Birchfield...'

Jane leaned back and closed her eyes, fighting hard to shut down the image of Charles fading away in the hospice, feeling again the sense of helplessness that had been building up for so many months: a helplessness she hid simply because she couldn't afford to show it.

Charles had been her rock; he'd understood the pressure she faced as the only senior woman in the division.

'Blokes bottle things up, Jane,' he'd told her over a late night builder's tea. 'We're not so communicative. We keep things to ourselves, work them out as quietly as we can. We might lie awake all night, worrying, but we'd never admit it. Women, though… well I know this is a generalisation, Jane, but women like to talk, it helps them. Polar opposites. Makes things tougher for you here, I know…'

He couldn't see the irony of the fact that he was so willing to share his worries with Jane. Men could talk to women. But not in the police force, which was why Jane had felt so blessed to land in the office next to Charles Aston. He'd never admit it, but she was pretty sure he felt a little bit blessed, too, being able to open up to her.

And now he was going to die. Jane leaned back in her chair and massaged the back of her neck, feeling her strength ebb away now she was alone. Her mother was mentally and physically fit, but angry and full of self pity. And Allan was becoming ever more withdrawn, so that going home was becoming more of an ordeal than going to work – even with all the extra responsibility she had taken on…

And now, she had to somehow find the strength to lead what looked like being her second murder inquiry – the biggest case Ashbridge had faced since Fiona Worsley was battered to death in the rubble of a redevelopment area. Two years later, Fiona was forgotten, and the scene of her murder was now buried under the first phase of the Boulevard development. And her still unrepentant killer, Laura Armitage, was locked up in Styal.

So, here we go again. Jane was already fairly sure that Irene's instincts were right. Jamie had been murdered, and tomorrow, Phil would tell her how.

She slowly and neatly wrote a few bullet points in her diary… CCTV? Jamie's father? cafe owner/manager? Allan and Jamie?

Allan… Jane first met him during the Fiona investigation, when he told her they were 'in a relationship' once. Now it seems, he also had a connection with Jamie.

Jane tapped her pen on the desk. Ashbridge is a relatively small suburb and he is the newspaper editor, so he's likely to know a lot of people. Something else to chew on. But that could wait for another day. Time to go home and hope he was asleep in bed.

Half an hour later, she was locking the car and yawning and walking up to her front door. She stopped half way up the short quarry tiled path, and tried to recall what had gone through her mind when she'd looked back at Irene's front door before Jag had interrupted her flow with his silly comment about vestibules.

Yes, that was it… we live and work and sleep and travel behind closed doors. Is it just for security, or privacy, or is it just a basic human instinct that we have a need to close ourselves in, shut ourselves away? And yet, most of us have computers and gadgets and high speed broadband that means we can reach out and send and receive messages across the whole world – and even view images taken in space. Is that now replacing human contact, driving us indoors to bathe in the light of computer screens?

And, if that's true, why then did Jamie feel the need to use an internet cafe?

Jane could hear the same traffic hum she heard outside Irene's house. She leaned against the front door. She'd learned to let her mind go free, exactly when it wanted to…

Is that what Jamie was doing? Using computers to shut himself off from people? Why had he started staying out later in the last few weeks? George Creasey had said the café owner always let Jamie stay on for a while because he was a regular. But what was so important that he needed to do that? Why did he need to go to that scruffy little dive to do it? Irene said he carried his laptop with him everywhere, and spent most of his time in his room. What was so special about the Pretty Cool Cafe?

Even though her brain was only working at about half speed, she was convinced Jamie Castleton had been up to something.

She quickly unlocked the door, closed it quietly, took off her shoes and headed for the kitchen.

She was so intent on writing down her thought process so it didn't get lost in tomorrow's madness that she didn't notice the envelope by the kettle with her name on it.

FIVE

'Still here George?'

'Apparently I am, yes, Phil. I get the impression you are an' all.'

'Jane told me to go home, but, you know... Well past your bedtime, though.'

'I know, but I've decided the beauty sleep wasn't working for me, so... How've you got on? Anything?'

'I've got a hunch, nothing more.'

'Well, your hunches are usually good. I always thought you should have bet on the horses. You'd do a damn sight better than I ever did.'

'I wouldn't bet on it.'

George groaned but Phil pressed on, moving a box of wine gums out of the way so he could perch on the end of George's desk. 'Truth is, George, I'm worried I might be losing it. Getting too old.'

George swivelled in his chair. He was a big man, but he looked shattered, the bags under his eyes even fleshier than usual. But he was famed for being the last man to leave the office most nights. He stretched his back, his blue shirt straining over his paunch, and reached for a wine gum. Phil noted with childish annoyance that he didn't get offered one.

'Come off it. You're the best in the business. Well, in Ashbridge, anyway… Come on, what's brought this on?'

'Thanks for the compliment, I think.' Phil fastened his coat. 'Probably just tired. Been a long day.'

'Yeah, it has at that. Get home. Throw a double Horlicks down your neck. That should do the trick. Wake up in the morning and it'll all be sorted.'

Phil laughed as he headed for the door. 'Fat chance. See you tomorrow, George. Don't work too hard…'

'Yeah, right. As if. Cheers my son.'

George watched as Phil walked away down the corridor, then popped another wine gum and turned back to his computer.

'Now then, Mr bleeding Gonzales, let's see what we can find out about you, eh?'

Jane finally gave in to the increasingly frequent yawns, gulped a glass of water, tiptoed up the stairs – avoiding the creaky step fourth from the top – and undressed in the bathroom so she was less likely to wake Allan.

She shivered as she cleaned her teeth, checking herself in the mirror. The jury was out, she thought. Not putting on the pounds, which was good, but one or two of the curves were becoming straight lines. Looking closer, she could see the blond roots showing through. Time for another appointment with Shelley at Top Cutz.

She also needed to make more time for the gym, then remembered saying exactly the same thing a few weeks ago, and having the same conversation with herself: 'How can I? I'm too busy running a division, and holding a relationship together, not to mention running off to see mum whenever I get a spare five minutes.'

Jane spat out the toothpaste, sipped some tap water, and dabbed her mouth with a hand towel, before dispensing a blob of moisturiser into her hand and giving her face a bit of love and attention.

Still shivering, she moved quietly into the bedroom, and stopped. Did Allan get so pissed he forgot to close the curtains? She eased them gently shut and climbed under the sheets, waiting for the goosebumps to subsidise under the cool sheets.

It was only when she turned on her side and stretched out her left arm that she realised.

Allan wasn't there.

He felt the first wave of tiredness on the outskirts of Birmingham, lulled into it by the sheer tedium of the M6 at night.

It made a change to drive at a steady 65 on any motorway these days, but it made it more difficult to stay alert. Normally that wouldn't be a problem: there were so many prats – ranging from company car drivers who thought they were invincible, to Formula 1 racing drivers behind the wheel of immense lorries; not forgetting the jokers in hats and driving gloves who drove at 50, oblivious to the angry faces, head shaking and colourful language behind them.

He'd foolishly thought he could make it to Lyme Regis in one session. He reached for the water bottle and took a swig, shaking his head as a very old and very loud Fiesta rattled past him like a tractor on rocket fuel.

The sat nav display was telling him – though not in so many words – that if he could stay awake until he reached Stafford, he might be lucky enough to get a room at the Travelodge.

Allan found that thought amusing.

But his tired smile faded fast. He was already having doubts. In fact, the minute he turned left out of their street, he was wondering whether he was making a massive mistake. How would Jane react? Was he just throwing his toys out of the pram?

He'd sat on the sofa for over an hour, trying to make his mind up, drinking coffee and loads of water to counteract the effects of two glasses of red. What swung it in the end was the very fact that he was indecisive; the fact that he couldn't make his mind up about something so important meant that something was wrong. So he needed space and time to come to a decision. Sorted.

Jane would be well pissed off when she read the note, but he'd phone her in the morning, and she'd understand.

He tutted as the first fat marbles of rain smacked into the windscreen. He flicked on the wipers, and forced himself to concentrate on the dark black road that stretched ahead.

Irene Castleton sat up in bed with the lamp on, her eyes closed in a futile attempt to soothe them. She was used to sleepless nights. In fact, she couldn't remember sleeping right through since Alec left her.

It had happened right out of the blue.

They'd been out playing darts, like they did once a week, every week; the only thing they did together. He'd won, as usual. He always seemed to get his eye in after three pints. Irene, on the other hand, found her faculties fading with each glass of Lambrusco. But the compensation was, by the time the game was over, she didn't care.

They'd lurched home, arm in arm, and she'd crashed out on the bed.

Next morning, he was gone. No note, no nothing. Part of her was glad. She remembered thinking it was what being released from prison must feel like. There'd be no more shouting in her face, no more putting her down, no more bruises, and no more apologising to Jamie for his dad's behaviour.

But the other part of her was fearful. And lonely. Jamie was quiet at the best of times, and he withdrew even further, dashing her hopes that she'd at least be able to build a strong relationship with her son. That's when the drinking really started.

Irene slowly, reluctantly opened her eyes. The glow from the street lamp formed a contorted rectangle that framed the bed. She heard the clank and roll of a milk bottle. Next door's cat.

She started as a faint thud came from downstairs. Then she remembered. Shirley was staying overnight.

Irene walked to the window, her head swimming with fatigue, and opened the curtains. Part of her was hoping even now that it was all a terrible mistake. But she knew it was hopeless. Jamie was gone.

And she was fairly sure she knew why.

Jane read the note again as she lay in bed.

> *'I've gone away for a few days. Thought we both needed a break. It hasn't been great, and I'm not sure why. I'm sorry I've been so crap. I just thought if we both had some time apart, it might help. I've got a bit of a gap before the next edition, so I'm heading for Lyme Regis. I'll be back soon and hopefully we can start again. That's the plan anyway. Love ya x'*

Despite, or because of, everything, Jane laughed. But it didn't last long. Then she screwed the paper into a ball and threw it at the bedroom wall. 'For fuck's sake, Allan.'

After a few calming breaths, she picked up her mobile, pressed 1 and Allan's number came up.

She hesitated: what was the point of phoning? He'd be driving. And why the hell should she? She moved to the bathroom for a glass of water and sat down on the bed to try and calm herself, the cool draught from the old sash window chilling her again.

It didn't take her long to decide. She turned the phone and the lamp off, got back in bed, pulled the duvet over her head and hoped for sleep.

Graeme Hargreaves was trying to concentrate.

It had already been an extremely long day of meetings.

Sue drifted past him in a cloud of perfume and a whisper of silk pyjamas and gave him the look.

Graeme covered the microphone on his mobile. 'You go, love. I'll just get rid of this, ok?'

She smiled and breathed a kiss into his neck, the gentle touch that always got him going, then closed the door behind her. Graeme shook his head and tried to focus.

'Yes, I heard, Paolo. Dreadful business. Anything you want me to do?'

'Police, they want records, server print outs, everything. I tell them everything in order—'

Graeme sat on the arm of the cream leather sofa, smoothing out a crease on his navy chinos. 'And it is, Paolo. Knowing you, I'm sure it is... Look, you have nothing to worry about. Some terrible accident, that's all... must have been, yes? So, come on, bad things happen... Yes, I know, but you've done nothing wrong... Have you?... No, it's fine... Just don't panic... You did the right thing to let me know.'

He reached for the pen and notepad on the coffee table and pulled it towards him. 'What can you tell me about him, Paolo?'

He listened, occasionally making notes, and tapping the pen on his teeth impatiently, then butted in. He'd heard enough.

'OK, ok… One of the regulars then… Leave it with me… Now just get some sleep Paolo, and we can talk tomorrow… Better collate what he was doing and email it to me. The police are bound to want to know, if they don't already… Yes, I'll call you… Around 10… Yes, yes… Relax, will you?… All right… Goodnight.'

He touched the screen to terminate the call.

Graeme poured a generous measure of his tipple of choice – Macallan Rare Cask Batch 1 – and leaned back in his Eames desk chair. He spun round slowly so he could look out through the triple glazed sliding doors across the bright lights of Manchester.

He felt the warmth of the whisky, and poured another as he analysed what Gonzales had told him.

That lad – Jamie Castleton. What was he up to? Seems he was a regular, then. Gonzales should have flagged that up. Someone had been hacking into the company's IT system, for God's sake.

George curled his long fingers round the glass, and hitched his glasses up his nose, frowning.

He'd built up a successful business, and had the lifestyle to go with it. Bullied mercilessly at school for being a 'speccy four-eyes' and studying hard, he'd never been a looker and usually ended up in the nets when football teams were being picked. He'd always been slim, too – or weedy, as his dad preferred, and he hadn't put much weight on since he left college with a diploma in business studies.

Ashbridge was a small town and he still knew most of the losers who had pushed him around at school. Most of them were on benefits. He didn't bear grudges. He'd moved on, unlike them. One or two had even impressed him by applying for a job with Greaves. They obviously didn't realise it was his company. Hadn't done their homework, and that was something no-one could ever accuse him of.

He smiled briefly, took off his glasses and massaged his tired eyes. then spun the chair through 90 degrees to face his glass topped desk. 'Now, Jamie. Let's see what we can find out about you, eh?'

Sarah would have to wait. But he couldn't.

SIX

JANE LEANED BACK AND frowned: 'Aconite? Sounds like, I don't know, something you'd find on a fossil hunt.'

Phil smiled. 'Aconite is a plant. It's better known as wolf's-bane or monkshood. The root is used as medicine. But it contains some poisonous chemicals. It's got all kinds of uses – some people take it for joint pain, finger numbness, cold hands and feet, pleurisy, that sort of thing. It's also used as a disinfectant, to treat wounds.'

Jane contained her inner smile: Phil was off one one, and once he got going…'OK professor, I get that, but how the hell could it kill someone?'

'I'm not saying it definitely did, in this case. I may be going down the wrong route, if you don't mind a bad pun… but the point is it contains chemicals that can seriously harm the heart, muscles, and nerves. Aconite is a poison that causes severe side effects, including – wait for it – the inability to move, heart problems, and death. It's so lethal, you can get symptoms in less than ten minutes, you can be paralysed, and stone dead in less than an hour.

'But—'

'One more point before I shut up… And, from what I've read about it, it can do its work and then be undetectable very, very quickly. No wonder they call it the queen mother of poisons. No wonder I haven't been able to find anything…'

'OK, thanks Phil, it's definitely worth more work. Couple of questions that immediately spring to mind, though… how would it have been administered? and even if it acts that quickly, you're not saying it's instant, so how does that explain Jamie apparently frozen in position, oblivious to what's happening to him?'

'Yes, I know. Like I say, Jane, I'm not there yet, but if he had been given a really high dose, maybe that would explain it.'

'Ok. But then, wouldn't it stay in the system for longer?'

She paused…

'What is it, ma'am?'

'In the system, Phil, maybe that's what this is all about… Anyway, I'll leave you to it. I'm getting the team together in about 20 minutes for an update. I won't share this with them yet. We need to be sure, so come back to me when you're ready. I asked Loretta to check out any CCTV outside that cafe, but she wasn't hopeful.'

'Loretta is always hopeful.'

'Especially where Mark is concerned?'

'So they say. I think they'd make a lovely couple.'

'You sound like their grandad!'

'I'm old enough to be.'

'True. But we soldier on. Thanks again, Phil, you're a bloody star, if you'll pardon my French. You may be antique, but you know how valuable they are.'

Jane leaned forward and her eyes met his. Phil knew what was coming, so he got in first.

'Boss, thanks for the kind words. I do appreciate it. Look, I know I said I wanted a chat about my departure. But shall we get this sorted first?'

'Are you a mind reader?'

'We've been together a few years now.'

'So you are a mind reader. Bugger!'

'Not exactly.' Phil hesitated. 'Can I ask, are you OK? I know you're worried about Charles Aston, but—'

'I am, yes. Since you ask, I am having a few problems at home, too.' Phil gave her his look, the one that said, you can talk to me… 'Allan left me a note. I saw it when I got home last night. He's taken it into his head that getting away from me for a few days would be a good idea. You know what? He could be right.'

'Sorry, Jane. But sometimes, it is for the best. And if you ever – well, I don't need to say any more, do I?'

'—need a shoulder to cry on… ? Right now, it's the least of my worries.' Jane laughed. 'So, I'll live. In fact, I slept like a bloody baby last night. Now go and find me a definite cause of death. His mum is coming in to do the ID later this morning. What are the chances of us being certain by then?'

Phil frowned. 'Just at the moment, not good. But I've cleared everything so I can concentrate on this one, so leave it with me for a bit longer, please, ma'am.'

'Come back to me just before 10 so we know where we are before Irene gets here.'

Jane held the door open as Phil walked out into the corridor, his bundle of papers under his arm. He definitely seemed more frail, a bit more rounded in the shoulder, maybe a few pounds lighter, too.

She called after him, remembering something. 'Oh, Phil…

I'll also need the forensics on my desk sometime today, please – anything from the search last night.'

Phil saluted like a trooper. 'Yes, ma'am.'

Sitting back at her desk, the changes in Phil reminded her how much of the subtle detail we fail to notice when we're with someone every day; the physical changes, yes; but also the changes in temperament. That was certainly true of her and Allan, and it was definitely true now, as Jane prepared to lead the Ashbridge CID in only her second murder investigation; for murder it most certainly, but unofficially, was.

The press office had been onto her already this morning, asking for any info they could release. Jane batted it away with the usual… 'we're in the early stages, too early to say.'

Jane reflected on what a mixed bunch they were. There was Phil, of course, and George, the Acting DI bruiser with a soft heart; DC Rossiter, still annoyingly young, pushy, and, yes, bright; Loretta Irons, recently drafted in from uniform branch after her help with the Fiona Worsley case; and Mark Manning, the IT expert Irons had the hots for, allegedly. And Jag, of course: hard working, and ambitious: but kept his personal life completely separate.

As she prepared to hold the first team briefing since Jamie's body was discovered, Jane realised she knew so little about them. How much had they changed over the two years since Fiona's murder?

She picked up her pen, ready to put her notes together for the team briefing, but she remembered Allan's note again and fought off the urge to call him. Maybe he was right: the job did always come first for her.

And maybe she was realising too late that she hadn't seen the change in him, too.

A few doors down the corridor, it was Jag's turn to make the tea, and he was doing it with his usual efficiency, even though his turn seemed to come round a lot quicker than the others.

Moraji had sneered when he told her he'd got the team's orders keyed in on one of his phone apps.

'Have you got mine on there as well?' she'd said.

Jag was hurt, but had laughed it off. He'd worked harder than anyone to become part of the unit at Ashbridge, and he was realistic enough to know that if he didn't pull his weight, his lack of experience – and his colour – was likely to count against him. He'd lived with what he called 'closed circuit discrimination' ever since he joined the force. He saw it not so much as racism, but the kind of mentality that comes naturally to people who feel they are part of a club, and resent any intrusion.

And if making the tea and coffee helped, he was ok with that, and Moraji should be too.

She'd been full of excitement when he got his breakthrough during the Fiona Worsley murder investigation two years ago. Jane had asked him to help her out with planning and organisation, and he'd jumped at the chance.

'You're going to be a detective? Wow!' She'd shouted and hugged him, then spent at least half an hour on the phone to her mother. Moraji took it for granted he'd get a pay rise, and she'd been crushed when he told her that he'd only earn more once he'd passed his exams and started going for promotion.

Now the reality was setting in, and his long hours were beginning to be an issue. Moraji was a qualified teacher and desperate to get back to work after baby Aarav was born last year.

They'd talked for hours about the right name for the boy, and eventually settled – rather optimistically as it turned out – on Aarav, which means 'peaceful'. But life had been anything but. He'd woken every night, screaming the place down, and with Jag working all the hours he could get, Moraji was carrying the burden, day and night.

Jag lined the mugs up on the wood-effect worktop in the corner of the office, spooning in the required amounts of coffee. Then he had to remember one spoon of sugar for Ross, two for Mark and George; and two teas for Loretta Irons and himself, white without. George – aka Crusty – insisted on bringing his own coffee, Douwe Egbert's Pure Gold, the jar bearing his name in black felt tip on a sticky white label. Jag poured and stirred, and took them round. Loretta – also known as Lorry – was served first, an honour that she always acknowledged with a slightly embarrassed smile and a mouthed 'thank you', even if she was on the phone. Which she was.

'...yes, yes, I know. We don't have any camera footage inside the cafe, but we are pretty sure there's a few covering the streets around it, so could you, would you mind just checking, please? Great, thanks, bye.'

She put the phone down rather too emphatically, leaned back in the chair, which always looked a bit small for her, and talked to the ceiling. 'God Almighty! You'd think I'd asked him for his credit card details. People need to get a life!'

Jag gave George his brew with a great deal of mock ceremony. It was their daily ritual, and the rest of the team did their best to ignore it, though Loretta thought it was quite sweet.

'Your coffee, Sir Crusty.'

'Thanks awfully, Jaguar, old chap.' George would then sip very cautiously as if tasting fine wine, and pronounce his verdict. 'A fine brew. Now bugger off and get me a custard cream you bloody slacker.'

Loretta rolled her eyes at Ross, who merely shook his head and carried on tapping at the keyboard, just as Jane strode in with Mark Manning, carrying the Samsung tablet that seemed permanently attached to his right hand.

Jane smiled, as Jag pointed at a spare mug with a question mark in his eyes. 'Tea, white without, for me, thanks Jag. And can we all pay attention just for a few minutes please? Time for an update. I've asked switchboard to hold calls until we're done, you'll be glad to know—'

She paused, flicking through her notes, then took a quick slurp of the tea Jag brought her. Mark declined the offer, and Jag finally got the chance to sit down and drink his.

Jane looked up and took a deep breath, as if she was waiting for a race to start. Which is what it felt like. Three, two, one…

'OK, let's try to summarise where we are… We have a young man, Jamie Castleton, who died suddenly while on a computer at the Pretty Cool Cafe on the High Street. It looked at first like he'd had a seizure, or something, but Phil says it was definitely not natural causes, and let's face it, it's not likely to fall into the category of accident…'

Ross sat up straighter, suddenly very engaged. 'So are we saying it's murder, boss?'

Jane looked each of them in the eye before replying. Everything depended on their commitment from this moment on. She liked what she saw.

'We can't say it officially, Ross, because Phil is still trying to establish what happened to the poor lad. But, strictly between us for now, yes – we are looking for Jamie's killer.'

She turned to George, who was leaning back munching his third custard cream.

'George, you were going to pay close attention to Mr Gonzales, the guy who runs the internet cafe?'

Loretta hid a grin as George tried to speak through a mouthful of biscuit and ended up coughing instead.

'Yes, ma'am,' he spluttered. 'He is just the manager. The business is owned by Greaves—'

Mark was interested straight away and started tapping at his tablet. 'The online betting company?'

'That's the one. They own a lot of property in and around Manchester, too, including several internet cafes, all of them with different names. Our Mr Gonzales is on the Greaves payroll.'

Jane turned to Mark. 'Do you know a lot about them, Mark? Is that especially significant?'

'Could be, ma'am. There's been a lot in the business press lately about how robust Greaves' IT systems are. It got me interested one weekend so I checked them out. Apparently, the company has at least doubled its turnover in the last five years, and insiders are asking whether their investment in tech has kept pace.'

'Meaning…?'

'Well, put simply, the more people who use it, the more strain it puts on their servers, and the more people who access the system to place their bets, the more likely that one or two will have the ability to hack in. They've got a lot of money moving through their system, straight into their bank – all of it done online. It's an easy target – like seagulls going for chips, ma'am. Their shares have dropped in value because of the press coverage, too.'

'Ok, interesting… So we have Jamie – a computer expert apparently – sitting in one of Greaves's own internet cafes, possibly taking the opportunity to hack into the internal systems of a betting company that's turning over, what, millions?'

'It's a possibility, ma'am, that's all.'

'That might explain his mother's comment about Jamie being up to something, and staying out late more than he ever did. But that cafe shuts early evening, doesn't it? So we need to know what else he was doing. George, what more do we know about Gonzales?'

George had timed his last custard cream to perfection, and now spoke without spitting shards over his desk. 'He's born and bred in Mexico. Moved here about 10 years ago. Bought out by Greaves around six years ago after he'd built up a tidy business at the Pretty Cool Cafe—'

Ross snorted. 'That has got to be the crappiest name for a cafe, ever.'

'—thanks for that. Moving on... Gonzales makes bloody awful coffee, but he knows his onions. He's been in computers more or less his whole life. Used to work for IBM as a technician. He never married, lives over the shop, seems to be his whole life. Nothing on record, ma'am, but there's something about him makes me edgy.'

Jane smiled and sat on the end of a table next to the whiteboard. 'Thanks George. Go with your instincts. Let's find out more about our Mr Gonzales. Now, everyone... Let's be clear, we need to be on our top game – all of us. Jamie was a young lad with his life before him. Whatever he was doing, and his mother is convinced he was 'up to something' – we need to find out, so let's get down to basics.'

Jane wrote on the whiteboard.

'Loretta – we want all CCTV coverage in and around the cafe, and I want you to go through it. Ross – start digging into Greaves, the company... history, the people who run it, any word on the streets about how it operates, as well as checking social media. Mark – you need to get into the internet cafe computers – especially the one Jamie was using – and find out what you can about what he was up to. George can get you the access we need.'

Jane watched as they took notes, and felt the energy levels picking up.

'Jag… can you contact Shirley, and check all is ok with Jamie's mum? She's due to bring her in for the ID at 10. I'd like you with us for that, ok? And George, can you publish your notes on Gonzales and Greaves so I can read it on the log, please?'

She paused. 'Ok, end of session. Thanks. We'll be taking a close look at Jamie's room at home later today, I hope. The main thing is I want everything you do and everything you find out on our shared log from now. We can't afford to lose any scrap of information. And remember, until I say otherwise… if anyone asks, and I mean anyone – this is not a murder investigation. Yet.'

George took a sip of coffee, and gave them his death stare, as Jane marched out into the corridor.

'Come on then, you lot. Get bloody moving!'

Paolo Gonzales hunched over his computer in his cramped back office, beads of sweat glistening on his forehead.

He'd been up since five, unable to sleep for the worry: a man dead, the police asking lots of questions, and Mr Hargreaves wanting a full report by 10 this morning. And his business closed down until the police told him otherwise. No punters, no revenue.

He frowned with concentration and gulped cold coffee as he absorbed the sequence of digits and code rapidly filling the screen. Jamie had been very busy during his two hour session, but where had he been looking?

Most customers came in to send emails to friends and family, usually overseas, so it was easy to analyse their data. It was a social thing for them – many of them had come to Manchester on casual contracts and they were a long way from home – so coming here was also a chance for them to chat, often in their own language.

But Jamie was different. He'd come in most afternoons, around 5 and usually stayed till closing time, though sometimes Paolo let him stay later – like last night. He was quiet, but friendly enough when you spoke to him. Never gave anything away, though.

Paolo had been curious. No, more than that, suspicious. When they were alone around closing time one night, Jamie had told him he did odd jobs for people, fixing computers, setting up WiFi, that sort of thing. And he always had a laptop bag with him...

Paolo quickly paused the scrolling display of code. Why hadn't he noticed? The police would want to know.

There was no sign of Jamie's laptop bag when they found his body.

Paolo's heart lurched when his mobile phone rang. He saw the caller's name on the screen. The office felt uncomfortably warm.

'Hello?'

'Mr Gonzales! How are you today? Let me get to the point, why are we still waiting for last month's instalment?'

'I'm sorry.'

'Your access comes at a price, Mr Gonzales. Let me make this perfectly clear. You need to pay what you owe within three working days.'

'The police have closed me down. No customers, so—' Gonzales chose his words carefully, explaining it was because one of his customers had died on the premises. 'Probably just a heart attack.'

'I see. You weren't closed last month, though, were you? Our records show your customers were very active on our sites. Obviously enjoying the... entertainment... we provide. And paying you for the privilege?'

'Yes, of course. OK. I will sort money.'

'Please, make sure you do... And if that guy was one of our customers, make sure you tidy things up. Have a lovely day.'

Paolo wiped a trembling hand across his brow, then stumbled across to mark his deadline on the wall planner above his desk.

He clicked the mouse and set the ticker tape of code flowing through the screen again.

A minute later, he stopped the scrolling and froze.

That boy had gone deep into the PC Cafe's systems. Enough to see that stuff.

'Shit!'

Gonzales thumped the desk hard, then pressed 'print'.

He heard the printer whirr into action behind him, and then immediately regretted it. If anyone finds a copy...

He could feel the panic rising. There was only one way out. He held his finger over the key that would delete all traces of Jamie's activity.

The dining chair creaked every time he moved an inch. The other guests spoke in whispers, making Allan even more conscious of the noise he was making. Still, the full English was to die for – probably literally. Allan demolished the last piece of bacon, and mopped up the egg yolk with a piece of toast.

The landlady was a very loud lady with a fresh face, a curly mass of brown hair, and a strong Irish accent, who insisted on being called Moll... 'No airs and graces here, love, just make yerself at home, you know'.

She'd welcomed him like a long lost friend when he'd apologetically rung the doorbell at 9am and asked if he could have a room for a couple of nights, 'And is there any chance of having breakfast now?'

No sooner had the words left his mouth than he was escorted past the cubbyhole that passed as the reception desk and into the front room.

'Ah just dump yer bag right there, me darlin'' cried Moll. 'What'll ye be wanting then? You look like a full English kind of fella to me.'

Allan agreed and was soon brought up to speed about how breakfast service worked at the Derry Rose Hotel. the buffet table piled up with small boxes of cereals he hadn't seen since school; jugs of various coloured liquids that resembled fresh juice but were anything but; pots of yoghurt; muffins, croissants, and a card on the table listing his other options – which included porridge, kippers, eggs your style and various combinations of egg, bacon, sausage, mushroom, baked beans, black pudding.

The small print at the bottom proclaimed that this establishment used locally sourced ingredients, which Allan assumed meant Moll making a regular trip to the Tesco he passed on the drive into Lyme Regis.

But he wasn't complaining now, as he looked out and saw the sun begin to burnish the giant boulders and ancient stone that formed The Cobb, in the distance.

Sneaking out before Moll could accost him again, he grabbed his bag and his room key from the hall, spread himself out on the bed, then reached for his phone.

It was time to talk to Jane, and he'd dreaded this moment since he set off from the Travelodge near Stafford three hours ago.

But now, he felt relaxed all of a sudden, no doubt helped by the overeating and the knowledge that the rest of the day was his own. When was the last time he'd been able to say that?

He sat up, pressed the screen and listened to the ringing tone... No answer.

Allan lay back on the bed and closed his eyes and decided he'd send Jane a text. Later.

Jane glanced at the incoming call message as her phone's vibration nudged it across her desk.

Allan. She pressed reject and carried on her desk phone conversation with Shirley, who'd spent the night at Irene's house.

'Sorry, Shirley, carry on where you left off. All quiet, you said…'

'I managed to get her to go to bed, ma'am. I could hear her moving around, but only in her room.'

'No suggestion of her going into Jamie's room?'

'I told her she mustn't and she said she wouldn't be able to face going in there anyway.'

'Good. Well done. Did you get any more out of her before she went up?'

'She kept going on about how he'd changed; become more serious, lately, whatever that means.'

'Well there is a possible angle involving online betting. The internet cafe where we found him is owned by Greaves. Jamie, with his technical knowledge, could have been hacking in from that cafe. Maybe felt safer doing it there.'

'Right. Oh! Sorry ma'am. She's coming downstairs, I'd better go.'

'Thanks Shirley. I'll send Jag round to pick her up just before 10, but we'll call you if anything changes on that. Can you make sure she's up to coming in to do the ID and let me know if not?'

'Yes, ma'am.'

'Ok, bye Shirley. And don't worry, you'll be back in your own bed tonight, I hope!'

'Don't worry about me, ma'am. As my boyfriend will tell you, I can sleep anywhere!'

Jane smiled as she put the phone down, but it faded as she checked her mobile.

Allan hadn't even left a bloody message.

She tried to damp down the anger building inside. It didn't happen often, but when the rage took hold, it was hard to hold it back. Last night, she was too tired to give a toss. 'Let the little boy go and play out for a while,' she'd said to herself. But now, maybe it was more serious than that. Maybe the life she'd dreamed of with Allan was just that – a pathetic dream.

She remembered the first time she'd gone for a drink with him. It was at that cool new wine bar in the converted cotton mill; what was it? Spinning Jenny's? She'd shocked him by asking for Sex on the Beach, and she'd loved him from that moment for his embarrassment, his obvious relief when she changed her order to prosecco, and the fact that he was pretty good looking.

That was just over two years ago, and he was also loving, kind, funny, modest – all the things she wanted but had failed to find. She could look after herself, but he was a big man, and he made her feel safe in his arms.

Two years…

Jane could feel the bubble rising again as she wondered for the first time… has he found someone else? She'd been engaged to Steve, then found him necking a girl young enough to be his daughter. History repeating itself?

Her thoughts were interrupted by a loud knock at the door. Steadying herself, she pressed Enter on the keypad. Forensic Phil walked in, and threw himself in the chair opposite, wearing a very satisfied smile.

'I think I've cracked it Jane!'

SEVEN

SHIRLEY HAD MANAGED TO coax Irene into a few mouthfuls of Weetabix and warm milk before Jag tapped on the door.

They stood in the hall, and spoke quietly, the morning sun bathing them in an almost ecclesiastical glow, thanks to the stained glass in the vestibule door.

'How is she? Is she ok?'

Shirley nodded as she reached for her uniform jacket on the hat stand. 'She's ok. Holding it together.'

'What about you?'

'Oh I'm all right. We chatted for a bit, mainly about Jamie.'

'Did you get anything new?'

'Not really. Doesn't sound like he had close friends apart from one guy called Martin she mentioned, or girl friends, but he was doing ok with his IT work, apparently. Anyway, Irene was getting really groggy so I packed her off, and managed a bit of a power nap on the sofa. Is someone coming to relieve me, do you know?'

'Yeah, Jane said, could you hang on for an hour, and the team will be round to go over the house. She wants to get the ID over first, before she gets Irene's ok for all that.'

'Right. Tell the boss I'll do a note for the log before I bunk off. You ready then? You wait in the car while I get her sorted. I feel so sorry for her...'

Jag instinctively reached out a hand; then pulled it back. She wouldn't want that. It was easy to forget that Family Liaison was just one part of Shirley's job: most of her time she was out on the beat, and Jag had already seen at close quarters how tough she was. He decided, correctly, that a touch of male chauvinistic sympathy wouldn't go down too well.

He turned away as she headed off down the hall, and sat in the car, listening to radio messages about shoplifting, minor RTAs, and domestics. He called in to let them know they were about to bring Irene in, and was beginning to get impatient, but then he saw Irene coming out with Shirley, and he realised he'd only been waiting ten minutes.

Irene had put on a long dark overcoat that made her look even more pale. But she held her head high and her back was straight.

Shirley opened the rear door for her, but she said she'd prefer to sit in the front. Jag smiled at her as she settled in, leaning over to help her with the seatbelt.

Shirley waved as they drove away, the concern etched on her face. Irene was holding herself together. But for how much longer?

'What do you mean, cracked it?'

Phil certainly had Jane's attention, and he was ready to give her chapter and verse on how Jamie died.

He leaned forward, spreading his notes out in front of him, opened his mouth to speak... and George marched in.

'Sorry to interrupt, ma'am.'

Phil didn't think he looked at all sorry.

'Yes, George?'

'Jag's just called in. He's on his way with Jamie's mother now.'

'Right, thanks George.'

He stopped at the door and turned.

'One more thing, ma'am... Gonzales just rang. He says Jamie always brought his laptop with him on his visits to the cafe. He's just realised – he says – that it wasn't there last night.'

'Interesting. OK, make a call to Shirley, ask her to check if it's in the house. Tell her it's not a search, because we haven't got a warrant yet; it's just a quiet wander round, making sure everything's in order.'

George smiled and called over his shoulder as he walked away, leaving the door open, much to Phil's annoyance. 'Understood, ma'am.'

Jane checked her Swatch – the black one with the gold bezel Allan bought for her birthday last year. She briefly wondered what he was doing and if she would see him again, then turned to Phil.

'Well, I'm really sorry, Phil, I don't think we've got time for this now. Irene will be here in ten minutes, and we need to be ready for her. Best not say anything to her, until we've had chance to talk it through, but let's see if we can keep her here a short time while you bring me up to speed, all right?'

Phil grabbed his notes, scraped the chair back as he stood, and said, rather unconvincingly, that it was fine and he'd brief her later.

Jane took a few of her Pilates breaths.

She remembered the Fiona Worsley case, and how besieged with information she was. It's so hard to step back and focus. The team were doing their jobs, but she had to be able to prioritise. She was the one to decide what was important, and she was determined to do this her way.

Charles Aston would expect nothing less. She could hear his voice…

'What the bloody hell am I paying you for Jane, but to take the lead? I keep telling you, trust your instincts. No bugger else will. Apart from me, of course!'

She stood to put her black Reiss jacket on, and checked herself in the mirror.

As she stepped out into the corridor, she paused at Charles Aston's office door, as she often did. She put a hand on the fake brass name plate: 'Thank you boss', she whispered.

'Oh I do like to be beside the seaside…'

Allan sang to himself sarcastically, dropping his head down into the wind as he walked in splendid isolation along the stone walkway of The Cobb, made famous by the film of the book, The French Lieutenant's Woman, by son of Lyme Regis John Fowles.

Allan had read in one of the leaflets he picked up at the museum on the other side of town that Meryl Streep braved stormy winds to walk over the dark stone boulders right to the end of the breakwater, looking enigmatic in her billowing cloak.

'Bet it was a bloody stuntman,' Allan muttered to no-one in particular, as the strong wind carried the first drops of rain forecast for the rest of the day. But he was determined to do it, and began hopping across the flat tops, where the black rock was streaked with seagull shit. 'Didn't show that in the movie, did they?'

Allan was peeved about the weather, but it was a minor gripe. Tomorrow was looking good for his guided fossil walk on the beach, here on what was known as the Jurassic Coast

– though there was nothing prehistoric about the property prices.

He turned his back to the wind and the town stretched out before him.

He'd also read that John Fowles had described the place as 'perched like a herring gull on a ledge, suspiciously peering both ways in Devon and Dorset.'

Allan failed to see the resemblance, decided against a selfie and took a panorama shot instead. He walked back towards Marine Parade, in search of a cafe/takeaway allegedly famed for its hog roast baps and its doughnuts, if you believed Tripadvisor.

As he walked, he wondered if and when he'd actually be able to talk to Jane over the phone, when she was in the middle of trying to sort out what happened to that lad, Jamie. He'd told himself after his nap – when he was not batting away the attentions of the loud but admittedly rather lovely Moll – that a text was his best bet. That way, he reasoned, at least she'd see that she was in his thoughts, even if she was too busy to talk to him.

He'd send the text around lunchtime. Definitely.

The rain was coming down harder now and Allan jogged onto Marine Parade in search of his midday snack. And there was the place, just over the road. With a sign on the door, black on yellow, 'Sorry folks. Closed today due to unforeseen circs. Back tomorrow!'

'Bollocks!' said Allan, grimacing an apology to a woman in a yellow mac with a yellow hood, red wellies, and a very wet black labrador, but she was totally unfazed.

'They do a very good pulled pork sandwich in the pub, if you're desperate.' She pointed in the direction of the museum. 'It's only a short walk that way.'

Allan summoned a smile and wiped the rain out of his eyes. 'Thank you, that's very kind. I'll give it a try.'

The woman in yellow smiled as Allan jogged off towards the pub with as much dignity as he could.

She called after him. 'Oh, hang on! I don't think they'll be open yet!'

But the man hadn't heard. She shrugged, then ran, cursing, as her dog scurried across the road nose to the ground as it followed an irresistible scent.

Graeme Hargreaves wondered what it was about IT specialists that made them think jeans and hoodies were appropriate office wear.

Still, he couldn't complain about the guy sitting on the other side of his grey steel desk. Not yet, anyway.

Adrian Cheshire was the best in the business, and for that reason had been parachuted in as head of department, after Graeme persuaded him to leave Google less than two months ago.

But now, it was time to find out what young Adrian was really about.

Graeme leaned forward, his right hand resting on a clipping from the FT. He slid it across the desk to Adrian. 'Have a read of that.'

'OK boss.' Adrian took a breath and concentrated on the trademark thin pink paper clipping. It was the first item under 'News In Brief'.

> *'Shares in online betting market leader Greaves are down 4.2 per cent, amid rumours that the company's internal systems have been hacked.*
>
> *'Greaves CEO, Graeme Hargreaves, reassured shareholders they had nothing to fear. "These are malicious scaremongering tactics by our rivals," he said.*

'It's disappointing, but not surprising. Our systems are robust and if there is ever a hint of weakness, be in no doubt it will be swiftly dealt with. The company is in a very healthy state, and we are looking forward to posting strong results at our annual meeting next month.'

Adrian looked up and frowned as he tapped a note into his iPad: 'I'll get onto it, sir.'

Graeme smiled but the words conveyed a touch of menace. 'You certainly will, Adrian. I want you to throw everything at this. Full inquiry. If someone is getting behind our security, I need to know who, how and where, and I need to know quickly.'

He paused, and the smile quickly disappeared. 'I don't need to tell you how damaging this could be if we don't stamp on it.'

Adrian sat up straighter, his dark eyes looking over Graeme's shoulder as he began thinking it through. He'd already realised that, at 27 years old, he was facing his biggest test yet. But this was the man who gave him his big chance in life, and he had no intention of letting him down. Graeme knew he had a tough streak himself, and that's why he was here.

Adrian massaged his fist. 'So, do you think it's more than just rumours?'

'I have to work on the basis that it is true. We can't afford to take chances. It's probably just coincidence, but this stuff has come out the day after a young computer nerd was found dead in one of our internet cafes…'

'Jesus!'

'—and the guy who manages it reckons the police suspect murder. So we've got some crisis management on our hands now.'

'Do you think there's a link?'

'Just makes me wonder, that's all. Who knows what we'll find when you start digging.'

'I'll start digging right now. Starting with that internet cafe.'

'Good.' Graeme sighed as his computer pinged. He turned to look at the monitor. 'There goes another 0.5 per cent off the share price.' He stood, the meeting was over. 'Just remember, in business – especially this one – everything and everyone is hard to believe. I want a daily update. I want this sorted. Understood? Nothing, and I mean nothing, matters more to me right now. Whoever is doing this needs to be found. You still do a bit of boxing, don't you?'

Adrian nodded. The slight kink in his nose, and the puffy right eye might be a bit of a giveaway. 'Still do the training, anyway.'

'You're built like a brick shithouse. So go and throw your weight around, ok?'

Adrian stood at just over six feet, head and shoulders taller than his boss, and a good deal more muscled. But as he looked in his boss's eyes and saw the strength there, he remembered what his dad always used to say when he was teaching him how to box: 'Show respect, but never be afraid… the bigger they are, the harder they fall.'

He knew he'd be the first to fall if he didn't get results. 'Leave it with me, boss. I'll find them.'

'You know what, Adrian? You'd better. Otherwise we're both on the bloody canvas.'

Graeme swivelled as his secretary buzzed him, announcing over the speakerphone that she had Mr Gonzales on the line. As Adrian closed the door, Graeme was leaning back in his chair, chatting into his desk phone as if he hadn't a care in the world.

'Mr Gonzales! Good. I wanted a word with you…'

Jane and Jag sat facing Irene across the canteen table, mugs of untouched tea in front of them.

Irene had held her composure right up to the moment Phil gently turned back the sheet that was covering her son's face. It was the trigger for a cry of anguish that must have been heard right through the station.

Phil had put an arm round Irene's shoulder and she had collapsed onto him, as he slowly eased her into his chair. They formed a protective circle around her as she wept, and Jag kept her supplied with tissues from a box on Phil's desk.

Still wearing her dark coat, she kept saying his name, over and over again, until at last, as her sobbing began to subside, Phil sat next to her and put a hand on her shoulder.

'You must have been very proud of Jamie, Mrs Castleton. I hope it is some consolation to know that he didn't suffer, didn't feel any pain. Please believe me.'

Jane and Jag exchanged glances. They both knew Phil was indispensable at times like these. An only son who stayed at home until his 30s to nurse his mum through ravaging cancer, he'd been through grief only ten years later when his wife Elaine died. Jane made another mental note to try and persuade him not to retire.

Now, though, he was back at his desk, and Jamie was locked away in a steel cabinet. waiting for what Phil expected would be his final examination – the one that revealed once and for all how he died.

Jane waited, the tea warming her hands, sensing that Irene would want to talk; needed to talk.

Finally, Irene sipped her tea and looked up.

Jane spoke quietly. 'Phil was right. You are proud of Jamie, aren't you?'

'Yes. We went through a lot, him and me.'

Jag chipped in. 'And it sounds like you both came through it.'

'We did… Jamie more than me. He lost himself in his computers. But he always had time for me…' Irene dabbed her eyes as Jag handed her another tissue from the box on the table next to him.

Jane studied Irene before moving things along, conscious that the clock was ticking. Whoever killed Jamie could strike again.

'Irene… you said yesterday that Jamie had gone distant, staying out late, not communicating. Did you work out why?'

Irene shook her head. 'I couldn't understand. He'd always been a loving son, in his own way. But, about six weeks ago, he started going a bit distant, staying out late…'

'Did he say where he was, what he was doing?'

'No. It was always – 'working late, mum' – but I saw him once when I was out at the shops – they were open till 8 on a Thursday, and he was with Martin; and they were arguing. '

Jag looked up from his notebook. 'Do you know Martin's second name?'

'Sutton, I think… yes, Sutton. He lives in one of them new houses. Moved out from Jesamond Street. I used to see his mum out and about. Not any more. Used to go to Holt School together.'

Jane leaned forward. 'What were they arguing about, Irene? What did you hear?'

'Jamie was having a right go at him. I couldn't hear what they were saying, but Martin was giving as good as he got. I thought he was going to hit Jamie. He was jabbing him, shouting, tried to grab his bag, that sort of thing.'

'Ok. When we came to see you last night, you immediately thought Jamie had been killed. Is that why you said that? Was it something Martin said that day? Is there anything else you can tell us? I know it's hard, Irene, but please think carefully.'

Irene sipped her tea: quick sips, like a bird, Jane thought.

'It was just… he changed so much, stopped talking. I'm – I was… his mother… I just knew something was wrong.

It was like, you know, he had done something bad and he didn't want me to know. He was never a good liar. I always knew.'

'Did you ask him directly?'

Irene looked indignant. 'Of course I did! He just said he had lots on his mind, about work.'

Jane reached out to touch her hand. 'Sorry we have to ask these questions, Irene. One more thing… we need to search Jamie's room, see if we can find anything that might help to explain what happened. Is that ok?'

Irene just nodded.

'Thanks Irene. I'll leave you with Jag now. He'll give you a form to sign, and there's a few bits of detail we need before we take you home. Would you like me to arrange for someone to stay with you, someone we can call?'

'There's no-one.' Irene took a deep breath. 'I'll manage.'

Jane left the canteen without looking back. Her phone pinged the arrival of a text. It was from the hospice.

'Please call us about Mr Aston. Thank you.'

Jane slammed her office door.

The man who took the call spoke with practiced calm. 'Charles's family are with him, and they asked that you be informed… He doesn't have much time left now. He's not in any pain. I'm so sorry…'

'How long, do you know?'

'It's so difficult to say. We think no more than a few hours. He is very weak. Please believe me when I say that he is comfortable and peaceful now.'

'Thank you for being straight with me. Please say thank you to the family for letting me know. Tell them – tell them I won't come. This is their time.. And… give Charles and them my love…'

Jane didn't give him time to say anything else. She disconnected the call, and tried to stifle the sobs that now convulsed her.

She wanted to be at his bedside, but his family wouldn't want that. She'd known this moment was coming. Told herself so many times, and convinced herself she would cope.

'Deal with it, Jane.' She could hear him saying it. She reached in a drawer for her tissues.

Her phone pinged again. Another text message.

'Just wanted to let you know I'm ok. But wishing you were here. Missing you badly already! Call you later xx.'

Jane sat down and sipped water, trying to quell the rising tide of anxiety that welled inside. She didn't care about lost pride, she just didn't want to be alone tonight. She tapped out a reply.

'Please come home Allan. I need you. jx'

Paolo Gonzales was still trying to shake off the effects of his whisky-fuelled night, and the substantial hair of the dog he'd had this morning after the phone call.

He thought he heard thunder. He unglued his eyes slowly and squinted at the sun from the sofa in his bedsit above the cafe. His pounding head would have preferred darkness. Then it slowly registered: it wasn't thunder. Someone was hammering on the door.

Mark Manning attempted a smile as Gonzales opened the door, despite the sight that greeted him.

Gonzales was a short barrel of a man, wearing only a grubby white vest and shabby jeans. He looked like he hadn't shaved for days, and when he spoke, he exuded alcohol and stale food.

'Morning Mr Gonzales! My name is Mark, Ashbridge Police. I'm here to take a look at your computer set up, if that's ok?'

Then, as Gonzales looked puzzled and scratched his chest.

Mark held up his ID. 'Mr Creasey did tell you I'd be calling?'

'Oh. Yes. Excuse.' He stepped back as Mark stepped in, his laptop bag in front like a battering ram. 'This way.'

Mark was in the cramped back office with Gonzales breathing heavily next to him, and he felt claustrophobic. He'd told Lorry about his fear of confined spaces, and she'd not been that sympathetic: 'Don't worry, love, I've got a king size bed.'

Mark dared to take a deep breath. 'Could you open a window, please, and is there any chance of a tea?'

Gonzales obediently wrestled the ill fitting sash window open a few inches. 'Only coffee. How you like it?'

George had warned him about the coffee. 'OK, just a glass of water, please, thank you. I'd better get on. Can you show me the computer Jamie was working on, please?'

'I get changed first.'

'That's great, thanks.' That sounded wrong, but Mark shrugged and took a look round. This was the back office then. A mess of papers filled the small desk, and a litter of cables trailed underneath, connecting the network computers. He could hear Gonzales thudding around upstairs as he sussed out the hardware.

Pretty modern, and some of it looked new. Probably part of the package when Greaves took over the place, he suspected.

Mark was surprised Ashbridge and Manchester could sustain so many internet cafes. Greaves owned six, and there were a few others. Interesting they should want to invest in dumps like this, but maybe it was just a way of acquiring High Street property. Internet cafes had done well after the first one opened about 20 years ago, but times had changed. Most people had some very powerful kit at home, and carried smartphones, so why bother?

Mark frowned. That was the nub of it. Why was Jamie even here? He wasn't sure what he'd find out today, but he was sure he'd find something.

Gonzales reappeared, a new man, wearing an open neck blue shirt and grey flannels. The smell was different but just as overpowering. Mark guessed he must have used a whole can of Lynx Africa, but the garlic on his breath was still winning.

'Ok, this way. I show you.'

Mark walked through; the windows giving any passers by a good view inside, he noted. And the work stations were close together. Not exactly private.

Gonzales held out the chair like a head waiter, and Mark sat where Jamie had been. He remembered the buzz of his first internet cafe in Bristol. Packed out with students from all over the world. And Mark. Must have been about 15 years ago…

'Thank you Mr Gonzales. If you could give me the access code so I can look at your back systems as well, please?'

Gonzales wrote down a sequence of upper and lower case letters and numbers and handed it over without a word, before walking out to the office.

Mark heard a phone ringing, which was good because that would keep Gonzales out of his hair – and his nose – for a while. He tapped a few keys to open up the operating system and got to work, against the background of Mr Gonzales's guttural grunts as he took the call.

Less than a minute later, Mark was plugging in one of his own USB drives, and setting the program running.

He sat back and sipped water, watching the cursor blink. Then he leaned forward as the code filled the dark screen.

Something caught his eye and he froze the action with the touch of a key. His hunch was correct.

'Got you,' he whispered.

Allan was in the pub, polishing off a meat pie.

He stared again at Jane's message: *'I need you'.*

There was no explanation; not that he needed one. Not so long ago, she could have said peel me a grape and he'd have jumped to it. Anyway, he'd find out why soon enough.

He read his reply: *'On my way. Back this afty xx'*

He scooped up the last chunk of pie and looked out from The Cobb Inn across the bay, as the sun shone searchlight beams on the sea. The clouds were still sucking up whispy dark columns of moisture on the horizon, but at least Allan could make it back to the B&B without getting another soaking. He hoped.

He turned away from the view, banged his pint pot on the bar, called out a thank you to the portly landlord, and checked his watch as he pushed out through the swing door onto Marine Parade.

His trusty Seiko Kinetic showed 11.25, which he guessed would mean an ETA in Ashbridge by the end of the afternoon. Allan groaned at the prospect of the M6 through Birmingham, and decided he'd better shell out for the toll route.

Allan walked as quickly as he could under the influence of a pint and a pie, and asked himself why he'd left Jane last night, and driven more than 300 miles, only to immediately hurry back because of a text message.

Halfway up the hill, he stopped for breath. The sun had found a proper gap in the clouds and the seagulls were arguing near the fish and chip shop. Below him, the gardens sloped down to Marine Parade.

'Get moving, Allan,' he muttered, and walked on, vowing to return one day.

EIGHT

PHIL WAS WAITING IN the corridor when Jane returned from the cloakroom.

It felt like all her emotional energy was gone. As she slowly regained a semblance of self control in the ladies, Jane remembered the words of her Uncle Bill – a DCI with a broad Yorkshire accent: 'The higher you go, the less you let your feelings show. You have to save it till you get home, love.'

Jane straightened her back and looked in the mirror as she obliterated the shock with wet wipes, mascara and a touch of foundation.

But it didn't fool Phil.

'You ok, Jane?'

Jane briskly opened the door and led the way in. 'Sorry to have to tell you, Phil, but I've just been told Charles is on his last legs now.'

Phil sat and puffed his cheeks. 'Oh God. How long…?'

'A few hours, maybe. They can't be sure.'

'No, of course. Are you going?'

Jane's lip trembled slightly but she held it back. 'No, he's got his family with him, that's what counts.' She sat down and fidgeted with her pen. 'Right, come on Phil. I know you were close, too. But we have to talk about Jamie. I'm already under pressure from region to go public. Is this definitely a murder inquiry? So… let's do Charles proud.'

Phil smiled sadly and ran a hand over his grey hair. 'I can almost hear him telling us to get on with it. Stop mucking about.'

Jane nodded and opened her notebook.

Phil got the message. 'Ok… I've ruled out aconite as the cause of death. I've looked into it and it just doesn't fit, sorry, despite my earlier confidence. So, I've had to go back to square one.'

'That's ok. Are you 100 per cent sure of what you're about to tell me now, though, Phil?'

'Yes, ma'am.'

'Good. OK, give me the condensed version, in a way an idiot like me can understand.'

Phil turned a few pages in his A4 notebook and caught the movement as Jane glanced at her watch.

'I'll make this quick, I promise… Right. Jamie died because he was injected with sux.'

'What?'

'Sux… proper name, suxamethonium chloride. It's widely used in hospitals, critical care, to paralyze patients before a life saving operation. In their hands, it's perfectly safe because it is only given when the patient is on respiratory support and has been given a sedative. But if not… it's not only lethal, it is fast acting, and fast to leave the system, too.'

'My God… so how did you—?'

'I'm giving you the quick synopsis, Jane, but I'm putting everything on the log today…

The point is, it acts within seconds, freezing every muscle, everything in the body. Given quickly through a needle, you'd only notice a light sting – the sort of skin tingle you'd get with prickly heat, which Jamie suffered from.

'Once it was in him, he'd lose the use of his fingers almost immediately…'

'Of course, his hand still on the keyboard.'

Phil nodded 'It's amazing stuff, and it's been used by anaesthetists for around 50 years. It was first used criminally in the 60s, by a doctor in America.'

Jane tried to steer Phil away from history. 'No doubt in your mind?'

'Not a shred. It's a tricky substance to trace, but once I'd found out about that doctor, it didn't take long to track down the techniques now being used in forensic science. The key to finding it is the two different elements that make up the drug. And I found the metabolites succinic acid and choline in tissue samples taken from Jamie.'

'That's brilliant work, Phil. Sounds like a tough one. I'd never heard of it.'

'It just meant thinking differently, boss. The way he died, it eventually clicked once I'd connected the idea of an injection with hospital treatment.' He looked up at Jane with an apologetic grin. 'I also racked up a hell of a phone bill, talking to a mate in America who's an expert on forensic analysis of these neuromuscular blocking agents, so it's not all my own work.'

Jane smiled. 'I'll send you the bill. So the big question now is, who would be likely to have a supply of sux..'

'And the obvious answer is medical staff. Or someone who works in a veterinary surgery.'

'Really?' Jane frowned. 'Well I'm not inclined to reveal any of this to the public. The last thing we need is anything that affects people's trust of the NHS, or their vet. But the other thing on my mind is the syringe. We need to find it.'

She stood and headed for the door. 'Thanks again, Phil. I'll read the full report later. But I've told you before, you can't ever retire, and this clinches it.'

Phil chuckled as he snapped his notebook shut. 'It may surprise you to know that I'm already thinking again. This has been such a learning curve for me. It's given me a new lease of life...'

They both acknowledged the irony with a grimace, but Jane raised a smile.

'That's the best news I've had all day, Phil. We need you. Anyway, time for me to make our murder inquiry official.'

'Second one, ma'am.'

'Yes, and I have the feeling this will be a lot tougher.'

'So what were you arguing about, Martin?'

Lorry had occupied most of the small red settee, leaving Jag struggling to find the elbow room to even get the pen out of his pocket, let alone write anything down.

Lorry leaned forward, elbows on knees, and he took the opportunity to extricate himself and perch on the arm.

Martin Sutton may have been one of Jamie's best friends, but he was less than communicative. Jag had tracked the family down to this address; a narrow three storey town house on an estate of identical homes, and he'd readily agreed to George's suggestion that he assist Lorry with the interview.

'Can't remember.' Martin sprawled in an armchair, legs wide apart, endlessly revolving a remote control in his hand.

'Really?' Lorry was keeping her cool, but for how much longer? 'Martin, can I remind you that Jamie is dead. You need to talk to us. He was your best friend, I'm told...'

'Yeah, he was a good mate.'

'So what happened that day. You two were really giving it out, weren't you?'

Martin yawned. 'Whatever.'

'I'm going to ask one more time, Martin. If you keep this up, you're going to be coming with us to the station. Is that what you want, eh?'

Martin tried to hide it by elaborately scratching his nose, but Jag saw the flicker of fear in his eyes, just as Lorry's mobile rang out, and headed for the door as she checked the screen.

'Can you carry on, please, Jag?'

Jag smiled at Martin, and put his notebook away.

'Listen, Martin, no-one's accusing you of anything, you know? We just have to ask these questions so we can work out what happened to Jamie. His death was really sudden and we need to find out why, talk to people who knew him. That's the only reason we're here, all right?'

'I don't know what I can tell you. Yeah, we had a barney, but that was weeks ago—'

Lorry walked back in slowly, pocketing her phone, and kept her eyes on Martin as she sat back down. Martin was a big lad, and judging by the tight t shirt, probably into weights she reckoned. But so was she.

'Look, we're trying to be nice. As far as we know, you're not in any trouble, so why not relax and start talking to us? Now, preferably… you see, Martin, I've just been informed by our Detective Chief Inspector that this is now a murder inquiry. So, think about that, and for the last time, tell me about the last time you saw Jamie, or you are going on a little ride with us…'

'Shit.' Martin's eyes were locked onto hers as he weighed up his options. He sighed.

'OK.'

Jag opened his notebook as Martin told his story…

'I'd seen him in that crap internet place on the High Street—'

Jag interrupted: 'The Pretty Cool Cafe?'

'Yeah, that's the shithole. I bumped into him, like, and I was, like, what are you doing in there? I mean, he's got all the gear at home, he's well into computers... Just taking the mick.'

Lorry wasn't pulling her punches today. 'Why should it worry you what he does in his spare time, Martin?'

'Because, like you said, he's a mate, all right? I was a bit worried about him. He looked thinner, and everything, so I asked him, and... I couldn't believe it.'

Jag looked up. 'What couldn't you believe?'

'He told me – straight up, no word of a lie – that he'd been hacking into these betting sites, making a bloody fortune, he said.'

'What did you say to that, Martin?'

'I told him he was mental. He'd get nicked.'

Lorry laughed. 'You're a real public spirited sort of guy, aren't you? You know what I think? You, my friend, are talking bollocks.'

Martin leaned forward, his fists clenched, but Lorry was unmoved.

'Come on Jag, we're going.'

Martin laughed. 'Yeah, about bleedin' time.'

'And you're coming with us.'

'What the f—'

Lorry lifted him off the chair with one hand under his arm.

'You're helping us with our inquiries. Is that alright with you, Mister Sutton? Don't worry, Jag will leave a note for mummy to let her know where you are. All right, Jag?'

Jag nodded and held the door open as Lorry marched down the path to his car, fired the remote to unlock it, then turned back and left a note on the mantlepiece.

As he closed the living room door behind him, he noticed a tote bag, partially hidden by a pile of DVDs near the television.

It was blue, with a logo printed in white. Jag moved closer, careful not to touch anything else.

Jag wrote a note and took a picture on his phone. The logo was in the style of a rubber stamp… Greaves Online Betting

The ops room was almost empty, but had obviously had a spring clean after Jane's confirmation that they were on a murder hunt.

The whiteboard had been cleared of the usual not very funny doodles, desks were tidier than she'd ever seen them, and even Ross seemed in the zone.

Jane sat on the edge of the conference table. Well, at least George and Ross were here…

'Where's Jag and Lorry?'

Ross grinned. 'In the showroom, ma'am.'

'What?'

'Jag and Lorry… car showroom?'

'That's terrible, Ross…'

'Sorry boss, but you have to admit – that's an awesome name for a double act. They're on their way in, with Martin Sutton. Lorry says he's a real piece of work. Should be here in ten.'

'OK. What's the story about the argument, do we know?'

George chipped in. 'Lorry reckons he's spinning a yarn, but I'm not so sure. He told her he'd been arguing with Jamie because he was bragging about making cash from an online betting scam.'

'Well that actually fits with what we already suspect. She must have a reason for questioning it. Any news on Greaves, Ross?'

Ross clicked the mouse and glanced at his monitor. Unlike the rest of the team, he had 'moved on' – his words – from pen and paper. Everything was recorded or tapped into his smartphone or tablet before being transcribed into text on his desktop. Jane hadn't a clue how it worked, but had relented in the face of his earnest argument... 'Boss, it saves time, I make less mistakes, and it saves paper.'

She snapped back into the moment as Ross scanned his screen. 'I started by getting the official line, and rang their PR department. They said rumours of systematic hacking are being spread maliciously by their rivals; their systems are robust, what's the fuss?: the usual guff. So next, I got on my bike to check out their HQ off Piccadilly. The reception area looks like a 5 star hotel—'

George snorted. 'I wouldn't know.'

'So anyway, I decided to hang around at the Pret a few doors down. I figured staff would use it at lunchtime...'

George again. 'What the hell's Pret?'

Ross sighed. 'You need to get out more, George. Pret... Pret a Manger? They do good food, to go.'

'Right. So it's a sandwich shop.'

Jane hid a smile. 'And you were right, were you, Ross?'

'Yes ma'am. They weren't difficult to spot. Loads of them had black t-shirts with the company logo. So I got talking to a group of them who were sitting near me at the window.'

George grumbled. 'All women, no doubt.'

Ross winked at him, annoyingly. 'Of course, George! Anyway, they were cagey, but I made out I was thinking of applying for a job, just wanting a bit of background.'

Jane approved. 'Devious. I like it. So... anything?'

'They must have thought I'd got no chance, the way I was talking, but after I'd warmed them up a bit, I said I was getting cold feet because of the press stuff about hacking, and there was a real change in the atmosphere then.'

'In what way?'

'There's obviously something going on, ma'am. They'd been really chatty and loud, but they dropped right down. Started talking about a new guy who's apparently been brought in from Google – and they reckon he must have had a massive offer to come to Manchester. Name of… Adrian Cheshire. They laughed at first, thinking he'd be interviewing me, but three of the girls said this guy had already started an internal inquiry.'

'Into the hacking?'

'Yes, ma'am. He's lined up interviews with all IT staff, asking for programming activity reports, screenshots, purchases, accounts, expenses, the whole thing.'

'They really opened up to you, didn't they?'

Ross shrugged. 'Used my charm, ma'am.'

Jane rolled her eyes in mock horror. 'Of course you did… But very well done.There's no doubt Greaves is taking this seriously, despite their public statements…'

'That's right, ma'am. And this guy Cheshire is a big hitter. I checked him out when I got back just now. He was top man in Google's development division, he was poached by Greaves only a few weeks ago, and says on his LinkedIn profile he's a middleweight boxer.'

'Best put George onto him then… But the timing of his appointment is interesting. It's either pure coincidence…'

George jumped in again. 'Or confirmation of a possible motive, ma'am?'

'Exactly. Thanks Ross. We've now got a viable lead. It's early days, but you've given us something to work on, which is excellent. So let's crack on. I'll talk to young Martin with Lorry when they get here; see if I can work out why Lorry doubts his story. Can you observe from the back room, please Ross?'

Ross simply said 'Sick', which Jane assumed meant he approved. 'Mark is still at the internet cafe, so we'll have another get together when he gets back, hopefully with the full team. We'll have to see how this goes, but don't worry, I'll get more resources if we need them. For now, I don't need to tell you, all leave is cancelled. And, to repeat, everything said in here is between us unless I say otherwise. Oh, and just so you know, I'll be doing a press briefing around 6pm, to fit in with the tv schedules. As you can imagine, I can't wait for that.'

Jane pushed herself up off the table. 'Thanks you two. I'm proud to have you both on the team.'

Ross surprised her by not being sarcastic. He just turned back to his monitor: 'Ta boss. Break a leg.'

George just grunted and lumbered off towards his coffee jar.

Jane needed time to go through the log to see what else had turned up, so she could prep her press statement, but as soon as she sat down and entered her password, her phone rang.

Shirley had stayed on at Irene's place pending the issue of Irene's permission for a search.

'Afternoon, ma'am. I just wanted to let you know the lads have taken away Jamie's desktop but there was no sign of a laptop, I'm afraid.'

'Shirley, thanks. Anything else turned up?'

'Well, he was into Star Wars and old sci fi movies. Quite a collection. No books, no diary. Nothing personal at all.'

'What? Nothing?'

'No, ma'am. One of the guys said it was like looking round a tidy office.'

'Maybe mum tidied up.'

'Well she promised me she hadn't touched it.'

'What about the bed?'

'No sign of sexual activity. They're checking the wardrobe now.'

Jane could hear doors being opened and closed. 'It struck me that all Jamie's clothes looked new, as if he really cared about his appearance. So, we have to hope Mark can get something off the desktop.'

'Yes, I think so… Oh, I spoke to Irene, and she said Jamie had a pretty big laptop bag he carried everywhere. Said she looked in it once, and couldn't believe the amount of stuff he was lugging around.'

'What sort of stuff?'

'She didn't know what it was, but from what she said, it sounds like storage drives and memory sticks, cables, the usual sort of stuff.'

'Frustrating that it's disappeared, but it's clear someone doesn't want us to find it…'

Jane checked her watch. 12.15. 'Shirley, you've been a hero. Get off home now, ok? You can write your notes in the morning, and thanks for sticking around. Much appreciated.'

'Ok, thanks, ma'am. I must admit I'm flagging a bit.'

'No wonder. See you tomorrow.'

Jane arched her back and stretched her hands, reaching for the ceiling. She thought of Shirley, going home. Her boyfriend worked nights at the bakery, so at least they'd have a few hours together. Chance'd be a fine thing.

Jane forced herself to log in. She was flagging a bit too, but it wasn't even lunchtime. She suddenly felt her age, then snapped out of it. 38 is not old… and anyway she knew this was just the start of a hunt for a murderer, and the adrenaline would keep her going.

Yet all she could think of right now was Charles Aston fading away. And the surprising realisation that she needed a few hours with Allan tonight. Maybe work didn't come first all the time.

As she clicked in and started reading Ross's notes, she had a random thought: what if someone could hack into police computers. What if someone already had?

She shrugged and reached for her hack-proof notebook: *'Talk Mark. IT security.'* Then turned back to the screen.

The more she read about Greaves, and online betting, the more she realised she would soon be signing in at their five star reception for a cosy chart with Mr Graeme Hargreaves.

Mark Manning was thinking exactly the same thing at roughly the same time.

Thanks to the malware he had used to sweep through the Pretty Cool Cafe network, he'd already seen enough to confirm that Jamie had indeed been hacking into Greaves from that computer.

He'd been clever, hiding behind a series of fake accounts. But not clever enough.

Mark sipped the last of the lukewarm water from the plastic cup, grimaced, and packed his bag. He'd thought about doing printouts in the back office, but now was not the time to alert Gonzales.

He found it hard to believe that Gonzales had not been aware. Either he had turned a blind eye because he and Jamie were in it together, or he couldn't be arsed to monitor activity on his own premises. Either way, he was stuffed. Even more stuffed if Greaves found out.

Unless, of course, Greaves was in on it, too. Or more likely, a rogue Greaves employee who was running the whole scam.

No, surely not… Greaves would have their own high level security, surely?

Mark felt the first stomach gurglings that were his ten minute lunch warning, and walked into the back office, checking the screen shots he'd taken on his tablet.

'Thanks Mr Gonzales, all done!'

No answer.

Mark opened the door that led upstairs from the back office, and called out.

'Bye, Mr Gonzales! Thank you!'

Heavy footsteps coming down the stairs... Gonzales looked shocking; white faced, his mouth hanging open, holding his chest, ragged breathing.

'What is it, Paolo?'

He slumped back onto the stairs, and Mark had to hold on to the rail to stop them both sliding down. 'Call ambulance. 999. Tablets... tablets...'

Martin saw his eyes rolling up into his head, and raised his voice. 'Where are your tablets, Paolo? Come on. Look at me! Tell me where they are..'

'Gone. Someone took—'

Then he fainted.

NINE

JANE SAT FACING MARTIN, with Lorry next to her, taking notes and with one eye on the ancient recorder, which had been known to cut out while a suspect was in full flow.

On the table, a jug of water and three glasses, none of them being used.

Martin sat back, with unconvincing nonchalance, his eyes fixed on the glass nearest him.

'So, Martin… we get what you're saying. But we still don't get why you reacted so badly to Jamie talking about his online betting scam. Why should that bother you so much?'

'I've already told you… '

'I know, but we need more explanation. Just to repeat, no-one is accusing you of anything, Martin. We need your help.'

He sighed and sat up a little straighter. 'Ok, ok… for the last time… We were good mates. I was worried about him. He'd never done illegal stuff before. I was shocked, like, tried to warn him off.'

'How did he react to that.'

'He was losing it, big time. Told me to get over it. No-one was getting hurt. No-one would know he was doing it. What's the problem, sort of thing… Can I go now?'

'Soon. Why was he telling you all this?'

'We were mates, for fuck's sake!'

Lorry leaned in. 'Cut that out, right now, sunbeam, or you'll be staying with us a lot longer.'

'Just gimme a break, will you? I don't know why he was telling me. We're mates, or is that too difficult for you to understand?'

Jamie smiled. 'No I get that, Martin. To be perfectly straight with you, what I don't get is… a) why you two were having a public barney on a busy shopping street about illegal activity when someone could easily hear, and possibly report it to us; and b) again, why your reaction was so over the top. I'm guessing that not very much would shock you, least of all, anything criminal.'

'Oh right, so I'm a criminal now, am I?'

'Well, are you?' Jane glanced at Lorry who slid out a copy of Martin's criminal record onto the table. 'According to this, you're not averse to a bit of petty theft, are you Martin?'

Martin sighed and rubbed the stubble on his head, then looked Jane in the eye for the first time. 'Yeah, that shit was years ago. I was just a kid. I swear I'm telling the truth! It's all I know. And it went loud because Jamie wouldn't shut up. I wanted him to button it, people would hear us, but he was so full of himself, like. He told me I could make a shitload of money, too, and he wouldn't take it that I didn't want to know.'

Jamie nodded. 'That's better. Thanks Martin. Interview terminated at 12.55.'

Lorry looked just as surprised as Martin.

'Can I go?'

'Yes, for now. You're not under arrest. You're just helping us, ok? But we will need to speak to you again, so don't go far, all right?'

Martin spoke quietly for the first time, and it sounded to Jane like a line he'd heard on the telly: 'I can't believe he's dead, you know?'

Jane stood. 'We'll find who did it.' She leaned in close. 'Whatever it takes.'

She noticed that Martin's hand shook slightly as he poured some water into his glass.

Jane forced one half of a cardboard, cheese and pickle sandwich down, with the considerable help of a mug of Jag's perfect tea.

As expected, Lorry had bent her ear all the way back to the office, questioning the decision to let Martin go so soon. Jane was quietly pleased Lorry was asserting herself. She needed people who were not afraid to pose questions. More often than not, they were the people who really cared, and it wasn't too long ago that Jane was challenging the decisions of her superiors as a new DC.

She'd listened to Lorry, then stopped at her office door, and surprised her by thanking her.

'You did the right thing, bringing him in, and you're right to be asking questions. I'm not totally convinced by his explanation, either, but we need him to think he's rolled us over. I want you to trust our instincts. Assign someone to keep a very discreet eye on him for the next two or three days. You decide who. Let's find out where he goes, who he sees. If he's innocent, or he's up to something, we'll find out. All right?'

Lorry flushed, even under her Goth inspired whiter shade of pale foundation. 'Thank you, ma'am.'

'No, thank you, Lorry. Great job today. See you for the team brief later.'

Jane never got to finish her sandwich. Mark called from the hospital to break the news about Gonzales.

'He'll live, ma'am. But no thanks to whoever nicked his medication. Christ, I thought he was a goner...'

'Blimey Mark... Is he well enough to talk?'

'Yes, the doc says they've stabilized him. He'll be sleepy for an hour, but after that should be ok.'

'Right, Mark. Stay with him. Make sure he doesn't get any visitors. We've only got his word his meds were stolen; he could just be confused. But I'm already getting a feeling this case is going to blow lots of stuff out of the water, so let's play safe. You can fill me in on your tech checks while we're waiting for him to come round.'

'Ok ma'am. Lots to talk about there, as well.'

'Great... Oh, and can you get me a sandwich from the vending machine? It's bound to be better than the crap George brought in this morning.'

Mark snorted. 'Of course. What filling?'

'Anything but cheese and bloody pickle, please. On my way.'

Adrian Cheshire stabbed a button on his desk phone.

'Chloe, can you cancel all calls and appointments for an hour, please?'

'No problem. Oh, just one thing...'

'Yes, Chloe?'

'Just something that happened earlier...'

Adrian sighed. 'Tell you what, why not come in and tell me to my face?'

The door squeaked slightly as Chloe timidly knocked and stepped in.

Adrian could do without the interruption, and Chloe wasn't known for her brevity, but he trusted her. 'Come in and sit down, and tell me what's on your mind.'

Chloe dragged a stray strand of red hair behind her ear, and smoothed out her grey skirt, keeping her knees together as she sat. Adrian had his back to the window, which meant she had a spectacular view over the Manchester skyline, looking north. The grey steel and concrete of the city looked like a cardboard cut out against the backdrop of hazy hills in the far distance.

Adrian waited. He could see she was struggling with the best way to phrase whatever was on her mind, but the clock was ticking and he had some printouts from the servers to read. Even so, he smiled and kept his voice moderate. 'What is it Chloe?'

Chloe's words came out in a torrent after the slow start. 'Well, I was in Pret earlier, getting some things for lunch, and there was a man sat by the window. None of us had seen him before, but he was very friendly and… nice. He started asking us questions; said he had the chance of an interview—'

'We're not recruiting. The memo only went out this morning.'

'I know. But I don't think anyone had seen it then.'

She had his full attention now. 'OK Chloe. Tell me more.'

'The thing is, he was asking about the hacking. Said he'd seen the papers. He was asking if there was any truth in it.'

'Was he now? And what did you say?'

Chloe lowered her eyes. 'I didn't say anything. He was more interested in the younger ones, you know, chatting them up. He was a bit of a looker… Anyway, a couple of the girls told him about you. Said you'd started an inquiry.'

'They said that? Hell fire.'

'I'm sorry, sir.'

'Chloe… don't call me sir, remember? Look, it's not your fault. I'll want their names, of course. Any idea who this guy was?'

'Never seen him before. He was young, sandy hair… Actually, no idea, sorry. But—'

'OK Chloe, thanks very much. Probably a journalist. They're all going to be snooping around now, looking to dish the dirt. It's what they do. Don't worry about it.'

'Well that was my first thought, But—'

'What?'

'As we were standing up to leave, I saw him reach into his jacket pocket for something and when his jacket swung open, I saw a badge.'

'A badge?'

'On a lanyard, like an ID badge.'

'Well lots of employees wear them these days.'

'But I saw it quite clearly, sir – sorry, Adrian. It was a police badge.'

'You're certain?'

'Yes, I am. I saw one just like it when mum and dad's place was robbed. The police came then.'

'Thanks Chloe, really appreciate you sharing this with me. Let's keep this between us for now. Did you tell anyone else?'

Chloe shook her head.

'Can you describe him?'

Chloe reached for her phone. 'I got a photo of him.'

'Chloe, you are amazing. Send it to me, will you? OK, leave it with me now, and thanks again.'

Chloe stood and walked to the door, the shafts of sun turning her red hair gold. Adrian called out.

'Don't forget… no calls for an hour, Chloe.'

She nodded and closed the door gently.

Adrian stood and rotated his head gently to relieve the tension. He needed to hit the gym today, work it out of his system. But no chance now.

He paced in front of the window and drank greedily from his water bottle as he turned things over.

A body had been found at one of the internet cafes, so maybe not surprising the police were sniffing around. But although Graeme Hargreaves would want to know, Adrian's priority was to work out if and how the hacking was happening. He wanted to present a solution to Graeme that would take the problem away. Telling him about the police could lead to a knee jerk reaction, and that was the last thing they needed. But if he found out from someone else, and Adrian had kept it from him…

Adrian stopped at his desk; his hand hovering over the phone.

Call him, or not?

Adrian shook his head, took a deep breath, snatched the papers stacked up on the printer, and started reading.

'You talk while I munch.'

Jane got as comfortable as she could on a plastic chair in a hospital corridor and attacked the prawn salad on brown that Mark had chosen for her. It was her favourite, but how did he know that?

Mark finished his Mars bar and reached in his bag for his Samsung tablet. Jane watched, as he jabbed and flicked until he found what he was looking for and turned the screen so she could see.

She managed to speak and chew at the same time. 'What am I looking at, Mark?'

'Ok, this is a picture I took of Jamie's computer screen at the internet cafe, after I had run my malware program—'

'Mal – what?'

'Sorry, ma'am. It's just a bit of software we use to get behind the barriers hackers put up to hide what they're doing. This proves that he was hacking into Greaves, ma'am.'

'Simple as that?'

'Yes, ma'am. This line here is an identifier for the Greaves portal, and you can see here the extra code that Jamie has added that gives him the access he needs to get behind it. Basically, it is like opening the door into the company's accounts office and taking their cash.'

Jane was nearing the end of her lunch. 'We'll need more than a photo, Mark.'

'It's ok, I have captured it on my own laptop to print out. We've got admissible evidence, ma'am. Thing is, I can't yet tell you exactly what he was getting out of it, but you can see there is a lot of activity… these short lines here, and here, and here, that indicate he was dipping in every few minutes. That suggests he was making brief hits, but frequently, and changing his IP address often, making it less likely he'd be identified. He was good, but…'

Jane dabbed her mouth with a paper tissue and sipped the orange juice Mark had also bought her.

'IP address?'

'Every computer has its own address, if you like. It stands for Internet Protocol and it's just a series of numbers. It gets complicated because when you use your own laptop, say, to connect to the internet using a different WiFi, your IP address changes. Which is perhaps why Jamie thought he was more likely to avoid detection if he worked from an internet cafe. But he went one step further, and changed the IP address many times, so the Greaves security system would be less likely to spot him breaking in.'

'So Jamie was a hacker, and presumably making a fair bit of money…'

'Yes, ma'am.'

'Have you accessed his bank account, credit card?'

'Yes, ma'am. but there's nothing unusual there.'

'More than one account, I suppose?'

'Yes, and it's very likely he was also using BitCoin from his other account.'

'Oh God.' Jane felt like she had been thrown into the deep end of the swimming pool. 'BitCoin… Go on Mark.'

Mark grinned. 'It's virtual money, basically. So you don't have coins in your pocket, they are stored in a computer file: think of it as a digital wallet…'

Jane felt herself going under for the third time, but was rescued by a moon-faced nurse who opened the door, gave them a gap toothed smile and announced: 'Doctor says you can talk to Mr Gonzales now, but no more than 15 minutes, please.'

Jane followed her, fighting against the memory of Charles Aston lying in the hospice, but Mark broke in, whispering before they went in.

'One other thing, ma'am. I'm thinking if Jamie was using this internet cafe, he may have been using others.'

'So we could be looking at a fairly big operation.'

'Yes, I think so, ma'am. And something else…'

'Yes?'

'I can't believe Mr Gonzales didn't know about it. It would have been easy to track this activity on the network. So he turned a blind eye, or he may have been part of the scam.'

'And the other internet cafes are also owned by Greaves. Someone found out. And now Jamie's dead…'

'…and it looks like someone tried to kill Mr Gonzales.'

Jane nodded. 'Or at the very least, wanted to scare him half to death…'

She paused, and turned so Gonzales couldn't lip read. 'Make a note for me, Mark. You and I need an appointment with whoever's in charge at Greaves.'

'That's Graeme Hargreaves, ma'am.'

'Whoever he is, get us in his diary. Fast. Oh, and thanks for lunch.'

She walked up to Gonzales, who was propped up in bed and looking washed out, held up her ID and smiled. For a minute, Mark thought she sounded more like a nurse than someone heading a murder hunt.

'Hello, Mr Gonzales, how are you feeling now?'

Eminem was echoing off the walls as Martin Sutton did his third set of 15 squat thrusts.

Sweat was running down his face, and he was pumped up. He loved Eminem, too – 'Lose Yourself' was on now, and that was on his Spotify playlist when he was working the weights at home.

The instructor yelled at them to move around, and Martin sprang down onto his hands for 15 press ups, one eye on the guy across from him who was trying hard to do everything quicker than everyone else.

Martin grunted: 'No chance, mate'. It was the last set, and he put everything into it.

The skinhead over the way fell on his back, his chest heaving as the whistle blew. Martin sprang up and jogged on the spot as the instructor turned the music off and led them into the wind-down stretches.

Twenty minutes later, he was showered, changed and signing up for next week's session.

He grinned as he threw his tote bag over his shoulder, and walked towards town. All that shit with the police was out of his system. It was too easy, really. Numpties, they were.

Bad news about Jamie, though. But he only had himself to blame. Should have kept his beaky nose out.

Martin enjoyed the fizz of adrenaline that lingered after his gym sessions, but the question now was...what do I do with the rest of the day?

A couple of girls he'd seen at the club were walking towards him: tight shorts and even tighter t shirts. He winked as they walked past.

'All right girls?'

The one with the bleached hair spat her chewing gum out. 'Yeah, you? What you up to then?'

'Looking for a bit of fun, I am.'

Her mate blew a cloud of smoke from her e-cig and pulled her mate away. She called over her shoulder as they walked into a nail salon: 'Best keep looking then, mate. See ya!'

Martin walked on, shaking his head, and stopped outside the internet caff. He read the notice, in black felt tip on white paper – 'Closed till further notice'. Looking through the window, he could see the computer where Jamie had been sitting that day.

The one next to his.

Martin turned as the 126 bus squeaked to a halt, and jumped on.

'Single to Deansgate, please, mate.'

It all happened too quickly for the police constable in jeans and denim jacket, who'd been watching from the other side of the street, and was now kicking the lamppost and reaching for his phone.

'Right, everyone, we've got some catching up to do. It's been a big day so far…'

Jane tapped her mug on the table and the chatter subsided. Ross signalled he was coming to the end of his phone call, and Jane took another gulp of tea while she waited.

Mark was sitting at Lorry's desk. George thoughtfully scratched his belly as he topped up his coffee cup. Jag sat with his notebook on his knee, and smiled at Jane.

'All set Jag? Notebook at the ready?'

'Always, ma'am. Ready when you are.'

Ross finished his call with his trademark, 'Cheers, mate.'

Jane cleared her throat.

'Ok, let's get on with it. I've got to do a news conference in an hour, so… Where to start? Mark: how about you kick off? Oh, and can you not interrupt with questions today. Save them for later, all right?'

Mark blushed slightly. 'So I've gone into the network at the internet cafe, and it's pretty obvious that Jamie was hacking into Greaves betting website, and creaming money off the top. It was easy enough for me to find the evidence of that, so Gonzales, the manager, must have known it was going on. If he didn't, he was an idiot. If he did, he was possibly covering up, or, more likely, was part of the scam.

'So the next bit of news… Gonzales collapsed in front of me at the cafe today. He was having some kind of heart problem, and said he needed his tablets, but someone had taken them. He's in hospital, and the boss and I have just got back from talking to him…'

'Thanks, Mark. So this is how it is. Jamie was engaged in criminal activity at the internet cafe, and it's very likely Gonzales was at the very least assisting him. Mark and I are of the opinion that if Jamie was operating his scam from one internet cafe, he was probably using others, so Mark is going to look into that.

'Meanwhile, Gonzales says he can't remember much about last night, when his tablets may have been stolen, because he drank a lot of whisky. He may have got confused, and he's certainly drugged up today, so we can't give him the third degree yet. However…'

Jane paused, and began writing on the whiteboard. 'We have to consider all options, however extreme: for example, that Gonzales found out what Jamie was doing, and bumped him off; that Gonzales was part of the scam, possibly with others –

remember Greaves owns these internet cafes; and that Greaves found out and eliminated Jamie, and tried to scare Gonzales off.'

Ross puffed out his cheeks. 'Christ.'

'Yes, I know. It's getting interesting, Ross. But we haven't finished yet. Lorry, your turn, please.'

Lorry updated on the interview with Martin Sutton, Jag's discovery of the Greaves bag, and summed up neatly at the end, to Jane's approval: 'In the end, we thought we'd gain more by letting Sutton think we were satisfied with his explanation about the argument with Jamie. Even though we're not. I don't trust him one little bit, so there's more to this guy that we need to find out. I put someone on the street to follow him around, but he hopped on a bus that terminates in Manchester and we lost him.'

'OK, thanks Lorry. Don't worry, we'll catch up with him. Now, let's move on. Here's what we need to do…

'George – can you get over to that cafe again and check it over. Take one of Phil's lot. We're looking for the tablets, signs of break in, or evidence of someone else on the premises last night, or this morning – someone could have got up there while Mark was on Jamie's computer. We're also still looking for Jamie's laptop, so can you double check that while you're there – there may be a sneaky hiding place we didn't find first time, though the chances are slim, and better do the usual trawls online, in case some joker put it up for sale.

'Ross – can you identify the premises Greaves owns that are internet cafes and make a visit, please? Just be a punter, check them out, get names – especially the managers. And show a photo of Jamie, see if anyone recognises him.

'Mark – you're going to arrange for us both to meet the boss at Greaves, and follow up on the techie stuff. That includes evidence of wider access into Greaves' system from other sites, if possible, plus we need to find where Jamie was squirrelling away his money.

'And Lorry – we need to keep track of Sutton. I'm with you: something tells me he's deeply involved. He was a friend of Jamie's, so who knows – he may be in on the scam himself. Or worse… Let's find out if he is a regular at these internet cafes – Ross, show his picture around too, ok?'

Jane turned to look at Jag, who still had his head down, writing fast to keep up.

'Jag? Will you join George and I at the news conference, please?'

Lorry's snigger set everyone off as they watched Jag carry on, head down, writing this down in his notes, too. Then he realised what he'd written and looked up, wide eyed. Moraji would go wild when he told her he'd be on telly.

'Me, ma'am?'

'Yes, Jag, you. With you on one side and George on the other, I know a) I won't forget anything, and b) there won't be any crowd trouble.'

This time, Jag was laughing, too.

TEN

ALLAN EASED BACK AND made the most of the space in front.

The M6 toll was carrying a fraction of the traffic that was clogging up the old motorway, and it was the first time in over three hours he'd been able to relax.

Driving always brought out what he was convinced was lumbago – not that he really had a clue what that was. But he remembered his dad nursing a shoulder and wincing, and he always said it was 'a touch of lumbago', so maybe it was. Anyway, it bloody hurt, and it was hurting now; the ache running from around his collar bone down to his elbow.

The first blue sign was a warning: 'Tiredness kills.' Half a mile later there was another: 'Services 2 miles.' Half a mile later, another heralded the presence of KFC, Costa and M&S.

Allan briefly wondered why there wasn't a sign saying: 'Fast food kills', but he turned off anyway, and started tutting as soon as he found his way into the car park.

The toll road was obviously empty because everyone was queueing up here for toilets, coffee and fried chicken. The car park was almost full. Allan ended up at the farthest point from the entrance, next to camper vans with annoyingly relaxed couples having a brew, and dog walkers furtively kicking their pets' turds into the long grass.

Once inside the gastronomic oasis, Allan couldn't wait to get out. He'd had the crazy notion of browsing M&S for some goodies with which to welcome Jane back home tonight, but that went out of the window when he saw that every aisle was like a manic game of Pacman.

His mood didn't improve either, when he queued up for a latte, and paid nearly four quid for a paper cup full of foam with scalding hot brown liquid lurking at the bottom.

Sitting back in the car with the door open, he rubbed his shoulder, and closed his eyes for a second. Half an hour later, he was woken by the slamming of doors of the campervan, and checked his watch.

3.20pm.

Allan yawned, listening to the deep steady rumble of cars rolling up and down the motorway a few hundred yards away.

He wondered what Jane would be doing now, and decided to text her.

'Hey, all ok? I'm about 90 minutes away, I hope. See you tonight. I'll sort dinner etc. Luv Ax'

His phone pinged straight away.

'Tough day, but I'm winning, thanx. Can't wait for etc!! News conf around 6. C u after that. So glad you're coming home xx'

Adrian Cheshire hunched over his laptop, managing to force himself to tap more delicately on the keys than came naturally.

He had extended his one hour of protection from calls and appointments to the whole afternoon.

Graeme Hargreaves wanted results, and he was going to get them a lot quicker than he expected.

Adrian had assigned two people he'd brought with him from Google as part of the deal with Graeme, to work on the investigation with him, and they were sworn to secrecy. It hadn't been that difficult to establish that breaches had been made.

The total loss was peanuts, at around £40k.

But the bad news was the impact on share prices and credibility.

And, to make matters worse, the company was being targeted from its own portfolio of internet cafes, which suggested to Adrian and his team that staff at the premises must have been aware. And even if they weren't, they'd be sacked for total incompetence anyway.

Graeme would go ape. Adrian sighed and gazed out of the window, searching for the thoughts that were forming and floating away, as he tried to compute the problem…

… a young guy is found dead at our internet cafe…hours later, our staff get a covert visit from the police… Graeme launches an inquiry into hacking at Greaves… I get a call that the cafe manager Gonzales is in hospital, with a copper on the door… all this for £40,000?

That was it. That was the point that was in danger of being lost. He shook his head: there's more to this; must be. Stuff the memo.

Adrian punched his deskphone: 'Chloe, can you get me five minutes with Graeme, please?'

'Sorry sir – Adrian… Mr Hargreaves is at a conference in Harrogate and won't be back till tomorrow.'

'All right, Chloe. Get a message to him for me. I need to talk to him, asap. On my private mobile, the secure one. And tell him to make sure he's watching the Manchester regional news around 6.30, or catch it on the radio. One of my mates at the Evening News tells me the police are giving a press conference about that lad who was found dead at the Pretty Cool Cafe.'

'Oh God! Really? Yes, yes, I will.'

'Thanks Chloe… I'm still do not disturb, all right?'

'Yes, no problem. I'll get that message to Mr Hargreaves, and then I'll be heading home. Any calls will go straight to your voice mail, if that's ok?'

'Of course, thanks for being my protector today.'

He smiled briefly as he heard Chloe laugh, then he put the phone down.

Adrian frowned as he hit 'save', then picked up a fistful of printouts and moved to the leather sofa by the window to go through them again.

There were only a handful of reporters in the conference room at Ashbridge Police Station, but one of them was from regional tv news, and she'd brought a cameraman, and a bored gum chewing guy with what looked like a pole mounted grey candyfloss.

Jag had set things up well, with Jane, George and himself side by side around a small table, a few chairs in a semi-circle, and a table at the side for the handouts – photos and a written version of the words Jane was about to deliver.

She'd done this before, but always felt a bit of stage fright, and always with Charles Aston at her side. She had George's solid and bulky presence this time, but even so, Jane felt hollow. She checked her Swatch, cleared her throat and glanced at her notes.

'OK, if you're all set?'

The diminutive tv reporter nodded and the cameraman moved slightly nearer, then gave Jane the thumbs up. Jane had managed to disguise her relief when she told her it was being recorded for both radio and tv, rather than going out live.

George was as supportive as ever. 'Oh that's good. Less chance of a balls-up, ma'am.'

Jane kept her head still, and tried hard not to stare at the camera. 'As you know, we discovered the body of Jamie Castleton at an internet cafe in Ashbridge two days ago. I'm here to tell you that we are treating this as a murder inquiry, and we will not rest until we have brought the perpetrator, or perpetrators, to justice…

'Jamie was just 23 years old. He lived locally with his mother. We are supporting Mrs Castleton through this terrible tragedy, as best we can, and I would ask that she be given time and space, and privacy.

'We need to speak to anyone who knew Jamie, or saw Jamie this week, particularly on the day he died. Any information, however insignificant it may seem to you, could be very important to us. Were you in the internet cafe or any other internet cafe that day? Was Jamie there too?

'Please call, text or message us through social media using the contact info Jag has added to our news release.

'Ok, that's it for today. We will keep you up to date as the investigation moves along, but I'm sure you understand that any information we do release will be limited. Thank you for your understanding.'

A hand went up. 'Stephanie Burke, BBC North West… Can you tell us how Jamie died?'

Jane stood and smiled. 'I don't want to say anything more at this stage, Stephanie. But anything you can do to help us spread our message today, would be really helpful.'

They could hear the questions being called out as they left the room, and Jane could sense George's disapproval. He was of the way of thinking that the press and police naturally get on like a house on fire – to use his own interesting metaphor, and that the more info they issued, the more likely they'd be to call in favours from the press when they really needed them.

Jane punched him on the shoulder as they walked up the stairs to CID.

'Thanks for being there, George. I didn't want to give too much away today. Not till we're sure of our ground. You ok with that?'

George produced a packet of wine gums from his jacket pocket. 'Care for some rubbery sugar, ma'am?'

Jane laughed. That was as close as George would ever come to saying she'd made the right call.

Then he turned to Jag, who was following close behind. 'I'm not offering you one, Jaguar.'

Jag winked at Jane. 'Why not?'

'You're not senior enough.'

Jane was still smiling when she closed her office door and leaned back against it.

Not a bad day's work. She nibbled a digestive biscuit left over from an earlier meeting and checked her phone. One message from Allan kept the smile on her face: he was shopping!

Nothing from the hospice, though. So maybe that was good news, in a way. She thought about phoning to check, but she'd told herself so many times today that she had to let go.

She heard the shouted goodbyes and called back as the team headed off down the corridor; the footsteps and the chatter suddenly shut off as the fire door closed behind them.

It was the time she and Charles would always meet to compare notes. He called it their 'dear diary sessions'. Jane stood at the window, her eyes filling with tears.

'Go Jane.'

Allan drummed the steering wheel with the flat of his hand as the radio presenter faded out Coldplay and handed over to the newsroom with the words: 'Today's top story – a murder investigation is announced in Ashbridge. This and more, coming right up.'

As the jingle played, Allan watched the procession of customers eyeing up the compost, tree ferns and fuchsias piled up on pallets outside the supermarket. He'd got the last place in the car park, just in time for the 6.30 bulletin.

'...Stephanie Burke, reporting from Ashbridge... Ashbridge Police have launched a murder inquiry after the body of Jamie Castleton was found at the Pretty Cool internet cafe in the town two days ago. DCI Jane Birchfield appealed for community support to help catch the killer...'

Allan listened, smiling, as Jane read out her statement, then the reporter cut in: *'DCI Birchfield refused to answer any questions, including how Jamie died. The cafe where he was found is closed down. This is Stephanie Burke—'*

Allan nodded, impressed, but his moment of pride was interrupted by tapping on his window, where a man in green overalls and a green cap was looking aggrieved.

'Are you going shopping, going home, or what? I've been waiting five minutes for a bloody space.'

Allan tried to behave. Zapping his car and heading for the entrance, he called back: 'I'm just about to go in. Won't be long, though.'

But his attempt at annoying niceness was wasted. The green man was already in his Ford van, lurching forward noisily to block off another driver who had also just spotted a car reversing out.

It was hard enough finding the way in, barred as it seemed to be by a maze of pallets and special offers. Inside was no different. Random piles of beer, chocolate, bananas, flowers were designed to tempt. And it worked.

Allan grabbed a green basket on wheels and rattled over to the beer mountain.

He'd been sorely tempted by a shop poster promoting a 'wine tour', bearing the invitation – 'discover all 32 bottles.' A guy in a gaudy floral shirt and rather short shorts moved in next to him and commented: '32 bottles? That should see me through the weekend, eh?'

'Yeah, maybe, but you wouldn't remember much, would you?'

Then he caught sight of a poster proclaiming the virtues of their wonderful supermarket team of 25,000 people. Allan shook his head and looked at the queue in front of him. So why was there only one bloody till open?

Fifteen minutes later, he was trying to get the keys out of his trouser pocket while balancing a shallow cardboard box containing his haul: milk, bread, deluxe sourdough pizza, bottle of prosecco, apple strudel, bottle of Malbec, bottle of Becks, and Jane's favourites – mixed nuts and a Bounty.

The bleached blond on the checkout with piercings and tattoos had smiled as she slid everything across the scanner at lightning speed. 'Someone's going to have a good night tonight, then, luv.'

Allan grinned as he unloaded into the boot. It was good to be back in the North. And he had the sneaky feeling the checkout girl was right.

Graeme Hargreaves laughed. 'Forty grand? Bloody hell. Those bastards are really in the big league, aren't they?'

But he soon regained his more natural demeanour after Adrian had summed up the real conclusion of his investigation.

'That was my first thought, too. It's peanuts. But then I

started to ask myself what we're missing. We now know there have been multiple hits on us from different internet cafes – all of them ours. Those guys had enough brains to get in, and yet they only take that much? They could have done us for millions…'

'Maybe, but perhaps they're not so stupid. A larger amount means it's easier for us to find.'

'Possibly, but when you break into a bank, you're not going to take a tenner, are you? It could be your only chance. You'd stuff your bag full and get out.' Adrian leaned forward as he spoke, the soft glow of his desk lamp reflecting off the polished surface of his desk. 'And now, we have a murder inquiry, boss. It can't be a coincidence.'

'So what are you saying?'

'There is more to this. That guy's death must be linked in some way…'

'But he only got away with £40k. That's not enough motive to kill him, is it?'

'Exactly my point. Except it might not just be him. Something else is going on, I'm sure of it. The police will be sniffing round, putting two and two together and making five, and before you know it, we'll be headline news and our share price won't be dipping, it'll have drowned in the deep end.'

'OK, Adrian… I get it. Cut the amateur dramatics. So what are we looking for, and what do you need from me?'

'Well, a little bird tells me a policeman has been chatting up a few staff over at Pret recently, so they're already connecting us.'

'That's not surprising, is it? Bloody annoying, and I bet my loyal employees were chattering like sparrows, but so what?'

'So, can you get someone to cover my admin stuff for a few days, so I can dig deeper?'

'Dig where?'

'I want to get to all our internet cafes, check their systems, see what I can find out. They were all being used by the hacker, or hackers. I want to see whether there have been any modifications to their own network – hardware and software. Should be easier to find out if there really is something else.'

'Maybe that's it – those cafe managers have been tampering with the system. Bastards. Right, get it done. And while you're there, interview the managers, then sack the lot of them; stick our confidentiality clause up their arses before you kick them, and shut every one of those places down. Let me know once done and I'll get the message out. We get rid of the problem. It's the only way we'll convince the shareholders.'

'And the police...'

'Yes. Them too. You've done well, Adrian. If I ever meet our previous head of department, I'll slaughter him. Where's the security? Jesus! Anyway, make sure you stay at least two steps ahead, ok? Having watched that press conference, I'm not exactly running scared of their DCI, are you?'

'My mate at the Evening News rates her. Said she did a cracking job on her last murder case. Definitely not a pushover. His words, not mine.'

Graeme's reply seemed to hover somewhere between sarcastic and hostile. 'Got mates and little birds everywhere, haven't you? Well, we'll see... Oh, and...'

'Yes?'

'Be careful...don't leave any papers lying around, all right? What was that programme... trust no-one...'

'The X Files?'

Graeme laughed. 'That's the one.'

'Don't worry. I don't.'

'Guess what? Neither do I.' Then the line went dead.

ELEVEN

ALLAN TURNED RIGHT AT the grim and grey Holy Trinity Church, and triggered a memory.

It was a happy one, even though he was wearing those hated, stupid grey shorts. He'd won a prize at Sunday School for copying out the Lord's Prayer and putting a fancy coloured border round it. Mum had pinned it up in the kitchen, and she and Dad were there in their best clothes, clapping as he shyly walked up the aisle towards the vicar, who looked like a white giant. The prize was a Bible, all posh with a black shiny cover and gold lettering.

Allan had hung onto it ever since, and he was sure God would forgive him for packing it away in a plastic box in the loft. Strange thing, he could remember the smell of it.

Now, though, he needed to sniff out a parking space somewhere within a two mile hike of his front door. His luck was in, and he couldn't hold back a smile of satisfaction as he parked on the opposite side of the road, just a few yards away. That girl on the checkout was right: it was going to be a good night.

He was leaning into the boot to repack the shopping that had inevitably spilled out of the box, when he heard a woman's voice, very loud: 'Oy! That's my space, mate!'

Allan sighed, cursed under his breath and turned slowly, to see Jane laughing. 'My God, Jane, I thought you were the woman next door! You bugger. Come here!'

He kissed her, pulling her with him to shelter from a sudden shower under the open boot door.

'I'm sorry, Jane, for leaving like that.'

She nuzzled into his neck. 'Don't be. Takes two, doesn't it? Let's go in.'

'Can you carry the rest if I get the bottles?'

'Frightened I'll drop them?'

'Listen, I'm trusting you with that deluxe pizza. It's a big responsibility.'

'Yeah right. Come on, I'm starving.'

The pizza was in the oven, the prosecco in the fridge, and the Malbec was open.

They sat close on the sofa, enjoying the silence.

Jane had brought him up to date on the Castleton case, and Allan told her they must go to Lyme Regis one day.

They sipped wine in the half light that leaked through the old pine panelled kitchen door. He stroked her hand.

Jane smiled and stretched her legs over his. 'That's nice.'

'You said you wanted me home because you needed me. It made me feel a bit weepy. And happy.'

'I meant it.'

He didn't want to spoil the moment, but he had to know. 'It also made me a bit worried. Was there a special reason? Has something happened?'

Jane put her empty glass on the coffee table. 'You know Charles Aston is in the hospice?'

'Yes.'

'Well, I got a call…' Her voice broke and Allan pulled her into his arms, stroking her hair.

'What's happened? Is he…?'

'I don't think so. His family asked the hospice to let me know that he didn't have long.'

'I'm so sorry, love. He's so special to you, isn't he?'

Jane nodded and Allan felt the warmth of her tears on his shirt. 'I couldn't go to see him. I knew his family wouldn't want that. I'm going to miss him so much. I know he'd want me to be strong, but—'

'I know. But you did the right thing, staying away. From what you've told me, I think he'd want everyone to let him go, peacefully. He couldn't be in better hands now. That hospice has got an amazing reputation. Treasure the memories now. It's not as if you'll ever forget him, is it?'

Jane sat up and reached for a tissue. 'No, I won't.'

'And let's be honest, no-one could ever forget you.'

'Hey, you.' Jane sighed and looked up. 'You'll have to cheer me up. I'm sorry, Allan, this was supposed to be…'

Allan did his best imitation of a stereotypical harrassed housewife. 'I said sorry outside and got told off. Typical… I drive 300 miles to get back, I go shopping, and I get home, and cook dinner. And what do I get in return? A ticking off… And then I have to cheer you up? I don't know why I put up with it, I really don't…'

Jane dabbed her eyes, and leaned into him. 'I love you, Allan Gary Askew. You do not have to say anything, but anything you do say may be taken down…'

'Trousers… And I love you, Jane Birchfield.'

Jane laughed, then sighed softly as Allan kissed her lips, her cheek, her neck, and stroked her thigh. Her breath was fruity with wine, her skin was so smooth…

Then the oven timer pinged.

They unwrapped themselves from each other.

Allan groaned. 'I was looking forward to that pizza. But right now it's a bloody nuisance.'

'Well dish it up because I'm hungry. We can always come back here for dessert.'

'No way… I've got us apple strudel for afters!'

Irene Castleton's hand trembled as she plucked up the courage to open the envelope.

It was from Jamie.

She'd gone into the bank that afternoon to check her balance, and hope there was enough to see her through, and they told her that her son had left a letter. The manager had come out and taken her into a private meeting room.

He'd spoken very quietly, and introduced himself as Brian.

'You've been a customer for many years, Mrs Castleton, and we all saw the news yesterday. On behalf of everyone here, I wanted to extend my deepest sympathy. Can I get you a cup of tea? Help you settle?'

She said yes please, and stared at the beige wall as she waited.

Brian pulled a chair round to be on her side of the desk, and Irene declined the offer of a Rich Tea biscuit.

'So, Mrs Castleton, Jamie also had an account with us…' Brian was obviously struggling how best to explain. 'Yes, and… well, a few days ago, he came to see me…'

'Did he? Why?'

'He didn't say very much…'

'No…'

'He just said he had a letter for you, but he only wanted us to give it to you if anything happened to him…'

Irene stifled a sob. Brian shifted in his seat, and slid an envelope across the desk to her.

'That's all he said?'

'Yes. I promised I would do as he asked, and I promised not to say anything to you, until... it was necessary.'

'What about the police?'

'Mrs Castleton... I will be calling the police first thing tomorrow, now that I am satisfied that you have received the letter. Please believe me when I say that Jamie seemed perfectly relaxed and calm when he came in. I asked him what he meant by 'if anything happened to him', but he just smiled and joked that he was thinking ahead. He made it sound as if he might be going away, or something. We had no reason to think it was anything other than a surprise of some kind. I know this must be a shock for you, but there was really no other way.'

Irene had picked up the envelope and cried. Brian asked a female clerk to sit with her for a while, and make sure she signed a receipt.

She'd been at home ever since, trying to distract herself with housework, putting off the moment. But now, she'd had a couple of glasses of wine, and it was taking the edge off her anxiety. She held the envelope to her heart, kissed Jamie's neat writing on the front – 'For Mum', and opened it.

It was a very short letter, but Irene still had to read it twice before it sank in. The bank manager was right: it certainly was a surprise of some kind.

Irene stared at Jamie's message.

'My God, Jamie; what have you done?'

Paolo Gonzales was flicking through a motoring magazine the nurse had brought.

It was three in the morning, everywhere was quiet, and he felt relaxed for the first time in months. It felt like a blessing from the Pope when they said they were keeping him in overnight for observation.

They'd given him better medicine than he'd had before; plus stuff to make him calm; and cups of tea. The food wasn't so bad, either – better than the Pot Noodles he lived on, anyway. But, best of all, he felt safe.

He smiled. They'd even put a guard outside the door. His family back home would laugh at that, big time.

He'd also had time to think. His brain was a bit fuggy from the drugs, but he thought his overdue payment had to be made by tomorrow. He could switch his phone on to check, but he didn't want to risk picking up any messages. Or being traced. Well, now at least he'd bought himself some time.

He'd told the police he had no idea who'd taken his medicine, and that he could have just got confused and forgotten to collect a prescription. He'd played the part of stupid drunk Mexican so well. The more he could delay, the more chance he had of getting on a flight back home to Mexico: and that new flat in Chihuahua City; paid for from the money he'd earned – the money they thought he was going to pay them. No hay posibilidad… no chance.

He'd been working towards this for a long time; sending money to his bank in Mexico. He smiled. They think they're smart. Think Gonzales is just fat oaf.

A wave of tiredness hit him. Leaning back on his pile of pillows, he tried to relax, dimming the lights using the controller at his side.

But one thought kept coming back… had they really sent someone round to steal his medicine? Was it one of their boys? He couldn't remember anyone coming in, but he had drunk a lot of whisky and crashed out early. Had he even locked the door? They were, he knew, capable of anything.

Now he was scared again. So many things could go wrong.

If it was them, they would kill him if they found him before he got on the flight in the early hours tomorrow night.

That boy must have died because he found something, and now the police would be all over his computers. What if they found out? What if Graeme Hargreaves found out?

Everything depended on surviving the next 24 hours. He tried to calm his breathing, but he felt claustrophobic from the pressure squeezing him from all sides, and the wave of panic that engulfed him sent his heart racing.

He was just about to press the call button when a doctor came in, wearing the royal blue uniform and a white surgical mask. He closed the door gently and stood slightly outside the glow from the bed light.

'How are you, Mr Gonzales? I saw your light was on. You should be resting...'

'Not so good. You come at right time. My heart...'

The doctor's eyes were smiling, and Gonzales calmed a little. 'OK, let's have a look, shall we?'

The doctor moved out of sight behind him. 'Oh yes, I see. We just need to adjust a couple of things, Mr Gonzales. Make you more comfortable, ok? Just give me a moment... There... Can you feel that?'

'Yes.' Gonzales felt the extra dose running into his body, and felt immediately sleepy. 'Yes, thank you.'

The doctor came back and leaned in close. His eyes were no longer smiling.

'Don't thank me, Mr Gonzales. I have a message from my employer. He wanted you to know this is what happens to people who don't pay their debts; people who betray him; people who lie to him.'

Gonzales' eyes widened in fear, but not for long.

The man stayed with him for a few moments, checked his pulse, and closed the door quietly behind him as he called out: 'Goodnight, Mr Gonzales.'

He nodded at the policeman on the plastic chair as he

walked past. But he was obviously playing a game on his mobile phone.

He didn't even look up.

TWELVE

JANE LAY IN A tangle of bedsheets, listening to Allan's breathing. She turned on her side to face him and the movement woke him. He slowly opened his eyes and smiled.

'Morning, ma'am.'

'Morning, constable.'

Turning on his back, he stretched out an arm and Jane accepted the invitation to wrap herself round him. He pulled the duvet over her shoulders and she felt herself falling into sleep again.

Allan kissed her head. 'Last night was amazing.'

'It was. We should do it again sometime.'

'Now?'

Her voice was muffled by the duvet. 'What? You'd rather have that than apple strudel?'

'Hmmm. I'll need to think about that.'

Jane head-butted him in the stomach, then threw the duvet back with a sigh and sat up, checking her watch.

'Got to go, love, sorry.'

'It's ok. I need to get in early today, too. Loads to catch up on.'

'OK, give me a lift in?'

'Depends.'

'On...?'

'What you're offering for dessert tonight.'

A bowl of muesli and a cup of coffee later, at just after 6am, they were on the road, turning left at the church, heading for Ashbridge police station.

Jane's mobile rang and they glanced at each other, eyebrows raised in mock shock.

'Here we go,' said Jane. Then... 'Morning George. Starting early today...'

'Yes, ma'am. Sounds like you're already in the car?'

'Yes, Allan's bringing me in.'

'Can you divert to the hospital? They've just phoned in. Gonzales died overnight. I would go myself but I'm taking a look at that internet cafe with a lad from forensics.'

'Shit. So there goes a prime witness and a possible suspect... So do we know if it's natural causes?'

'They're not sure yet, ma'am. I've called Phil, just in case, and he moaned a lot, but said he'd get there if you need him.'

'Good work, George. Should be straightforward. Be there in about 10 minutes.'

She disconnected and looked at Allan. 'We interviewed this guy last night; he was in a private room; George got our lads doing shifts on the door...'

'What was wrong with him?'

'Heart condition.'

'Well, there you go... couldn't be helped.'

'Maybe... Do you mind dropping me off there?'

'Course not. And... I meant to say this last night... you know I'll help if you need it.'

Jane put a hand on his thigh, and Allan smiled. 'Especially if you do that.'

Jane waved as Allan drove off after dropping her at the main entrance. He'd smiled when she kissed him on the cheek.

'Take care, Jane.'

'You too.' Then a slight frown as she'd reminded herself she had at least two days' work to get through today, even without Gonzales. 'It's going to be a long day. I'll see you when I see you, ok?'

'Yeah, don't worry. I'll be late home too.'

She watched his car vanish into the tide of traffic already heading towards Manchester, breathed in a lungful of chilly early morning air, and walked quickly through the sliding doors.

Much later that night, Jane would tell Allan today had been a significant day.

But right now, sitting at her desk going through the log notes, she was worrying about it melting into a confusing blur.

First, there was the news that it had taken forensics all of 20 minutes to find additional prints in Gonzales' flat, and another half an hour back at the station to identify them. Jane authorised the arrest on the initial charge of theft, and Lorry and Jag were given the honour of bringing Martin Sutton in.

But there was no-one home, and Jane had to decide: circulate a description and hope for the best, or throw everything at it and go public. That was ok if he was acting alone, but a signal to clear all traces if he was working with others.

Second, she was still waiting to find out whether Gonzales had died naturally. The hospital said he'd been sat up reading into the early hours, but had seemed relaxed and comfortable. Time of death had not been established yet. There were no indications of anything out of the ordinary in his room, and his drip was intact. PC Sykes had been outside from 2 till 6am, and had seen nothing to arouse his suspicion. Even so, she'd asked Phil to take a look at the body.

Third, Ross had logged that he was on his way to the internet cafe on Deansgate, reminding Jane of Mark's confidence that the betting hack was unlikely to be confined to the Ashbridge site. So who knows what that would throw up…

Tapping her pen on the desk, she pressed the button that shone the message 'do not disturb' outside her office.

'OK Jane, think,' she whispered. She wrote JAMIE in the middle of a sheet of A4 and circled it, then began writing down connections, names, possibilities, ideas; drawing lines where links could exist.

As the page filled with bubbles and connections, one word kept cropping up – BETTING. It linked Jamie with Gonzales and Greaves, and possibly Sutton.

Jane pressed her temples with the tips of her fingers… what if Sutton was actually in on it with Jamie? Mark Manning was certain Gonzales must have known about the hack, so was he part of it too? or was he going to shop them, and Sutton decided to stop him, or scare him off?

If Sutton did steal Gonzales' medicine, he was sentencing him to death, even though he may not have meant to. But Gonzales had survived, thanks to Mark and the hospital… until the early hours of this morning, that is…

Jane's train of thought was shattered by her deskphone. She cursed herself for forgetting to divert it.

'George, what is it?'

'Mrs Castleton received a letter from her son, after his death.'

'What? When?'

'The bank rang. Said Jamie left it there a few days before his death, to pass on if anything happened to him. He seemed fine, relaxed, they said.'

'Bloody hell... what's in the letter?'

'Bank couldn't say. They didn't open it. Lorry's with the mother now. She told her Jamie's put £40,000 in an account for her.'

Jane needed to let that sink in. 'Forty grand?'

'Yes, ma'am. Jamie wrote that it was to say thank you for bringing him up. He was sorry he wasn't with her, but he didn't want her worrying about money any more. Lorry's photographing the letter and sending it over.'

Jane paused, remembering her uncle Bill's words: 'You set the pace, don't let the pace set you.'

'All right, George. We need that letter in our hands, so Lorry needs to borrow it. Find out where the money is. Meet you back here later.'

'Yes, ma'am.'

Jane sipped water and stood at the window. She'd spent five minutes on the phone with the Chief Constable of Greater Manchester, assuring him they were already identifying leads and making good progress. And it was true. But was it going in the right direction?

She knew it was always easier to be led by events, and take the wrong path. Do that too soon in a murder investigation, and you were in trouble.

She clicked her fingers as she glanced again at the mind map. No thinking time, just pick something. One word stood out... 'BETTING'.

Snap decision. Time to change the focus, see what happens. Maybe Jamie wasn't the centre of it all.

Jane picked up the phone...'Morning Mark. I want that appointment with the boss at Greaves, today or tomorrow... Hargreaves, that's it... As far as he's concerned, we just want his help, all right?... And I want you with me, remember?'

Ross stretched his legs and spun round in the chair, smiling broadly at the girl with long black hair and skinny jeans, who was tapping on one of the other computers.

'Hi.'

'Hello.'

'Sorry, can I ask, what is your accent?'

The girl sighed. Not that line, again. 'I am Polish.'

'Ah, ok.' Ross wheeled a little closer, but she held her hand up.

'Please. I am busy with this.'

'It's just... I was wondering if you had seen this man before...'

Ross held out Jamie's picture. The girl looked but shook her head. Ross showed her a photograph of Sutton. 'Or him?' This time, she hesitated, just enough for Ross to feel hopeful.

'Maybe him.'

'Recently?'

'This week, for sure. About lunchtime. Couple days ago. OK now?'

'Was he using a computer? Or just having coffee?'

'He was there, on computer next to you.'

'Thanks for your time.'

Ross wheeled back to his own workstation, and sent an email to George, cc Jane.

'One positive ID of Sutton at Greaves's Deansgate gaff. This week, daytime. Nothing on Jamie as yet.' He looked out of the window and a big guy with a crew cut and an expensive suit caught his eye.

He seemed to be looking straight at Ross, but then he turned away and checked his mobile.

Ross shrugged, and carried on with his message: *'Only one other punter in here. Makes me wonder why Greaves took them on. Sutton may have used a workstation. Maybe grab info off that? Off to Salford next.'*

He pressed send, tilted himself back in the chair and turned as a buzzer signalled someone else was coming in.

Ross quickly mimed being busy browsing, and raised an eyebrow when crew cut walked over and sat down next to him, straightening the creases on his trousers.

Ross noted that, even under his suit, his biceps were thicker than most people's thighs. He wondered whether he ought to recognise him, maybe from one of the Manchester night clubs. His eye was puffed up slightly, as if he'd been in a fight. A bouncer, then...

Ross tried to maintain his trademark cool, but he was relieved the Polish girl was still there. And even more relieved when the guy spoke, held his hand out, and seemed friendly.

'Good morning, I'm Adrian Cheshire.'

Ross gave the handshake his best shot but his slim fingers felt like they were trapped in a slowly closing vice.

'Nice to meet you...'

'I recognise you. You're with Ashbridge Police, aren't you?'

Ross was impressed; almost thrown. But he refused to show it. 'Yeah, spot on. And you are?'

'I'm Ops Director at Greaves; you know, that company you told some of my colleagues you were hoping to work for?'

Ross kept a straight face. 'Just doing my job, Mr Cheshire.'

'We all are, Mr...?'

'Rossiter. My friends call me Ross. Anyway, how do you know me?'

'We have loyal employees, some of whom aren't easily misled, even on a coffee break. My PA was one of them, and she was so taken with you she took a picture. So... Ross, how would you feel about telling me what's going on?'

'What's going on is that we are investigating a murder: a murder that took place in one of your internet cafes.'

'I understand. But not this one.'

'No.' Ross hesitated. He could feel himself being drawn into telling this guy more than he should, and Jane would go ballistic.

'Right. So you're here because…?'

Ross chose his words carefully. 'Simple reason. We're trying to find people who may have known Jamie, and it struck us that if he used the Ashbridge site, he may have visited others in your empire. Pretty standard stuff.' Ross smiled and showed the picture. 'This is him. Ever seen him before, Mr Cheshire?'

'No I haven't.'

'Now it's my turn… can I ask what you are doing here?'

Adrian smiled, and Ross swore later he almost liked him. 'Doing my job, Mr Rossiter.'

Adrian checked his watch and stood. 'Glad I bumped into you.' Then, just as he turned away, he stopped, and leaned in. 'I'm here for one of my regular site visits. Can I suggest that you contact me, at any time, if you want any more information about the company and our activities. There's really no need to go undercover. Here's my card. I mean it. Call me.'

He walked away, tapped on the back office door, and went in without waiting for a response.

Ross put the business card in his shirt pocket, and tapped out a text copied to Jane, George and Mark.

Just met a big guy at Greaves, Adrian Cheshire. And I mean big! He recognised me! Wants us to call if we need anything. Thought one of you might take him up…

He added the number, and hit send.

At that same moment, Adrian Cheshire was calling Graeme Hargreaves.

'I just found that copper at Deansgate, the same one who was at Pret yesterday.'

'What in God's name is going on? Does he think he's got a part in Spooks or something?'

'Couldn't get anything out of him, but I gave him my card. I saw his badge and he's just a DC. Told him to get in touch.'

'Bollocks to that. I'll get in touch… What's that DCI woman called again?'

'Jane Birchfield.'

'Well it's time we met. Leave it with me. And don't forget what I said. I want to know what you find out, when you find out. Give me an update first thing tomorrow, ok – just in case I need to impress Ms Birchfield. I don't want her catching me out, all right?'

'Will do.'

Adrian switched off and felt the sheaf of notes in his inside pocket. His report was pretty much done, and Graeme was not going to be pleased.

He turned to the Deansgate cafe manager, who was trying to look busy sorting papers on his desk.

'Now… Joseph, isn't it?'

Joseph looked up, nodded and folded his arms.

Adrian slowly unfolded two sheets of paper and laid them side by side in front of him, then opened the conversation that would lead to his third dismissal of the day.

'OK Joseph, there has been a fair bit of hacking going on from this site; directly into the Greaves system. I note that your job description tasks you with monitoring activity here, so I presume you were aware of that…?'

Jane mulled over the Sutton situation in less than a minute, then put a note round on the system ordering that his description be circulated straight away, initially only to the Ashbridge uniform section.

When Lorry handed over Jamie's letter, she said George had asked her to pick up the work on Sutton's description.

Lorry was all for full publicity. 'We'd catch him quicker if we got it on the news, wouldn't we ma'am?'

'I don't want the media getting hold of it yet, Lorry. Think it through. if it's on tv and radio now, we not only give Sutton the advantage of knowing we're after him, giving him time to scarper; but if he's working with others, we alert them too. They could shut up shop and make it difficult to track them down. We could blow one of the best leads we've got out of the water. And it's thanks to you that we're onto him, isn't it? Better this way…'

Lorry took notes. She was keen to learn, and already thinking about her next promotion. 'Oh yes, I can see that. Sorry, I didn't mean to-'

Jane held up a hand. 'It's ok… Well done, Lorry. Thanks for the letter as well. Interesting times. Happy?'

'Oh yes, ma'am, thanks! It's great to be part of the team and I love the extra responsibility.'

'It's good to have you on board. You're a quick learner.'

Lorry smiled and crossed her legs, as if she was settling in for a chat. 'What do you make of the letter, ma'am?'

Jane smiled. 'Let me read it. I think we all need some thinking time. Remember not to rush into anything. Every step we take has a consequence.'

'Oh, yeah, definitely.'

'Right. Better get that description out before Sutton emigrates?'

Lorry sprang out of the chair, full of nervous energy. 'Oh! Yes! Sorry, I'll do it now.'

She was just about to slam the door behind her, when her head peered round. 'Thanks, ma'am.'

'Bye Lorry, thanks.'

Jane poured a can of sparkling water into a glass, and was just about to sip when her deskphone rang. The LED screen told her it was Doreen on the front desk, aka Dizzy Doreen.

'Hi Doreen.'

She sounded even more hyper and distracted than usual. 'Hello, yes, sorry to bother and all that, but I have a call from you—'

'You mean for me…'

'What? Oh yes, sorry… God! What a day!'

'Just tell me who it is Doreen.'

'Yes. It's… hang on a minute, I wrote it down… yes, here it is: it's a call from Mr Hargreaves' office at Greaves Online. He's the boss, you know!'

'Ok, that's good, thanks Doreen.'

'So shall I put it through?'

'Well that would be helpful, thank you.'

'All right, any time. Here it is!'

Jane reached for her notebook and tapped her pen as she listened to Doreen pressing myriad buttons. Finally, another voice…

'Am I speaking to DCI Jane Birchfield?'

'You are. Who is this?'

'My name is Lucinda. Mr Hargreaves' PA. I'll put you through now.'

Jane wrote a note… *'Cancel Mark call to Hargreaves.'*

His voice was pleasant enough but he was clearly in a hurry. 'DCI Birchfield. Nice to talk to you. I thought it best if we spoke rather than doing this through our PAs…'

Jane thought: Chance'd be a fine thing. Jane said: 'That's fine. How can I help?'

'Would you be free to meet me here tomorrow around 11?'

'In connection with…?'

He laughed briefly. 'We both know, don't we? There has been a murder at one of our sites, and you're clearly interested in my company because one of your boys has been paying us unannounced visits. So, as we have nothing to hide, why don't we skip the skullduggery and sort this out between us? How does that sound?'

Jane kept her tone of voice formal, deciding not to rise to the bait. 'Sounds good, Mr Hargreaves. As you can imagine, we will leave no stone unturned. I had in any case planned to call you today to arrange for us to meet up.'

'Great minds.'

'Can we say 10.30 tomorrow, your office. I'll bring a colleague, Mark Manning, who is a little bit more savvy about IT than I am, if that's ok.'

'Of course. Look forward to meeting you. Heard lots of great things about you.'

Jane paused, slightly thrown; but was that his intention? 'That's a nice change. See you tomorrow.'

Jane thanked the heavens she'd had a night in with Allan last night, because today was entering the category of manic. She quickly logged the appointment, copied Mark in, and allocated 30 minutes prep time for later: whenever that may be.

But now it was time for the call she'd been putting off all morning. Part of her said that Charles must still be hanging on, otherwise the hospice would have called. The other half of her brain told her the hospice wouldn't call; it was up to his family if they wanted to let her know.

All the crisp formality and control of her phone call with Hargreaves had gone now.

The knot in her stomach grew tighter as she keyed in the number.

THIRTEEN

ALLAN HAD NEVER REGRETTED investing his pay off to become owner, editor – and sole employee – of the Ashbridge Free Press; the paper he set up after nervously accepting early retirement from his old editor; the warm hearted, alcohol infused Sidney.

His office on Western Avenue was on the first floor of a block built three years ago on the old abattoir site. Most of his fellow tenants had come and gone, including the one he missed the most… the enigmatic Michelle, who looked like a model, and ran the equally enigmatic Agence Elise.

She left a year ago, and Allan had finally plucked up the courage to ask her what she did. His illusions were shattered when she told him in a pronounced Birmingham accent that she sold cleaning products.

Her space on the first floor had been taken by a guy who did telephone and wifi related installations, but the best news was that the ground floor had been taken over by the excellent

Betty's. Its window justifiably proclaimed 'Best Butties Int' Bridge', which Allan thought could be successfully defended in a court of law. He had to admit the cakes were pretty amazing, too.

Now, he was at his desk with one of Betty's Bakewell tarts and a mug of coffee, scanning the rival Times paper to see if he could spot any opportunities for a new angle on a story.

They'd devoted most of the front page to the Jamie Castleton murder, and Allan made a note to rib Jane about the fact that she was their page 3 girl…'Police Appeal – Can You Help?'

The Free Press was distributed to shops and offices on Fridays and Saturdays, which gave Allan an extra day's news gathering advantage over the Times. But he was running out of time for this week's edition, and he still had the best pages – front, 2 and 3, to fill.

He couldn't avoid covering the murder in some way. But which way?

Then he remembered Jane saying that Greaves owned the cafe where Jamie died – information he could easily have got from other sources, using their local knowledge. The Times hadn't mentioned any of that.

He would never drop Jane in it, but this would be safe enough; as long as he made sure the paper's on-call solicitor read the story before it was printed, anyway.

Allan started a web search, and saw a link to a piece about the company's share price being hit by hacking rumours. Interesting… and could be the angle, although Allan didn't want his paper to always look for the negatives. After all, the profits came from the advertisers.

He used his fingers to scoop up the last crumbs of Bakewell from the paper plate, cleaned up with a wet wipe, and began following the web trail.

As usual, it didn't take long to get sidetracked, and he soon found himself on Jamie Castleton's Facebook page, without really knowing how he got there. Jamie had used it mainly to promote his business, including a mention of the work he'd done for Allan on his server and network.

Allan shook his head. Jamie was a nice lad, and very good at his job.

He scrolled back to the top of his page and couldn't resist having a nosey at Jamie's friends list. It wasn't going to fill his paper with exclusives, but it was his lunch break, and… result! He saw a face he recognised, and clicked to see his page. Yes, that was the guy. He works out at the same gym; bit of a psycho; edgy, pumped up; headphones on; always checking his phone…

So that's his name… Martin Sutton.

Lorry was having a good day. First, there was Irene's letter, then the important job of circulating Sutton's description, and then a nice chat with the boss.

She was in a good mood, even though all this made her late for lunch in the canteen with Mark. She was miffed that – after climbing two flights of stairs, two steps at a time, she was there before him. Mark showed up five minutes late, by which time she'd seen off two sausage rolls. But she smiled and nudged his knee under the table with hers, as he sat down, just as she was about to give up and go.

They'd been a couple for two months. Lorry had been completely thrown when Mark asked her if she fancied a drink after work. It was one in the eye for her mum, who said her Goth look would turn most men off. Truth was, mum didn't want a man taking Lorry away from her. In any case, she'd had to lighten up the dark Goth make up a bit anyway, after getting her transfer into CID. Now Mark was calling round a few nights a week. And mum actually liked him, which was a first.

Mark leaned in. 'How are you, lovely? Can I get you anything?'

Lorry dabbed a finger on her plate to mop up some stray sausage roll pastry. 'I haven't got long. But, go on… get me a sponge pudding, will you, darling?'

Mark came back with her order, and a plate of egg and chips. He loved his food, too, and it showed. 'Sorry I'm late. Working flat out on the tech stuff on the murder. You?'

Lorry listed the things she'd done, then keeping up the stage whisper level of their conversation whenever they were on police time… 'Being honest, I reckon we know who did it.'

'What? Who?'

'One of his mates, name of Sutton. Jag and me went to see him, and ended up bringing him in. Looked guilty as sin. My theory is they were both doing that betting hack, then Jamie ripped Sutton off, and Sutton killed him.'

'Yeah… it's possible… Have you told the boss? What does she say?'

She winked. 'Not yet. But I've circulated his description, so it won't be long before we drag the slimy creep back in here.' Lorry put her hand on his, and whispered. 'Imagine that, babe… my first murder case, and I'm the one who nabs him!'

Mark smiled and carried on eating, with Lorry helping herself to chips, narrowing her eyes as Mark told her: 'I'm going on an interview with the boss in the morning.'

'Who with?'

'It's just gone on the log. The boss at Greaves… Graeme Hargreaves. She wants to find out how much he knows about the hacking. I was going to phone him to make an appointment, but he called the boss before I got chance, so it sounds like—'

'—he's keen to talk…'

'Yep. The boss wants me there to help out with any techie stuff.'

'You'll be great. Wish I was coming.'

'You might be interviewing that guy... Sutton, by then.'

Lorry's dark eyes glinted. 'Yeah. He's the murderer. I'm sure of it.'

Forensic Phil had seen enough of hospitals in his time, what with his mother and his wife's illnesses.

He'd vowed he wouldn't set foot in one again, unless he was wheeled in on a trolley.

But here he was, being messed about by jumped up, smooth faced bureaucrats disguised as doctors, utterly sure of themselves, and adamant that their judgement was flawless. Which meant that no, Phil could not examine the body.

One particularly obnoxious guy told him. 'You see, he was in the Cardiac Unit, and it appears he had a heart attack. It's hardly a police matter, is it, hmmmm?'

The fact that the death was linked to a murder inquiry was apparently of no consequence to any of them.

Jane had promised to take it up with the Chief Exec, but that could take hours.

'God help the bloody patients,' he said to no-one in particular, as he marched out to his car.

Shirley French was in a hurry.

She was determined to cram in a jog and a gym session before her shift started. Her boyfriend Shane thought she was mad, but Shirley couldn't take that from a man whose only real exercise was going to watch football, and lifting his right hand to pick up customer calls at the call centre in Salford. He said it paid better than the bakery, but she reckoned it was just easier work; sitting on his backside all day.

Shirley checked her pace on her running watch – 7 minutes for the first kilometre – and, with about 2k to reach the gym, decided to kick on a bit. She'd done a 5k park run in under 30 minutes, but that was six months ago, and work had been getting in the way since then.

She reached the gym, breathing hard, swiped her card and went up to the fitness centre, enjoying the fact that there was no need to change out of her t-shirt and Lycra leggings.. Everything else was in what she called her Tardis belt, which had room for keys, her phone, money, and a notebook and pen.

After a quick hello to the girl on duty, she helped herself to a cup of water and began her routine.

It was mid-afternoon, and very quiet. Only half a dozen people in, unfortunately including one guy grunting and heaving as he tackled a set of weights, which he then dropped with a crash. He had headphones on, and was rocking his head to the music, oblivious to the noise he was making.

Shirley inserted her card into the chest press machine, and adjusted the load. Three sets of ten here, then it's the lateral pulldown, then the leg extension, then some free weights, stretches and the return run home.

She checked her action in the floor to ceiling mirror, and tutted as she noticed the weightlifter, hands on hips, giving her the eye.

Shirley was aware of her good looks, and proud of her slim figure. She was also aware of the effect she seemed to have on men, who seemed much more keen to talk to her than friends who weren't so slim, blond haired and blue eyed. The shallowness and the injustice of it really wound her up, and she was keen to stay in the background whenever she went out with girlfriends, because she knew how hurtful it must be.

She'd hardened up after a couple of years coping with some real bozos and some pathetic chat-up lines at the station, but her mum was right – 'You care too much, Shirl.'

And this creep looked like a perfect example of the sort of leering pig she loathed. The kind who thinks he's God's gift because he has biceps bursting out of his tight t-shirt.

Shirley finished her set and moved to the next machine. She could see him following her with his eyes, and yes, my God, he really was licking his lips slowly and obviously.

She thought there has to be a law against this, then reminded herself she was a PC with martial arts training. She *was* the law.

She forced herself to concentrate on her routine. But 20 minutes later, as she was doing her last hamstring stretch with the belts, she saw he was still looking.

This time, she stared back, and there was something in his eyes she found disturbing. This was far more than the usual come to bed look. Shirley was used to that. But this… It felt more like 'come here and I'll do disgusting things with you'.

She felt the revulsion building, and gave him another hard stare as she walked away.

He just smiled and winked, and called out: 'See you next time.'

Shirley ran the 3k back home three minutes quicker, and stayed under the shower a lot longer than usual.

Ever since Jamie's letter, Irene Castleton had been unable to decide how she felt any more.

She'd bump into people at the Nisa store down the road, and one or two would try to be neighbourly: 'How are you coping, dear?'

But Irene didn't know what to say. Tongues would wag if she told everyone she was all right, and a lot richer. Equally, she wasn't the sort to milk the sympathy. So she'd stuck to a standard reply, which she thought was safer: 'It's a very difficult time, but I'm coping, thank you very much.'

And it was true. She felt she was coping. Not that that made her feel better. In fact, she felt guilty she wasn't grief-stricken.

Everyone expected her to crack up now she was on her own. She could imagine them saying it…'That boy was the light of her life. She'll go downhill now, just you wait.'

Irene had spent most of her life telling herself that no-one can go downhill for ever. There must be a climb up sometime.

That big detective woman had written out a copy of Jamie's letter before she took the real one away. Irene read it again.

The bank manager said Jamie had opened a savings account for her, and he'd explain it all next time she went in. She could go in any time, even without the original letter, because he knew who she was.

But Irene didn't want to rush it. Another feeling mixed in with the rest was fear, as she tried to imagine how he'd made all that money.

As she'd said to Shirley French, the liaison officer: 'A mother knows… He changed in the last few weeks. Hardly talking, hardly smiling.'

Shirley had asked what she thought he was up to, and Irene had immediately regretted it, but she said, without really thinking: 'Something illegal.' Well it had to be something bad, for him to change like that, didn't it? Shirley had just said it was a natural thing to think like that, but that sometimes people can get depressed and anxious when there's no obvious reason.

Irene wasn't so sure about that. She remembered the depression that hit her after Alec walked out all those years ago, leaving her to bring Jamie up.

And here she was, alone again. But thanks to Jamie, this was a different kind of alone.

Irene had already started spending the money in her head: some new clothes, a few bits of furniture, and maybe a cruise?

Everyone said lots of single people do cruises and there's always someone to talk to, and lots of things to do.

Irene had another thought. For the first time in her life, she could be selfish.

There was no-one else to worry about, no responsibility. Just the chance of enjoying what time she had left.

And then, the guilt hit her again, and she felt the tension headache creeping across her forehead.

How could she even think like this? What would people think of seeing her spending money like water? Her new life was all thanks to Jamie. And look at the price he'd paid to give his mum a bit of security.

A mental health counsellor had told her years back, after she'd been abandoned by her husband: 'You won't find any answers in a glass of wine, Irene.'

But Irene was tired of thinking, tired of turning everything over. She wiped her eyes on the sleeve of her blouse, poured herself a large one, and told herself she'd go to the bank tomorrow.

Shirley thought about Irene as she drove into the car park behind Ashbridge Police Station.

She was still thinking about her as she signed herself in on the sheet at the back entrance.

'Penny for them, Shirley.'

'Oh, hi Ross. Y'alright?'

'I'm cool, yeah. You look a bit out of it.'

'And a good afternoon to you too.' She smiled. 'Yeah, I keep thinking about that poor lad's mother...'

'Mrs Castleton?'

'Can't imagine how she's feeling. Keep thinking I should go round. Do you think the boss would mind?'

'Probably not, but depends what your other boss – that dictator of a sergeant – has got lined up for you.'

'I'll go round in my spare time if I have to. I'm worried, Ross.'

'You care too much.'

'And you sound like my mum.'

'Crap. No-one has ever said that to me before.' Ross grinned and ran a hand through his hair. Shirley could see the black roots showing, then averted her eyes as he turned to face her again. 'Have you heard about our manhunt?'

'Are you taking the pea eye double ess?'

'Me? Shut up. No, it's true. Lorry's circulated a description of a suspect.' Ross did a really bad impression of a cowboy drawl. 'Y'all better git some shootin' irons, cos this is a manhunt.'

'Who is it?'

'Dunno. I've only just got back from a tour of internet cafes, as you do.'

'Now you're making me jealous… Hey, I'd better go and see what the Sarge has got for me. See you later, Ross.'

'See you, manhunter.'

Ross took the stairs two at a time, before Shirley could react; his metal heels clicking loudly. Shirley walked into the office. She was the first in, so she stopped at the sarge's desk where he always left notes for the next shift, and picked up a bundle of paper.

It was the usual stuff… dodgy looking middle aged male seen several times near school playground; a few shops on East Street reporting shoplifting, possibly by the same gang; and the poster Ross mentioned…

FOR INTERNAL COMMUNICATION ONLY: We want to interview this man in connection with the murder of Jamie Castleton…

That was as far as she got. Her eyes strayed automatically down to the colour picture.

She threw the other papers back on the desk and ran up the stairs to CID.

It was only when she got there she realised she'd forgotten the code to get in. George, Lorry, Ross and Jag looked up as Shirley yelled at them to open the door.

Jag stepped aside as she walked in.

'I know this guy! I saw him today at the gym!'

FOURTEEN

ALLAN WAS HALF ASLEEP on the sofa when she got home.

Jane had been buzzing most of the day, but now all she wanted was space. She pushed the thought away as she turned her key in the front door, wondering whether Allan's loving mood would survive many more of her late nights. If not, she may have more space than she bargained for.

So she felt something approaching relief when he got up and hugged her.

'Thanks, that's just what I need.'

'Knackered?'

'Totally, but not in a bad way.'

'So, positively knackered…'

'What about you? Got your edition sorted?'

Allan certainly seemed attentive tonight. He asked about Charles, and Jane told him there was no change. She managed to dodge his questions about work, then happily obeyed his orders to get changed and relax, while he sorted supper.

By ten, she was the one half asleep on the sofa.

Allan turned her round so she could lean back on his chest. He stroked her hair, but spoiled it by asking if she had any more news about her day.

Jane instantly felt the bubble of adrenaline grab her stomach, and sat up, surprising herself about how keen she now was to talk about it.

'We're moving really quickly. We are already looking for someone.'

'Really? For Jamie's murder? Wow.'

'Don't get too excited. We're pretty sure he's involved, but that's as far as it goes.'

'Who is it? Can you tell me?'

Jane smiled and sipped her tea, remembering how Allan's local and personal knowledge had come in very useful last time. 'Well, after your help during the Fiona Worsley case, how could I not?'

'True. I wish I could be of more help now. I did know Jamie briefly, when he did that work for me.'

'I know. You told me.'

Allan looked hurt. 'I do remember… You don't think I forgot, do you? No, don't answer… Anyway, about this suspect…'

Jane reached down to her bag, pulled out a poster and gave it to him.

'His name's Sutton.'

Allan's eyes widened as he saw the picture. 'You're kidding me.'

'What? Don't tell me you know him?'

'Good grief! No I don't, but I know where you can find him.'

He told her about the gym, and Jane forgot her tiredness as she talked through what Shirley had said earlier.

'We sent a couple of uniforms round to his house again

tonight, but no sign of him. His mum said he's always out, and she hasn't seen him since breakfast.'

'Do you think he knows you're looking for him?'

'He knows we suspect him of involvement, and that's motive enough to lie low. By doing that, he sort of confirms it, doesn't it? But he was confident or stupid enough to be at the gym this afternoon, so…'

'So…?'

'So maybe he'll be there tomorrow as well.'

'Reasonable assumption.'

'So why don't we nab him there?'

'Why not?'

Jane kissed him on the cheek. 'How about a teeny glass of red before bed?'

Allan frowned. 'You're up to something.'

'Well I was just wondering…'

'Yes?'

'Well, you're a big man…'

'Flattery will get you everywhere. And…?'

'How about you going to the gym tomorrow afternoon? I have the feeling Shirley will be there, too…'

Forensic Phil was propped up in bed watching the TV, and wondering what BBC4 was thinking of, buying in these slow Scandinavian crime series.

He found it hard to believe that detectives said so little, and never smiled. And why did they bother shooting it in colour when just about everything was grey and dark?

He decided life was too short, fired his remote at the screen and leaned back into his pillows.

Lying there in the sudden silence, looking up at the ceiling in the dim glow of the radio alarm, that familiar feeling of loneliness crept in like a burglar.

Phil sighed and closed his eyes, softly saying his night-time mantra…'you are doing fine… there's nothing wrong with being alone… just one day at a time… today was a good day.'

It sometimes helped, but not tonight.

The idea of retirement, and leaving behind all the people he knew through his long career, suddenly sounded ridiculous. Why had he told Jane? What would he do with his life? Sudoku? Singles holidays? Reading the paper in the library?

The Jamie case had given him a new zest for the job; a feeling he thought had gone, because he arrogantly thought he'd seen it all.

Phil pulled back the sheets and sat on the edge of the bed.

That was the point… there's always something new to learn.

He looked in the mirror and talked to himself: 'Yes, even at your age.'

And the Jamie case wasn't over yet. Now there was the death of Mr Gonzales to assess.

Phil moved downstairs and mixed a mug of Horlicks. It was supposed to help you sleep, but his brain was working overtime now.

Why was the hospital being so cagey? Was it just down to the usual internal politics? More than likely, but wasn't it a very strange coincidence that the last man to see Jamie at the Pretty Cool Cafe was also dead?

He had to get the chance to examine the body. And there was no way they could delay any longer.

Phil pulled his laptop towards him and switched on.

It was time to make the most of all that age and experience.

FIFTEEN

THE SUN WAS SHINING and the office was buzzing about Jane's plan to corner Sutton in the gym.

George was already irritable with Ross and Lorry, who seemed to be in competition for the assignment. 'For Christ's sake, button it!'

Lorry looked as guilty as a naughty schoolgirl, but Ross just grinned. 'Sorry, George. I just like winding Lorry up.'

'Well pack it in, will you? I need to concentrate.' He stared at his screen, then sat back and slapped his forehead in mock surprise. 'Well, would you Adam and Eve it? We finally got access to the CCTV footage.'

Lorry immediately perked up. 'That's great, when can we go through it?'

George narrowed his eyes. 'What do you mean, we? You're going through it.'

'But what about—?'

'I'm not sending either of you to the gym. I'm going. And

you two can have the honour of sitting quietly looking at the CCTV records.'

'But I brought him in, in the first place, George!'

Ross chipped in, laughing. 'Yeah, come on George. I just can't see you in a gym, somehow.'

Lorry was not amused. 'Come on, it's not funny. George, please…'

George sighed, and tried to look sympathetic. 'Sorry Lorry.' Ross sniggered, earning him scathing looks from both of them. 'The CCTV footage is important, too. Think about it. All we need is to see Sutton going in that cafe and coming out at the right sort of time, and we've nailed him. So, come on, get busy. Finish your jobs for this morning, and you can have a nice sit down in front of the telly later.'

Ross blew Lorry a kiss. 'I've always wanted to watch daytime tv with you, Loretta.'

George hid a smile. 'Now come along children. Behave. I've got to chat through the operation with the boss now. No more buggering about. We've got a killer to catch, remember?'

Allan spent the whole morning writing copy, editing contributors' copy, proof reading copy, and laying out the remaining news pages.

He was square eyed by lunchtime, but quietly pleased with this week's edition.

He'd decided to hold off till the last possible minute to decide the main story. Options were news of a couple of big retail names signing up for the Boulevard development – an exclusive he'd got from a contact at the company; and the hunt for Jamie's killer – with the possibility of an arrest this afternoon if all went well.

He'd stayed up late with Jane, drinking red wine and talking about the case. She trusted him not to break stories, but involving him in an arrest was a new one…

He'd surprised himself by agreeing so enthusiastically. It was deadline day, after all. But, thinking it through as he tried to sleep had relaxed him. All he was doing was being there after lunch, doing his normal workout, then texting Jane if and when Sutton came in. Oh, yes, and being prepared to rugby tackle the bastard if he started anything, though Jane assured him Shirley was more than capable of taking anyone out of action.

The reward could be another exclusive, too.

Allan stretched his aching back. So, two hours to go. Enough time to check the advertising pages. But first, one of Betty's butties had got his name on it.

The smile on Graeme Hargreaves' face seemed genuine enough, but Jane caught a glimpse of the steel behind his eyes as they shook hands in his office.

But then, you'd need a lot of steel to build a business like Greaves from nothing.

The other guy Ross had met was there, too, wearing a suit that seemed too tight just about everywhere.

Again, though, Adrian Cheshire came across as naturally friendly.

Jane and Mark sat together on a black leather sofa as Hargreaves poured coffee, looking relaxed in an open-necked shirt.

He and Cheshire sat in armchairs on the other side of the polished glass table.

'Thanks for fitting in a meeting, Mr Hargreaves.'

'Graeme, please. And Adrian.'

'Yes… Jane and Mark.'

Graeme leaned forward and looked Jane in the eye. 'We're glad of the chance to talk it through, Jane. Adrian has done a lot of work on this, and – if you're happy – I'd like him to explain where we are as a company.' He turned and smiled at Adrian. 'Go for it.'

Adrian glanced at his notebook.

'Well, obviously, the boy's death was a tragedy, and we can't comment on that. But we are sure he was the one hacking into our online betting server, at a cost to the company of £40,000.'

Jane hid her sudden interest by writing *'Irene £40k'* in her notepad. Adrian carried on, unperturbed by the sound of Mark tapping into his tablet.

'We know that access to the betting system was done from all our internet cafes, not just the one in Ashbridge. And we know it was one person because there was a pattern in the amounts taken, and the transactions were from only one location at a time.'

Mark looked up. 'So no evidence of a team working together.'

'Exactly. And we were able to track down the first transaction to... erm, Jamie Castleton's computer at the Ashbridge site. He seems to have used the same one, every time. We are satisfied that he was the hacker.'

Jane glanced at Mark, then turned to Graeme. 'Thank you. So does this mean the hacking has now stopped?'

'Yes it has.' Graeme held up a hand. 'And before you ask your questions, could I add that I have taken the decision to immediately close all our internet cafes, and shut down online betting temporarily ahead of a relaunch, giving Adrian here the chance to put in the security systems that his predecessor obviously failed to do.'

Mark sat a little straighter. 'Would you be willing to share the technical detail with us so we can verify that Jamie was the hacker?'

'Of course, Mark.'

Jane was thinking back to something Adrian had said. 'Can I double check… can you tell us how long the hacking has been going on?'

Adrian licked a finger tip and flicked through a few pages. 'Almost exactly a month.'

'And he – presumably Jamie – was touring your internet cafes to do this?'

'Yes, I have to say he wasn't very sophisticated in the way he tried to disguise himself,'

Mark murmured. 'Almost as if he wanted to be found out…'

Graeme was obviously wanting to move on. He shuffled in his seat. 'Well, that's for you to decide obviously. We just wanted to share what we've done and try to demonstrate our full co-operation with your inquiry. We have no prior knowledge of Jamie—'

Jane spoke more sharply than she intended. '—Or Mr Gonzales?'

'Well he's our employee, so obviously…'

'Did you know he died in the early hours yesterday?'

'No I bloody didn't. How?'

'The hospital thinks heart attack, but we want to check.'

Graeme looked at Adrian. 'We can dig out his personnel file, can't we?'

'Yes, I'll check first to see about family who need notifying. He was from Mexico but he may have relatives here.'

Jane nodded. 'We'll also need the names of your internet cafe managers, please. So, I think that's all for now. Thank you both for your time. If you could share that info with Mark, and send any personal details about Mr Gonzales direct to me, that would be helpful.'

Back in the car, with Mark driving, Jane was still trying to decide whether she could trust Graeme Hargreaves.

He, meanwhile, was at that moment having the smile wiped off his face.

Adrian was never sure how Graeme would react to anything, but he always said he preferred people who levelled with him.

He waited till the boss was back behind his desk, then cleared his throat.

'I've got some more news.'

'Well don't keep it to yourself, man.'

'Ok… I've found evidence of access to the dark web from the cafe where Jamie was found, and the one in Deansgate.'

'Dark web… probably people playing about with digital currency.'

'Yes there is a little bit of that…'

Graeme looked up. Adrian wouldn't waste his time, and it wasn't like him to build up to something. He'd normally spit it right out, but right now he was looking upset. 'Go on, tell me the worst. You're one of the few I'll take bad news from.'

'They've been getting into hard porn. And I mean, seriously hard porn: extreme, perversion, kids…'

'Jesus…'

'It gets worse… Looks like Gonzales was part of it.'

'Shit. And he died yesterday.'

'Yes.'

'Chances are he was bumped off, is that what you're saying?'

'I don't know. But it's possible.'

'When you say he was part of it, what exactly does that mean?'

'He wasn't making the porn, but the access went through him, suggesting—'

Graeme sprang out of his office chair, turned away and yelled at the window. '—that the dirty bastard was raking it in, on company time! If this gets out… I've just shut down our whole online betting service so we get the shareholders back onside, show them we are in control. But this… Christ!'

Adrian had been preparing for this all morning: he knew it would be seen as his knockout punch, but in his view, it was the only way.

He walked over and they stood together, looking out across Manchester. Close up, he could hear Graeme's ragged breathing. He'd never seen him look so deadly.

'We can't bury this. We have to tell the police.'

Graeme's breathing slowed as he clenched and unclenched his fists. He closed his eyes. 'I know. And they'd better track down who's behind this filth quick. Because if I get there first, I'll kill the bastard.'

Irene had refused to open the envelope containing the savings account book at the bank. She told them she had already had one shock from Jamie, and wanted to be on her own for this.

The bank manager had said he was always there, but of course he wasn't today, so Irene had to put up with a junior who couldn't shut up.

But she'd said it was ok to take it now. The account had been opened, and all they needed was a sample of her signature. And that was it.

She'd decided to extend her trip by stopping for a coffee at Betty's. Everybody said it was nice coffee and cakes there, so Irene went in around 12, ordered a cappuccino and a rock cake, and sat by the window.

She looked up as a big bloke came in and joined the queue for takeaways. His dark hair and heavy face reminded her of Alec. She wondered what he would be saying if he was sitting with her now: 'let's get a new car'. And she would have been a mug and said yes, as usual.

She broke the rock cake into bite size pebbles. By the time she'd finished, the big man was on his way, carrying a white paper bag and a disposable coffee cup.

Irene took another sip of coffee, and opened the envelope. Inside was a maroon booklet with the name of the bank in gold letters. She opened it slowly, and saw the opening balance… the numbers under the £ column were like a foreign language: 40,000? She'd been living on £300 a month since it changed to Universal Credit.

She flicked through the pages, noticing how thick the paper was and how stiff to open.

Then she saw a piece of paper had been slipped into the centre pages.

'The man is called BEAVIS. I've left a trail. Tell police for me. Love you mum. Jx'

Irene made a choking sound, scraped her chair back and stuffed everything in her bag before pushing out of the door at speed. A guy in a business suit in the takeaway queue shook his head and resumed studying his phone.

She'd only gone a few steps when the big man appeared in front of her.

'Are you ok?'

Irene leaned against the wall. 'Just… had a shock. Be ok…'

Allan frowned. She looked pale, her chest was heaving, and he could see her hand trembling.

'Want me to call an ambulance?'

'No… I'll be fine…'

Allan pointed at Betty's. 'Shall I find you somewhere to sit down in there?'

Irene's breathing was coming back to normal, and she managed a smile. 'No, thanks dear. I'll just get home.'

'Where's home?'

'Oh, it's about ten minutes walk.'

'Sure you're alright?

Irene nodded, patted his arm, and Allan remembered seeing her picture in the Times that morning.

'You're Mrs Castleton, aren't you?'

Irene stopped, uncertain. 'Yes.'

'I'm Allan, editor of the Free Press. I saw your picture in the paper, the other one. You see… I met Jamie when he did some work for me not long ago. He was a great lad and very good at his job. I'm… very sorry.'

Irene began weeping. Allan didn't know what to do, and mimed reassurance as Betty's lunchtime customers glanced their way on the walk back to work.

'I didn't mean to upset you…'

Irene sniffed. 'No, it's not that. It's just… you're the first person I've met who knew Jamie.'

'I got on well with him. He was very serious about his work. Very professional; thorough. I liked that.'

Irene held his hand, and he felt hers shaking. 'Thank you. Makes me feel happy to hear nice things about him. Not had that before…'

'Well, I'm sure others thought highly of him too…' He suddenly remembered his promise to be at the gym by two and he still hadn't signed off the advertising pages. 'Erm… are you ok, now? Can I get you anything? Oh, here's my card. Call me anytime.'

Irene squeezed his hand and looked into his eyes. 'Thank you, Allan. I will.'

He watched her walk steadily to the end of the street, but then she stopped and turned to look back.

As he waved, he saw her look down at her bag and hesitate.

Allan jogged up to her. 'Are you alright?'

Irene felt she could talk to this man, and she hadn't been able to say that about any man since Alec left. He had kind eyes, and he knew Jamie, so… 'I've had a shock. I don't know what to do.'

Allan steered her back towards Betty's. 'Come on, let's sit down in here and talk about it over a cup of tea.'

Irene finished her story by producing Jamie's note. Allan noted how neat the handwriting was. 'This is definitely Jamie's writing?'

'Oh yes, same as the letter he left for me.'

'And you have never heard him mention anyone called Beavis?'

'No, like I said, he hardly spoke to me in the last few weeks.'

The talking seemed to have done her good. She couldn't work out what sort of trail Jamie was referring to, until Allan suggested it must be something he'd done on his computer. Allan's big headache was whether he could use any of it as a news story. He knew it would be picked up by the nationals, which meant he'd earn a few quid. But it wouldn't help Irene's state of mind to splash her over the front pages. And the police didn't know about the Beavis note, so he'd have to spend time explaining it to them… and the clock was ticking to print deadline.

The clock… he checked his watch. 'I've got to get back to work, Irene. Can you give me your phone number, and I'll call you tomorrow? See if I can help. I need a bit of time to think anyway.'

He walked her to the end of the street. She patted his hand. 'Thank you, Allan. It's been so nice to talk to someone…'

'No problem. Thanks for trusting me. I'll call you tomorrow, alright?'

Back in the office, he felt guilty for even thinking of running a story after Irene had poured out her troubles. Maybe next week, though…

He looked at his watch again, saw his gym bag by the door, and wondered what on earth was going to happen next.

SIXTEEN

ALLAN FELT THE NERVES in his gut as he walked slowly up the stairs to the gym.

Helping the police with their enquiries had taken on new meaning, and sounded exciting, when he chatted the plan through with Jane last night. All he had to do was send a text as soon as Sutton arrived, and be there as an extra body just in case help was needed. 'Just do your usual workout, and be discreet when you text me. Oh, and Allan... don't try to be a hero, ok?'

Sounded easy enough, under the anaesthetic of two glasses of red, but it felt scary enough now.

Pushing through the double doors, he swiped his card and headed towards the free weights zone, scanning the room as he stopped at the water dispenser. He counted four people on treadmills, one bouncing around helplessly and far too quickly on the Nordic skier, and a plump man being coached on how to do the plank without resting on his stomach. But no sign of Sutton.

Allan knew this could be a waste of time. If Sutton doesn't turn up, he'd have lost at least an hour on his deadline day.

He willed himself to relax, and let his mind wander. The gym had a different atmosphere during the day. Allan was normally here in the early evening, with the other workers, and the radio music was upbeat. It felt more like a hotel lounge now.

He chose a spot which gave him a view of the entrance, picked a couple of weights, and did a set of bicep curls. By the time he'd done his next set of squat thrusts with dumbbells, he felt so hot he was wishing he'd worn shorts instead of his sweatpants.

His stomach lurched yet again as the door swung open. A guy walked in... or rather swaggered, bouncing on the balls of his feet, muscled chest and arms stretching against his t-shirt, headphones clamped on.

And he was heading Allan's way...

Allan recognised Sutton when he was just a few strides away. Their eyes met, and Sutton nodded without changing his disinterested expression. Allan raised a hand in greeting, and did a couple more squats as Sutton began crashing around setting up what looked like very heavy bar weights.

Turning his back, Allan mimed checking his phone, then scrolled down to Jane and sent a one word message... *Yes.*

It pinged back straight away, and it sounded so loud that Allan flinched. But no-one took any notice. He remembered Sutton was probably deafened by his own music, anyway.

Jane's response; *'10 minutes max. ok?'*

'Yep, fine.'

Allan had never known 10 minutes take so long.

Fortunately, Sutton was oblivious to everyone else, and just hammered his way through routines with grunts, occasional gasps, and crashes as he dropped the weights. Allan began to hope that Jane was sending some muscle, as back up for Shirley.

His heart sank when she walked in alone. He'd hadn't been expecting her to stride in wearing uniform, and carrying a stun gun, but he did expect more than Lycra shorts and a close fitting t-shirt – even though she did look stunning.

It obviously had the desired effect on Sutton. Jane had told him about Shirley's first meeting with him, and Allan saw his smile as he clocked her in the mirror. Shirley was bending over adjusting a cardio machine, and Sutton dropped his weights so he could enjoy the view.

Sutton caught Allan's eye and winked: 'Fancy some of that, mate?'

Allan faked a smile: 'Too young for me.'

Sutton laughed without humour as he strutted towards Shirley: 'Never too young for me, mate.'

He called out: 'Knew you'd be back. Couldn't stay away, eh?'

She turned and held a blocking hand up towards his chest: 'Just back off all right?'

'If you fight me off, it'll just make it… harder; know what I mean?'

Allan took a few steps forward, giving himself a clear run at Sutton. If he built up enough speed, he could at least flatten him for a while. But Shirley was unmoved, staring him out. 'Well if you do want to make it harder…'

Sutton smiled, but not for long.

She sprang him quickly, spinning Sutton round, pinned his arms behind his back, and left him face down on the floor within a couple of seconds.

Sutton yelled and thrashed like a giant netted salmon. Shirley flashed a look at Allan and he ran over and put all his weight into sitting astride Sutton's back.

But Sutton was fighting back, and he could feel himself being lifted off the ground.

Allan saw two PCs built like tanks burst through the doors and run towards them. Next thing he knew he'd been thrown to one side, and he felt the dull pain as his head hit a corner of a padded bench. Opening one eye, he saw one of them kneeling on Sutton's spine while the other pulled his hands behind him and cuffed them.

Allan sat up, rubbing his head, as they dragged Sutton upright, just as a really large guy in a grubby looking overcoat walked up to them.

He sneered at Sutton. 'Martin Sutton. We'd like the pleasure of your company at Ashbridge Police Station, if you'd be so kind.'

'What the fuck for?'

George Creasey looked round the gym. Not surprisingly, they were the centre of attention. 'Language… You've been telling us porkies, young man. Let's go.'

George tilted his head towards the door, and the two uniforms marched him out.

He smiled at Shirley. 'Bloody hell Shirley. Remind me to be nicer to you.'

Shirley laughed, ran a hand through her hair, and smiled at Allan. 'And remind me to be nicer to you. Thanks for sitting on him.'

Allan just rubbed his head, grinned like a schoolboy, and blushed.

Jane replaced the receiver and nodded at Phil.

'All good. We've got Sutton, and no harm done, apart from a bump to the head for Allan.'

'Is he ok?'

'He's always bumping his head… Anyway, Phil you were talking about Gonzales. How did you get on at the hospital?'

'Spoke to a mate of mine who's a friend of the registrar.

He's agreed to let me have a look. Word is they're not 100 percent sure.'

Jane tutted. 'Very reassuring. If the police took that attitude…'

Phil nodded. 'Exactly. I don't know about you, but it seems more than coincidence, doesn't it? Two people involved at the same internet cafe?'

'I'm hoping we can shed a bit more light now we've got Sutton nailed on as being present at the time of death. But Gonzales…how and who?'

'Well I hope to help with the how.'

'How soon, Phil?'

'Tonight, with a bit of luck..' He smiled. '…And no interference from smug gits with stethoscopes.'

Jag was greeted enthusiastically, but only because he was carrying a white box which they all knew contained a selection of cupcakes, courtesy of the boss.

Jane laughed when he offered her first choice, and heard Ross and George booing.

She pointed at George. 'I expect better from you, Creasey.'

'Sorry. You know I give my all, ma'am – especially if there's cake.'

Jane turned to the others, as they tried to eat without wasting any precious crumbs: successfully in Lorry's case.

'I just wanted to say thanks for a good job. I'm pleased with today, and with progress generally. I'll talk while you eat…

'We've got 24 hours with Sutton before we need to charge him, and we need to make the most of that. So I'll make this quick. We know he went into the cafe a few minutes before Jamie died, and we know he was in the flat upstairs the night before Gonzales collapsed in front of Mark, saying his tablets had gone missing.'

Lorry finished her cake first, and jumped in. 'It doesn't look good for him, does it, ma'am? I just had this feeling…'

'Let's just say I'll be interested to hear what he has to tell us, Lorry. But meanwhile, we also have confirmation from Greaves that Jamie was working alone, and earned 40 grand from the betting hack – the exact amount he left for his mum—'

George said: 'So if Sutton wasn't a hacker, it's an even bigger coincidence that he was there when Jamie died.'

'Yes, George. He was hinting last time that he may have been involved in the betting hack. We now know he wasn't… Let's see if we can use that to trip him up.

'Moving on… Mark and I met Graeme Hargreaves and Adrian Fisher. They've decided to shut down all their internet cafes and get rid of the managers. And they're stopping online betting site for a while, so they can rebuild a secure version.

'Also, Mark has suspicions about the print out Gonzales gave George on the day Jamie died. He's checked out some of the websites Jamie was supposedly looking at, and they are all just news and entertainment stuff.'

George grunted. 'Well, he was a young lad… Still, wouldn't surprise me if Gonzales doctored it.'

'Mark just can't believe someone as computer orientated as Jamie would while away his time in an internet cafe looking at stuff that most people browse through at home. So, Mark is doing a bit more work to get behind the security at the PC Cafe.

'Finally – Phil has got permission to examine Gonzales. I need hardly tell you that if it's anything other than natural causes, we're looking at a double murder enquiry, and I may need to bring in some help, but let's wait and see.'

George stood to sweep chocolate crumbs off his shirt front into a waste paper basket.

'Oh, and George – don't forget I need someone to keep an eye on Irene. Phil's checked the handwriting on the note Jamie left her, and it looks genuine, but that's a lot of cash and it's illicit earnings… we need to make sure she doesn't do anything stupid.'

George grumbled. 'Yeah, like going on a shopping spree with Greaves's cash.'

'Exactly. Now that really would go down well in the media.'

Jane had noticed Ross looking thoughtful, tapping his pen on his teeth. 'Come on Ross. What are you thinking?'

'What if he'd told his mum he was going to leave her £40k. Pretty good motive to knock him off…'

Lorry tutted. 'Come off it. His own mother?'

Ross gave her the smug smile that always annoyed her, and shrugged his shoulders.

Jane turned to leave. 'Ok Ross. We can't exclude any possibility just now. But we'll keep that one on the back burner for now… Right George. Let's go and talk to Mr Sutton.'

Ross sighed theatrically as the door closed behind them. 'So now I've been put on the back burner, have I? I'm hurt.'

Lorry laughed, then noticed Jag staring at his computer. 'Hey Jag. What are you doing? You haven't said a word to us all day.'

'George wanted me to carry on looking at the CCTV footage, a couple of days before and after Jamie died.'

'Found anything yet?'

'I've just found Sutton looking through the café window a day later, then jumping on a bus. I'm trying to find out which bus so I can try and pick him up at the other end.'

Ross groaned. 'You poor sod. Now that should definitely go on the back burner.'

Sutton checked his watch as Jane and George sat down.

'Do I need a solicitor?'

George looked up. 'I don't know. Do you?'

Sutton shook his head. 'Right smart arse, aren't you?'

Jane tapped the table with her pen. 'At the moment, you are helping us with our enquiries… so let's get on.'

George ran through the formal stuff in a dull monotone, never taking his eyes off Sutton.

Jane slowly opened her notebook and pulled out two sheets of paper, which she glanced at before placing them on the table, face down.

She looked up as George pushed the record button. 'Remind us, Martin, why you were arguing with Jamie in the middle of the High Street.'

'Oh for – I told you, he was doing some kind of betting hack, and I was warning him off.'

'Were you hacking as well?'

'Sometimes.'

'From the same place as Jamie? The Pretty Cool Cafe?'

'Yeah.'

Jane turned over one of the sheets. 'OK… take a look at this. It has been produced by the company that owns that cafe.'

She pushed it across.'Allow me to explain. These lines show beyond all doubt that only one person at a time was hacking into the company system. It's the same pattern at all the other internet cafes they own. So, you see, Martin – you can't have been hacking with Jamie, because he was operating alone.'

Sutton puffed out his cheeks and leaned back in his chair; the arrogance returning. He stared at Jane: 'Amazing. And you brought me back here just to tell me that did you?' He slapped the table hard and leaned in. 'Did you?!'

Jane raised her eyebrows and turned to George. His cue to step in.

'Carry on like that, matey, and I'll have you for threatening behaviour. On top of everything else.'

'Oh yeah? Well, there isn't anything else. Can I go now?'

'Oh no. You see, we are investigating a murder. We can keep you 24 hours, and I've no doubt we'll be allowed to add another 12 to that, no problem.'

George shuffled a few papers, giving time for that to sink in.

'So… what were you doing at the Pretty Cool Cafe the night Jamie died?'

'No comment.'

'Interesting… Next question: what were you doing in Mr Gonzales' upstairs flat the night before last.'

'Is this a joke? I… wasn't… there.'

'We've got fingerprints that prove you were. What were you doing there, Mr Sutton?'

Sutton looked down at the papers on the table and shrugged his shoulders. 'Ok, all right. I had a drink with him. So what?'

'Really? So you were lying—'

George was interrupted by a knock on the door, and Lorry came in, looking apologetic. George noted her entrance for the recorder.

Lorry said: 'Sorry ma'am, but there's a phone call for you, and you really need to take it.'

George recorded suspension of the interview.

Jane glanced at Sutton. 'Take five, Mr Sutton. But don't worry. We'll be back soon.'

She walked quickly to her office, asking Lorry to relieve Ross in the viewing room, to keep an eye on Sutton. 'Who's on the phone?'

'It's Mr Hargreaves, ma'am. Says he has some urgent information.'

Jane struggled to keep her voice steady.

'You are 100 per cent certain?'

Graeme Hargreaves was as businesslike as ever. 'Adrian accessed some of the web addresses he and his team had traced, using whatever program it is. Think sick and perverted. Then double it. We're talking children; young children, for God's sake.'

'My God…'

'And whoever these charming people are, they've been using our cafes at Ashbridge and Deansgate to get in.'

'Any way of identifying who is producing this stuff?'

'Adrian tells me there are multiple layers of encryption, and many random and numerical web addresses. Which is an IT guy's way of saying he hasn't been able to track them down.'

'Can I send Mark over so he can talk to Adrian?'

'Yes, I'd welcome the chance to team up. Apart from the damage to the company if this gets out, it's damaging me. I thought nothing could surprise me anymore. I was wrong.'

Jane eventually finished the call and slammed the receiver down as if it was contaminated. She felt anger and disgust welling inside her.

Her phone pinged. A text from Allan: *'Hi. Please call me. I have news Ax'*

Jane glanced at her desk calendar, and her reminders for today included phoning the hospice, and phoning mum. Meanwhile, Sutton was waiting in the interview room, she had to get Mark over to Greaves, and talk to Phil later about Gonzales.

Jane quickly numbered her tasks in priority order.

Allan was bottom of the list.

Allan inched his way home after joining the procession that was heading out of Manchester on the Ashbridge road.

This week's edition had gone to the printers, and they'd given him his favourite slot first thing in the morning. It meant he'd be relatively fresh when he signed off the final proofs, as compared with desperate for opening time/home if he'd had to do it tonight.

He'd resisted the temptation to persuade Irene to talk to him on the record. The main story was about the retailers coming to the Boulevard scheme, under the headline 'Big names give big boost to Ashbridge'.

He was happy enough with the story, but, as soon as everything had gone off to the printer using the secure Cloud Jamie installed, he found himself preoccupied with Irene's cryptic message. Allan enjoyed cryptic crosswords, and his mind was now set on solving the clue…who or what was Beavis, and what was the trail Jamie was talking about?

It was only when he arrived home just after 7 that he remembered he hadn't heard back from Jane.

Opening the door to the empty house took him back a few days, when he'd felt sufficiently pissed off with life to drive off to Lyme Regis. He tried to tell himself she was on a murder inquiry; she's bound to be stressed, and late home, and he should damn well make allowances…

Anyway, he wanted to tell her about the gym, and meeting Irene. So if that meant a quiet couple of hours with a ready meal and a glass of red wine before she got home, he just might be able to cope.

First things first, though. Allan sat at the kitchen table, opened his laptop, and typed Beavis into the search engine.

Jane arched her back and stretched her hands out towards the ceiling.

Everything was aching, and she felt the prickles of tiredness behind her eyes as she logged out of the system.

It was 9pm, and, however tired she felt, she wouldn't normally think twice about staying on into the early hours.

But now she felt the added pressure of Allan, no doubt waiting at home, watching the clock.

Then she wondered if she was using him as an excuse; that she really did think everything could wait till tomorrow. .

There was certainly plenty to be done. She ran through her list as she walked downstairs.

Phil was sure Gonzales had not died of natural causes, and there were strong similarities with Jamie's death; Sutton had been detained overnight for more questioning tomorrow; Mark was going to spend the morning at Greaves, checking out the betting hack and the hard porn access; and Jag would hopefully be uncovering more of Sutton's movements on CCTV.

Jane stepped out into the brightly lit car park. So far, it all seemed to be pointing at Sutton. But something about him made her question it, and she wished she could put her finger on what it was.

That was part of the problem: too much information means too little thinking time.

She smiled to herself as she pulled out of the car park onto the empty street. So that was settled. It really was ok to go home at 9pm, just to get some thinking time.

Two hours later, when she and Allan were still talking about developments in the case, she concluded she may as well have stayed at work.

It was as if he'd been bursting with news. She'd given him Brownie points for making her a sandwich and handing her a glass of Malbec, but he was talking at her about meeting Irene before she'd even made it to the sofa.

She'd tried a bit of sarcastic rhetoric. 'Oh hello darling. How was your day? You must be exhausted…' But it had gone completely over his head.

By the time he'd finished his story about Irene, though, he had her full attention.

'Blimey, Allan, are you sure you don't want a job with us?'

'No, you're alright, I'll stick to meddling.'

'Have you got all this written down somewhere?'

'Yeah, do you want me to send it? Like a statement, you mean?'

'Sort of... ' Jane frowned as she remembered the news from Hargreaves that had shaken her up. 'Look Allan... that stuff about Beavis. Please don't follow up on it. Leave it to us, will you?'

'I will, but I've already tracked down a few local Beavises, and—'

She spoke more sharply than she meant to, and Allan looked baffled. '—Well don't do any more.' She paused, softening. 'Sorry, Allan. Please trust me; the inquiry has taken a new twist. I can't talk to you or anyone else about it yet, but believe me, you do not want to get involved.'

'What sort of twist?' She held out a hand and he took it. 'Jane? What's wrong?'

'I just don't want this inquiry to spoil our lives, Allan. The more we find out, the messier it gets. And the more time we all have to put in. So, if you must know, I'm worried you're going to start resenting me coming home late. And on top of that, I'm now worried that the more you know, the more it will affect us both.'

'But—'

'I need you, Allan. I don't need another detective. I need you to keep me sane. To stop it getting to me; to make me laugh.' She smiled ruefully. 'I don't think you realise how important you are.'

Allan puffed out his cheeks. 'It's ok. I get it. Hmm. You've never said that to me before. It's... nice.'

Jane laughed. 'Nice? What else do you expect from a nice person like me?'

Allan winked. 'Well, you know…'

'No. Tell me.'

'Shall we go to bed?'

'I'm not tired.'

'Even better.' He held out a hand and pulled her up into his arms. 'Come on.'

Hargreaves' news about hard porn, and the memory it had provoked, came back as she cleaned her teeth. She tried to fight it away, but she was shocked it still hurt so much. It had happened 25 years ago, but the shame and revulsion felt exactly the same.

She felt shaky as she climbed into bed, hoping Allan had dozed off while he'd been waiting. She'd never felt less like having sex.

But as soon as she lay down, he moved in close, kissing her ear, cheek and mouth gently as he stroked her stomach, slowly moving his hand towards her thigh. Then he stopped, propping himself up on one elbow. 'Jane… you're shaking. Are you ok?'

She wanted to tell him what happened, but she'd kept the shame locked away for so long. She opened her eyes and tried to smile. 'Sorry. I just got over tired. Don't worry. Do you mind if we don't tonight?'

'Course not.' There was the pause, and Jane knew what was coming next. 'You're working too hard.'

'I know. Night Allan.'

She bounced as he dropped heavily onto his back, then turned over.

SEVENTEEN

Ross punched Jag on the shoulder as he walked into CID.

'You been here all night, mate?'

'Yes, most of it.'

'What? You need to get a life.'

Jag smiled politely. 'I know. But I like my job.'

'Fair enough. Anyway, I did ok at poker last night, thanks for asking… Hey, you should join us. Just me and a few mates, at my place. Next week?'

'Oh no. I'm no good at cards. Thanks though.'

'Oh well, one day, maybe? Anyway, have you found anything? I'm assuming you've been staring at CCTV footage all night?'

'Well, you know you told us about that lady who said Sutton was at the cafe on Deansgate?'

Ross snorted. 'Lady! Sorry, mate, yes, I remember.'

'Well he was. I tracked him down using the bus route he took from Ashbridge and we've got him going in there.'

'Ok, that's good. But how does that help?'

'I am thinking it will help the boss and George when they talk to Sutton.'

'See if he lies, you mean?'

'Yes, and I also have found another man – I think it's a man – going into the Ashbridge cafe where Jamie died.'

'They reckon half a dozen were in there that afternoon, so…'

'Yes and I can see them on CCTV because George gave me their descriptions, But this guy – he was not on that list.'

Ross moved to look over Jag's shoulder. 'Show me.'

'There.'

'Sweet. I hate to be a killjoy though, mate, but we'll never identify him. All you can see is a baseball cap and a coat.'

'It will be difficult. That's what drew me to him. The fact that he looks like he's trying not to be recognised.'

Jag stood up quickly as Jane walked in, and, noticing her tense expression, Ross moved rather guiltily to his own desk.

'You wanted a word, Jag?'

'Yes, ma'am. It's the CCTV footage…' Jag repeated what he'd told Ross, and ended by showing her the image of the unknown man. Ross shook his head. No way were they going to identify the guy.

'Can we zoom in closer?'

'Already done, ma'am, and it's very interesting… See?'

'What am I looking at Jag?'

'The trousers and shoes, ma'am. They are unusual.'

Ross moved in quietly and peered over their heads, as the image was magnified even more.

Jane smiled at Jag. 'Good work Jag. He's wearing scrubs.'

Jag turned to grin at Ross, who forced a smile as he quickly sat down again and punched the power button on his computer.

Jane spoke to both of them. 'Can you get to work on this now? Put every bit of detail on the log, Jag, so I can look at timings. Ross, can you take a close look at the image? See what else you can spot – approximate height, weight, skin colour, anything that might help. The trousers look blue, so check if that's significant. Might be different colour coded outfits for doctors, nurses, support staff… Then start searching for this guy… anyone fitting that description, with clothes like that, working at the hospital, or a clinic—'

'Or a vets, boss. And off duty at that time?'

'Good, Ross, yes. I'm back in with Sutton in a few minutes, so text me if you get anything definite, and we can see if there's any connection between them, alright?'

They nodded.

'Thanks you two. Ross, don't forget to brief George. And Jag?'

'Yes ma'am?'

'Excellent work. I saw your car was already here when I got in. Thanks for putting the time in.'

As the door swung shut and self locked behind her, Ross winked at Jag.

'You two should get a room.'

Jag looked blank. 'A room? What for?'

Ross sighed. 'Oh never mind…'

Sutton had again declined the offer of a solicitor.

As expected, he denied using the internet cafe on Deansgate, until George showed him a still from CCTV clearly showing him walking in.

'Yeah, so what? I took a quick look at the dump once, that's all.'

George had given him his most disarming smile. 'But, mate… we've got a witness says she saw you in there, working away on a computer. Even showed us which one, she did.'

Jane had left most of the talking to George this morning, but now she stepped in.

'So what were you doing in there? We know you weren't betting. Why go all the way into town, just to use a computer?'

Not surprisingly, Sutton clammed up again.

Jane checked the clock: they had another five hours before they either let him go, or applied for a 12 hour extension. She decided to let him stew a bit longer.

It turned out to be a good call.

Phil had left a message on her desk. *'Gonzales killed same way as Jamie. Carried out same tests as before and found traces of same substance. Full details on log by afternoon. Phil'.*

Jane knew she'd been off the pace this morning after only an hour's sleep last night, but she felt fully awake now.

The CCTV image flashed into her mind... That guy was wearing scrubs. So he was most likely a doctor or a nurse, no doubt with access to medical supplies, even if he had to steal them. The cap and the coat suggested he knew he'd be easy to identify, and that he was on a work break with no time to change out of uniform.

And Jamie and Gonzales both died from an overdose of a powerful drug used by hospitals.

Her instinct about Sutton was right. She'd remembered as she lay in bed last night, trying not to think about pornography, that one of the team – maybe Lorry – had described him as a knucklehead who wasn't even clever enough to lie properly.

And that was true.

Jane looked at Phil's note again, and felt that familiar surge of excitement as she sensed a breakthrough.

Sutton still had a lot of questions to answer. Something told her he wasn't the killer. But was he into perverted porn?

George seemed keen to talk, which was a bit unusual.

'I still don't get it, ma'am. Why would a crappy little betting scam like that be worth killing two people? And they both look like a professional job, too.'

'I know. We've got means and opportunity, but we're a bit short on motive.'

'We'll never pin this down unless we work out why. There's got to be something else. An angle we're missing.'

'Any ideas?'

George scratched his belly thoughtfully. 'I'm not famous for having ideas.'

Jane smiled. George was building up to something. 'Come on. Let's hear it.'

'Well, ma'am – if you insist… Jamie was a clever lad by all accounts; especially with computers.'

'True.'

'So I got to thinking… are we looking at it the wrong way? What if he was up to something else, and leaving clues for us. You told me this morning that note to his mum said something about following the trail…you know, the one she showed to Allan?'

Jane stared over George's shoulder, trying to remember something Mark had said at the meeting with Hargreaves. Yes, that was it… 'Almost as if he wanted to be noticed.'

'Sorry, ma'am?'

'It's ok George. I was just remembering a comment Mark made on the same lines. We now know that some people have also been accessing hard porn from two of the cafes. My first thought was that Jamie was one of them. But maybe he found out it was happening…'

George clapped his hand on his knee. 'And the bastard behind it found out. There's strong motive, right there, ma'am.'

'And we may have the killer on CCTV.' Jane stood quickly, suddenly energised. 'Right George, let's see what else we can get out of Sutton, then I want to throw everything at finding that guy on CCTV.'

'Yes, ma'am. And I'll bet you a fiver Sutton's one of the dirty bastards doing the hard porn.'

'I'm not taking that bet on, George. I reckon you could be right. Let's go.'

Ten minutes later, George was sipping his coffee in the interview room; enjoying Sutton's suffering, and Jane's technique.

Her news that Gonzales was dead, and it was another murder enquiry, had obviously shaken Sutton up, though he tried to hide it behind his usual show of anger.

'I haven't killed no-one!'

Jane threw him off balance by calmly nodding. 'You know what? I don't think you have.' Then, just as the cocky smile had made its comeback, she hit him with an inspired guess: 'Did you know Gonzales was running a hard porn subscription service?'

Sutton hadn't seen it coming, and the look on his face told them everything they needed to know.

George had never seen Jane so wired, as she pressed on. 'What happened? Did he demand more money from you to watch it? Is that why you went to see him the night before he died? Is that why you stole his tablets, knowing that without them he would probably die? You may not have killed him, but you had a damn good try. You're looking at a very serious charge here, Martin. Maybe it's time you talked to us…'

'I want a solicitor.'

George pushed the phone across the table. 'There you go, son. Press that button that says 'DS' and you'll get a duty solicitor. We'll wait for you.'

Back in Jane's office, George grinned. 'Blimey, ma'am, where did that line about Gonzales come from?'

Jane didn't reply. She was staring at a note on her desk.

'Ma'am?'

When she looked up, the colour had gone from her face and her voice sounded hoarse.

'I've just got a message. Charles Aston died half an hour ago.'

Mark Manning and Adrian Cheshire had to shuffle to one side to squeeze into the lift together.

Mark sucked in his stomach as best he could, conscious that, unlike him, Adrian was broad in the right areas. But, as he told Lorry later, they'd got on well… or, in his words, 'like brothers in IT arms'.

They'd had a productive couple of hours, comparing notes on dark web track and trace techniques. Mark was gratified to learn that police procedures stood comparison with anything the private sector had come up with. The only difference was that Adrian had access to what seemed limitless resources. And Mark didn't.

He felt confident, but at the same time, faintly out of his comfort zone, as they headed up to the top floor of Greaves' chrome and marble multi-storey palace, to meet the main man.

Adrian must have sensed his tension. 'You'll like Graeme. He doesn't like bullshit, so just tell it as it is, and he'll respect you for that.'

Mark nodded as the door pinged, and slid open, revealing what looked like the deck of a cruise ship: teak floorboards, chrome rails and white furniture. Mark stopped to admire the view across Manchester, but had to move quickly as Adrian was heading towards a large set of white double doors.

'This is the private way in,' he explained. 'He knows that if I use this door, it's confidential stuff he doesn't even want his PA to know.'

Adrian tapped a code into a keypad and the doors swung open to reveal, for the second time, the biggest office Mark had ever seen.

A disembodied voice called out: 'Adrian. Good. Come in, come in.'

Mark looked round, and realised why he hadn't spotted Hargreaves. He was wearing dark trousers and a dark shirt, and had obviously been sitting on a dark leather sofa.

He looked quite small, too. Though most people were small compared to Adrian. But his smile was genuine and the handshake very strong. 'Hi, you must be Mark. Good to meet you, and thanks for working with Adrian on this. I don't need to tell you how important it is to me that we cooperate fully.'

He pointed to the sofa and armchairs that occupied one corner of what looked like an entire floor of Mark's nearest Ikea.

There were bottles of water, and a pot of coffee, and a big plate of shortbread biscuits Mark would have had to himself, given the opportunity.

Graeme waited while they helped themselves, then looked at Adrian. 'Ok, where are we?'

'Well there's no doubt Gonzales was in on it. We found that the different terminals accessing the porn were used at certain times and on certain days, and we traced card payments to an account Gonzales had tried hard to conceal, coinciding with those times and days. Mark might want to chip in here…'

Mark cleared his throat. 'Yes… so Gonzales was being paid by people accessing porn at the two internet cafes, but we are sure the manager at Deansgate was unaware this was happening.'

Graeme shook his head. 'Why is that not a surprise? Sorry, Mark, carry on.'

'We were able to hack into a dark web browser Gonzales was using for payments into his account. But we haven't yet been able to get into the account to see whether he was a middle man, paying a fee to the provider of the porn, or whether he was the provider as well.'

Graeme couldn't hide his disgust, and Mark warmed to him. 'Forgive me, Mark, but it's just as well he's dead. It saves me killing the bastard… I mean, do we seriously think he was filming the porn as well? I can't believe it.'

Adrian bit on a shortbread biscuit, and Mark took that as an invitation to tuck in.

'To be honest, boss, I can't see it either. From what we know, it looks very much like Gonzales was paying out for the service, and trying to make money selling the access. And he was making good money. We can't prove all of it yet, but we'll find a way.'

Mark nodded. 'It's just a matter of time, Mr Hargreaves. We've got various tools we can use to get behind the layers that are built to protect dark web users. And an avenue we have yet to explore is Gonzales' phone and email records. We haven't gone into those much so far, but it's a different story now… There must be some contact with the person producing the porn. And one more thing… thanks to Adrian's help we've been able to confirm that Gonzales falsified the details of Jamie's final session.'

'Falsified?'

Adrian took over. 'Yeah, he printed out a browsing history from another user's PC. We checked and it's an exact match to the machine next to Jamie's on the day he died.'

'OK, so the fact that he covered that up…?'

'Suggests that Jamie may have been onto something.'

'Like the fact that Gonzales was feeding porn to perverts.'

'Exactly.'

'Good work, guys. Whatever you need, just ask me, either of you. This is absolute priority.'

He shook hands and stood up, walking back towards the double doors. Mark remembered wondering about how someone who seemed so slightly built, could be so powerful.

But he still regretted not eating a few more shortbread biscuits.

Graeme called out to them as they waited by the lift. 'Nearly forgot, Mark. Say hi to your lovely boss for me, will you?'

Mark nodded and smiled to himself as he stepped into the lift. He certainly wasn't referring to Forensic Phil.

The empty feeling in Allan's stomach had nothing to do with hunger.

He couldn't get away from the feeling that he was the one doing all the giving, being understanding, trying to make the relationship work. Whereas Jane's top priority was work. He wasn't even sure if he came second.

With time to brood on the slow drive to work, he'd decided that last night was a microcosm of everything that was wrong. He remembered he got home first, made her something to eat, poured the wine, chatted about his news… And the only time she'd come to life was when he talked about doing some research about that name Beavis. Even then, all she did was put him down… keep away from it, she'd told him.

They couldn't even have sex for the first time in weeks. She'd seemed up for it, and he certainly was; but he'd felt her flinch when he stroked her, for God's sake.

So there they were at breakfast, being polite, and Allan sensed they were both relieved when it was time for goodbye pecks on the cheek, and have a nice day.

Allan felt the indignation building inside, and he was already dreading going home tonight..

He stared at the screen showing 45 emails waiting to be read, including the usual letters to the editor from the usual suspects. He decided to ignore them for now, and opened a new tab. He had just keyed in 'Beavis', when his mobile slid across his desk on vibrate.

It was Jane. Allan tried to sound upbeat, but knew he'd failed.

'Hi Jane, you alright?'

Her voice sounded very unsteady. 'Allan… Charles Aston died today…'

'Oh God. Jane, I'm so sorry.'

'Can you come and pick me up?'

'Now? At the station?'

'Yes I know it's unusual but I need to get away; have some time with you… Sorry, I know you're probably busy—'

'Don't be daft. You're the one who's busy. I can be there in 20 minutes.'

'I've got to have another little chat with Sutton first, Can you meet me in a couple of hours? See you at the car park entrance… and Allan?'

'Yes?'

'I'm so sorry about last night. I've been badly shaken up – not just about Charles. And I want to talk to you.'

'Oh, ok… All right, Jane. Don't worry, and I'll get a bite to eat and see you later.'

Allan ended the call, trying to fight off the belief that whenever he had doubts about their relationship, he was always the one to end up feeling guilty.

Then he remembered what his mum used to say: 'That's the devil talking, Allan.'

He was hoping the devil would leave him alone for the rest of the day. But what the hell did Jane want to talk to him about?

EIGHTEEN

JANE SWITCHED HER PHONE to silent, and wished she could do the same for her brain.

The headache was worse today. It felt like a tight band, squeezing her. She massaged her temples with the tips of her fingers, her mind flicking channels... Charles, Allan, Sutton, the secret she thought she'd buried.

It almost felt like betrayal, when she'd only just heard that Charles had died. It was the news she'd been expecting, so maybe the shock wasn't so deep as it might have been. She knew he, of all people, would understand. But that was exactly why she missed him so much.

She wondered if she would have confided in him about her secret. But even if she hadn't, he would have sensed something was wrong, and encouraged her to talk.

Allan wasn't like that. He was afraid of feelings, and confrontation. She had no idea how he would react to her news, but she knew she had to share it with him before it poisoned them both.

She checked her watch. It was time to concentrate on work – something Allan said petulantly that she'd always been able to do.

Jane topped up her water bottle from the dispenser in the corridor. George – faithful, solid George – was waiting outside CID. He'd known Charles longer than anyone, and had brushed away a tear with his sleeve when Jane told him. She'd make sure he was next to her at the funeral next week.

'Come on George, let's do this.'

'Any more lucky guesses to surprise me with, ma'am?'

'Maybe… It won't surprise you to know that I think it's time we turned the screw, George. I'll give you a one word clue: Beavis.'

George smiled. 'Music to my ears, ma'am.'

Sutton was wearing his cocky smile as they sat down, no doubt feeling confident after a chat with the duty solicitor, the middle aged, greying Mr Browning, who always managed to look tired.

George did the introductions and switched the tape on, then glanced at Jane.

She put her elbows on the table and held Sutton's gaze for a moment. This was the pre-arranged cue for George to pay close attention to Sutton's reaction.

'Ok, Martin. We've talked about Mr Gonzales being murdered, and reminded you that you may face serious charges in connection with stealing his tablets.'

'Yeah, I know all that. It's bollocks.'

'Well, we'll come back to that later. But now you can help us with something else… I take it you must be very familiar with the name Beavis.'

It was a direct hit. Sutton's eyes widened, then he licked his lips. Jane noticed his hand was shaking slightly as he ran fingers through his hair.

Jane spoke quietly. 'What can you tell us about him, Martin?'

Sutton looked at Browning, who picked up his pen for no apparent reason, and looked bored. 'Perhaps you could give us an indication of why this is relevant?'

'Certainly. Your client's friend Jamie left a note for his mother, mentioning that name, and saying we should follow the trail. Now I'm not an expert, but from Martin's reaction, the name Beavis clearly is of some significance in this case. Which, I will remind you, is a double murder investigation.'

Browning leaned into Sutton and whispered. Sutton looked scared for the first time since he'd been brought in.

'All right, yeah. I know the name.'

'Who is he?'

'I don't know him, I just know the name, alright?'

Jane sighed. 'Look Martin. You've got a choice. Help us with our inquiry and it will look a lot better for you. We'll find this guy with or without you, so you need to think. Jamie was your friend—'

Sutton shouted: 'And now he's dead, isn't he? Jesus!' Jane picked up the meaning of George's raised eyebrows. 'Are you frightened of Beavis, Martin? Of what he'll do to you?'

He'd lost any semblance of control now. The fear was written in his eyes, and he spoke quickly.

'Gonzales told us about him. Said he was the real deal, doing all sorts of stuff, and Gonzales said he was paying him money every month, and he said he would be a dead man if he didn't pay.'

'Why was he paying Beavis?'

Sutton stared at the table.

'Come on, Martin. There's no need to be scared.'

'Oh yeah? What do you know about it, eh? He'll fucking kill me...'

George leaned forward. 'No he won't mate. He'd have to get past me first, and that's not going to happen. Talk to us, help us, and we'll look after you.'

Sutton whispered to Browning, then looked up. 'So, if I tell you what happened, we've got a deal, have we?'

Jane smiled. 'Like I said, Martin; you help us, and it will look good for you. But how much you get back depends on how much you give us. So, I'm sure Mr Browning would advise you to tell us everything you know… tell us the truth.'

Sutton took a deep breath and placed the palms of his hands on the table in front of him.

'Ok… Jamie was hacking into the system at Gonzales' place: that's where the betting thing started. But… he couldn't stop. Once he'd got in, he kept looking for stuff. He was like that… anything to do with computers. He found out Gonzales was getting porno videos and people were paying him for it.

'He said he found it by accident, but he said he was going to find where it was coming from, and then he'd tell the law cos he thought it was disgusting. He told me, you know, that day we were shouting in the street? And he said to me… *'you'd better make sure you're not looking at that stuff, because I'm going public with this.'*

'I told Gonzales one night, and that's when he said the name. He was bricking it – said he'd have to tell Beavis, cos if he found out from someone else, Gonzales would be a dead man.'

George looked up. 'He said that, did he?'

Sutton nodded, and his eyes suddenly filled with tears. 'I told Jamie to back off because of Beavis, but he wouldn't. Then a few days later, Jamie was dead. He wouldn't listen…'

For a moment, the only sound was the low hum of the tape recorder.

Sutton quickly wiped his eyes on the sleeve of his hoodie, and sat back. He tried to look defiant again, but the teary eyes ruined the effect.

Jane broke the silence. 'Thank you, Martin. You did the right thing. Can you confirm that you were one of the people viewing these… videos?'

'Yeah.'

'Can you tell us who else was?'

'Didn't know their names. Gonzales said the others came in at different times.'

'Did Jamie track where it was coming from?'

'Don't know. Don't think so.'

'Why did you go and see Gonzales the night after Jamie died?'

'I wanted to know if he'd told Beavis what Jamie was doing.'

'And had he?'

'He was off his head: whisky… said it was fuck all to do with me.'

'Is that when you stole his tablets?'

Sutton and Browning had another whispered conversation: 'No comment.'

'Ok Martin; Mr Browning… if you're going to withhold vital information, there's no deal. Either you tell us everything, or you are on your own. So think about that in your cell tonight. Tomorrow is your last chance. We'll give you a few minutes to talk to each other, then someone will take you downstairs.'

Out in the corridor, Jane told George she was taking the rest of the day off.

'Going anywhere nice, ma'am?'

'Just having a bit of time with Allan. It's been a while.'

'What are you thinking about Sutton?'

'That he took his tablets, but he didn't kill Gonzales. He's obviously scared out of his wits by Beavis. So let him stew in his cell tonight.'

'So we find Beavis, and we solve two murders, ma'am.'

'I think so, yes, George.'

Jane kissed Allan on the cheek as she settled in the passenger seat, but she sensed the tension behind his smile.

They both needed to get this over with. She smiled back, trying to lift his mood. Ironic, really, since she was the one dreading this. 'Shall we drive up onto the moor? I feel like a bit of air. Then maybe call in for a pint on the way home?'

Twenty minutes later, they were sitting on a bench at the viewpoint, looking across the tops of the pine trees towards Ashbridge. Jane remembered this was where Allan had held her in his arms for the first time. But there was a barrier between them now.

They'd made small talk about the view, then Allan turned to her, frowning. 'The suspense is killing me, Jane. Have you brought me up here to tell me it's over?'

'What? No!'

'That's a relief.'

'I thought you were getting fed up with me, not the other way round… No, I said I had something to tell you. I've never told anyone before. It's something I've lived with most of my life, and I'm ashamed of it. I've been putting off telling you, because… well, it's pretty disgusting… but now… the investigation…'

Allan's expression was a mix of puzzlement and concern. 'It's not good to keep things inside.' He paused. 'Disgusting? Christ, Jane, what's been going on?'

Jane cursed her stupidity. Now he thought she was shagging someone else. She briefly wondered why she could cope with confronting villains, yet struggle to communicate with the man she loved.

Allan could see the anxiety on her face, and he took her

hand in his. 'I know I can be a tosser at times – I'm not as tough as you... But I want you to tell me. Now.'

He looked so tense. Jane put her hand on the back of his neck and kissed him with a passion that caught both of them by surprise. They pulled apart guiltily as a car parked up near them with a scrunch of gravel.

Allan smiled and took her hand again. 'They caught us, like school kids—'

His smile faded as Jane turned away. 'Jane? What have I said?' He saw the frown on her face, and it seemed like a shadow had been cast over her. Her hand gripped his tightly. She let go and spoke slowly, as if she was having to force the words out.

'I was 15 years old. Never been with a boy. Never wanted to, and no-one asked me. Went home after school and did my homework, like a good girl. That's what I was – what mum and dad always said... 'Our Jane is such a good girl.' My favourite subject was English, and he was my favourite teacher. Mr Harrison. Everybody liked him. He was young, good looking...

'He liked me, and I really liked him.' Her voice became bitter. 'And respected him.

'I stayed behind after school a few times for extra tuition. It was just flirty at first. After a few weeks, he started touching my hand, my face... nothing much, but enough to get me excited. I was flattered. I was plain Jane. No-one had ever shown any interest in me till then.'

She sensed Allan's discomfort and turned to him. 'I know this is hard to hear, and it's going to get worse, sorry – but I've got to tell you.'

Allan just nodded.

'So... it went from there. The little touches turned to kisses. I started going round to his house instead of seeing friends. And then... and then... he started getting more physical; touching me, his hands all over me, getting more and more… intimate. I didn't mind too much at first, but every time I went to see him, I knew what he really wanted to do to me; even though I was under age – or because I was under age…'

Jane sighed. 'He never shagged me, but we did pretty much everything else. I suppose so he could always deny he'd actually had sex with me. I know it was wrong, but it was bloody great doing something wrong. But one night, I found out what a monster he was…'

She glanced at Allan. His face gave nothing away but his arms were folded tight against his chest. Jane took a deep breath, as the memory churned inside.

Then the words spilled out. 'It turned out he was into child porn. I was supposed to stay overnight with him. Told my parents it was a sleepover. I was watching tv and he went into another room he used as an office. He was gone for a while, so I went to see where he'd gone, and… he was watching a disgusting porn film – a child forced to do oral sex on a brute of a man.'

'Oh God, Jane, I can't believe—'

'—And while he was watching, he was jerking himself off.' She felt Allan flinch but she couldn't hold back. 'This man, this teacher that kids looked up to and loved – that I looked up to! – was just a dirty filthy pervert. He didn't even know I was there. I ran out of the house and walked the streets, crying my eyes out.'

'I felt so dirty.' She looked at Allan through the tears in her eyes. 'I feel dirty now, just remembering it.'

Allan hugged her, pulling her in so tightly he could feel her heart thumping. 'It's horrible, but… You did the right thing, telling me. But why on earth didn't you tell anyone?'

The feeling of disgust was still there, but it felt like an enormous knot had been untied inside her. 'I couldn't, Allan.

If I did, I'd have to tell them I was seeing him, and that he was being... intimate... with an underage pupil. I didn't dare tell my parents. It would have killed them.'

'So what did you do?'

'Bottled it up... for 25 years. Managed to change my study options so I didn't have to see him again. Stopped talking to my parents. Mum never understood why, and I can't blame her. We've been like strangers ever since, and I've never plucked up the courage to tell her what happened. Stayed away from friends, and found it difficult to trust men ever since.'

If Allan was flattered, he didn't show it. 'I can't believe you had to deal with it on your own. It must have been terrible.'

'Yeah. Not so unusual, though. That's what gets to me now. It's still going on. Young girls and boys being exploited, treated like animals to satisfy sick perverts. And this case we're on... that's what brought it all back. It's why I had to tell you, after last night. When we were going to bed, it just hit me again. I'm sorry to put all this on you... I just wanted you to understand.'

'I do, of course I do. I'm just sorry you've had to suffer in silence for so many years. You're a tough lady...'

Jane laughed ironically as she was blowing her nose, and the sound effect made them both laugh. 'Not so tough, and not much a lady. If I was really tough, I would have told everyone at school what happened. Made him pay. That's what I do now, isn't it? Make people pay for their crimes...'

'Maybe. It's easy to get everything right when you look back, though? I'm glad you told me. Makes me feel closer to you.'

Jane's voice sounded small. 'Really?'

'Yes. But I'd like to kill that teacher...'

'I know...That's what scares me now. It looks like Beavis is the head of a hard porn production unit that is selling child abuse videos. Just the name, Beavis, makes me feel violent. But

I can't let it affect me. That's why I wanted you to stay away from it.'

Allan let out a great sigh. 'And all this time, I never realised what you've been going through. What does that say about me?'

Jane looked into his eyes and smiled. The tears felt cold as they dried on her cheek. She held his hand. 'You couldn't have known, could you? All you need to know is that there's no-one else I'd rather spend my life with.'

Allan wiped a tear away. 'Same here.'

Jane glanced over his shoulder and saw a woman in the car, chewing, and looking at them curiously. She'd never bought into the idea that simply talking about problems helps them disappear. But she was converted now. And, she realised suddenly, she was very hungry.

'Come on you,' she pulled his arm as she stood up.

'Where are we going?'

'The pub. Have you forgotten already?'

As they walked back to the car, they saw the woman in the car had company. The man was reading a newspaper; the woman was now staring into space, emitting great clouds of vapour from an e-cigarette through the open window.

Allan grinned at Jane across the car roof. 'Nice to get out into the countryside for a bit of fresh air and fun, isn't it?'

They were still laughing as they drove down the steeply winding road through the trees, towards Ashbridge.

'What a difference a day makes...'

One of her favourite songs was on the car radio, and Jane's renewed energy and sense of purpose on her way into work convinced her the lyrics must be true.

Allan's love and understanding last night had reinforced her conviction that he really could be the rock on which she could build her life. Suddenly, she didn't feel so alone. It was some compensation for the sense of loss she felt now Charles had died. But what surprised her the most was that she had, for once, not been afraid to show her vulnerability.

It made her wonder if she'd been trying to play the ballsy female copper too long. Maybe her sensitivity and intuition were the things that really gave her the edge. Even so, she knew the next few days was going to be a test: could she – after what she went through all those years ago – be dispassionate and objective as she hunted Beavis down?

She thought it unlikely he was the man in scrubs Jag had found on CCTV. But then again… Jane had discovered that so-called respectable professionals were just as capable of depravity and greed as anyone else.

As she parked in her usual space behind the station – still reluctant to use the bay marked Chief Super – she wondered whether they would find Beavis hiding behind, what was the phrase?… a cloak of respectability.

George reported that Ross had no luck identifying the man in scrubs. He'd checked hospitals, clinics and vets, and no-one had reported anyone missing from duty that afternoon, and no-one could identify him from the fairly fuzzy still from CCTV.

Lorry and Jag had assembled more than 300 people and companies with the name Beavis. using local phone directories, online listings and social media accounts.

Jane told George she wanted Mark on the case. 'If Beavis has got any sense, he's likely to be hiding behind lots of security. Jamie was trying to track him, so can you get Mark to go back into Jamie's activity at the internet cafe, and see if he can pick up the trail he left for us?'

'Lorry thinks Sutton knows more than he's telling us.'

'I'm sure that's right, George, but Lorry needs to get away

from the idea that Sutton is the answer to everything. Speaking of which… shall we go and have another little chat with him?'

George smiled. 'I'll go and get us a coffee, ma'am.'

Allan hesitated before making the call. He'd promised Jane he wouldn't get involved, but he'd also promised Irene he would be there for her.

What harm would it do to just call her and see how she was?

He jabbed the screen, and she answered straight away.

'Hello, Irene. It's Allan; from the newspaper. We met the other day.'

'Hello Allan. This is a nice surprise. I thought you'd forgotten me.'

'No—'

'I know you're a busy man, but why don't you come and have a cup of tea?'

'Thanks, I'd like that. Is everything ok? Nothing's happened, has it?'

'No, I'm alright, I suppose. Just worried about what happens next. I'm a bit frightened.'

Allan didn't want to get drawn in over the phone. 'Tell you what. Why don't I pop round now? I've got an hour to spare.'

He was there in ten minutes, and completely thrown when Irene hugged him on the front doorstep, then fussed over him with tea and Victoria Sponge cake as they settled at the kitchen table.

While he was making short work of a generous slice of cake, Allan began to fret about whether he would be able to live up to Irene's expectations. She was obviously lonely, and needing support – emotionally, as much as anything. He wanted to help, but…

'You certainly like your cake, don't you?'

'Oh… yeah. Thanks. It was lovely. Erm… Irene… you said on the phone you were frightened. Can you tell me why?'

She hadn't started on her small slice of cake, though she had speared a piece with her fork. She paused. 'I'm scared of having all that money. I'm scared of Beavis, and what he might do.'

'Do you think Jamie might have left a trail that only you could follow? You're his mum, after all.'

'No, I shouldn't think so. It'll be about computers; it always was with him, and I don't know the first thing about them.'

Allan knew he was straying into police territory, but he couldn't stop. 'And are you sure he never mentioned anyone called Beavis? Or a company he did work for?'

Irene replied quickly: perhaps too quickly, Allan thought. 'No, I can't remember anything.' She leaned towards Allan. 'Can you help me?'

'I'm not sure how.'

'You're an editor. You must know people. Maybe you could find out who he is.'

Allan wondered if Irene was as vulnerable as he first thought. 'That could be a problem for me. You see, my partner is the head of the local police, and she doesn't want me getting involved.'

He thought she'd be shocked, but he wasn't prepared for the anger. 'What? So all this concern for me… You're just snooping for your wife, aren't you?' Irene stood so quickly she knocked her chair over. Allan looked up to see her shaking hand pointing at the door. 'What a fool I was to think someone really cared about Jamie, and wanted to help me. Well you can just get out!'

'Irene – I do care—'

'No you don't. You're just trying to get information.'

Allan stood and smiled, trying to keep his voice calm. 'I promise I'm not. She doesn't even know I'm here. I want to help you. I meant what I said about Jamie, too. He was a good lad.' He walked round the table and put a hand on her arm. 'Come on, let's just sit down, shall we?'

Irene looked so beaten. She sat, shoulders hunched, staring at her hands. 'I'm sorry I shouted.'

Allan grinned. 'That's ok, I'm used to it at home. Now, how about another piece of cake?'

As they talked, Allan realised she hadn't worked out that the money in her account was the result of criminal activity. Jane had already told him that Shirley had been round to explain it to Irene, but it obviously hadn't sunk in. Either that, or she'd decided to spend it anyway.

He expected Jane had already contacted the bank to make sure she couldn't make withdrawals, so Irene might be in for another shock.

More importantly for Allan, he was trying to calculate how much of a news story he'd be able to get from talking – or rather listening – to Irene. He'd already pictured one splash headline… *Grieving mother gets a fortune she can't spend.*

He realised Irene had stopped talking. She was looking scared again. 'What is it, Irene?'

'I've just remembered something.'

'Oh yes?'

'I used to work in a betting shop.'

'Round here?'

'It was a long time ago. In town… The thing is, the man who owned it was called Beavis.'

NINETEEN

They'd already done a seven hour shift, and it was only early afternoon.

Charles had always told her she was too maternal about her team. She could hear his voice now, as she walked towards CID: 'For crying out loud, they wanted to be bloody sleuths and we're paying them to do it!' Jane smiled – she missed his over the top indignation.

Walking in to start the briefing, she could see what he meant. Apart from George, they had built up a young team, and, by the look on their faces, all of them – including world-weary George – were clearly relishing the challenge.

Jane filled them in on this morning's interview with Sutton. 'His story is that Jamie discovered hard porn access, by accident, while he was hacking into Greaves' betting website. Mark is already looking into that. Jamie told Sutton he was disgusted, he was going public with it, and he was pretty sure who was behind it all. Someone by the name of Beavis;

which, as you know, tallies with a second note Jamie left for his mother, Irene.

'Sutton was one of the people who were viewing this porn – which apparently is extremely hard core. He says he panicked when Jamie told him, and told Gonzales, who was paying Beavis for the videos, and then getting payments from punters, no doubt at a tidy profit.

'Sutton says he panicked again when Gonzales told him that he – Gonzales – would have to tell Beavis someone was onto him. Sutton didn't want his name made known to Beavis, and he certainly didn't want his porn access to become public knowledge. That's why he took Gonzales' tablets – to scare him off, he says.

'Next thing he knows, Jamie is dead. He's convinced Beavis killed him, because Gonzales told him about Jamie. Now, Sutton is scared that Beavis might come after him.'

George grunted. 'Not much chance of that. He's going down for this.'

Lorry shook her head. 'Bastard – sorry ma'am.'

Jane raised an eyebrow. 'It's ok, Lorry. I think we all feel the same. But we have to be careful we don't let the nature of this case affect our judgement. We are investigating the murders of two people, and we need to keep level heads. Everything by the book, ok? So, anyone got anything?'

Jag raised his arm. 'I have been looking at CCTV at the hospital, ma'am, during the early hours of the morning when Gonzales died.' He paused, looking embarrassed.

'What is it, Jag? Something wrong?'

'Well… there is a doctor going into Gonzales' room, and coming out about five minutes later…'

'Wait. I thought we had someone outside all night. No-one mentioned seeing a doctor.'

'No, ma'am… Perhaps if I show you?'

Everyone moved to get a view over Jag's head as he flicked rapidly through the footage, clicked pause, then play. 'So there is the doctor, coming down the corridor…'

George pointed a finger at the screen. 'Where's the copper? Should be in that bloody chair!'

Jag moved the cursor and pressed play again. 'And here he is, coming out, ma'am.'

Jane was furious. 'Bloody hell! Who is that? He's on guard duty and he's staring at his bloody phone. Not even looking up, never mind checking and challenging. I want his name and I want him in my office, as soon as we've finished here.' She lowered her voice and put a hand on Jag's shoulder. 'Well done, Jag. My first question is… does that doctor bear any resemblance to the guy in scrubs we found on CCTV outside the cafe?'

'Can't be certain because the angles are different, but he looks similar in height and build. As you can see, he kept a head covering and a face mask on, too.'

Ross frowned. 'That's suspicious for a start. If he was just checking up on a patient, why keep them on after.'

Jane nodded. 'OK, let's crack on. Jag… please find that copper and let me have his name. Then do what you can to manipulate the images. Anything to help us identify that doctor, and anything that might show if he was carrying anything, or a distinguishing mark.

'George, can you organise the whole team to track down people called Beavis who may have had a connection with Jamie, or his mother, or Gonzales, or…'

She stopped. Another angle suddenly leapt out at her. George waited, signalling to the others to stay quiet. Then, when she turned to look at him again: 'Or what, ma'am?'

'—or any commercial or personal links with Greaves, the company, and Graeme Hargreaves, the boss.'

'You think they might know each other?'

'It's a long shot, George. But it's strange that Beavis should choose fairly obscure internet cafes to market his filth: both owned by Greaves.'

'He's probably selling it all over the world. Maybe these are just his local outlets.'

'Yes, but Manchester is a big city. Surely it would be easier, if not safer, to sell this stuff direct. Why work through someone like Gonzales?'

'To embarrass Greaves?'

'I wonder, George… But we definitely need to see if there are any connections between Hargreaves and Beavis.'

Mark Manning posted another whole gingernut into his mouth, and was half way through it when a sequence of binary code on the screen caught his attention.

He'd been struggling to retrieve info from the hard disk of the computer Jamie used at the internet cafe for most of the day.

He'd finally swallowed his pride and messaged Adrian Cheshire at Greaves, to see if he could help unlock the deep deletion that Gonzales had executed. He'd emailed back straight away with a link to a program he had developed during his time at Google.

'No matter what they do, Mark, they always leave a trace,' he'd written. 'There's not much that can get past us now. Hope this works for you, but let me know if not.'

Mark was impressed. He likened it to a friendly virus – though the criminals it trapped would use a different adjective.

In the time it had taken him to brew up and raid the biscuit tin in CID, the results started trickling in. At first, it seemed an odd and random sequence of code. But that in itself drew him in. Someone as computer literate as Jamie did every keystroke for a reason. It was just a case of understanding. And, always in the back of Mark's mind, was his final message to his mother, in which he talked about following the trail.

He felt a shiver up his back as he realised he was looking at Jamie's last computer session. He must have died only minutes later. Mark wondered if he'd known he was going to die that day.

Mark sipped his tea and frowned in concentration as he tried to make sense of the sequence of numbers.

He tried to imagine what he himself would do, and that's when the series began to make sense. Jamie was leaving a message, and each sequence of numbers represented elements of that message. That had to be it.

Mark stretched across the desk for his ASCII character code table, and began translating.

Graeme Hargreaves and Adrian Cheshire stood side by side watching the view over Manchester turn from full colour to monochrome, as the light faded and the rain clouds sped in from the west.

Graeme was clearly in no mood to talk about the weather. He'd been snappy all day, and had just offended his partner Sue, in front of Adrian. She'd called in, dressed to kill, to see if he wanted to go out for dinner.

Adrian had to hide his embarrassment when Graeme just called over his shoulder: 'For Christ's sake, Sue! You just don't get it, do you? I'm a bit busy running an international business, as it happens. So, no thanks. I'll see you later, all right?'

Adrian didn't risk looking at her. He just heard the soft click of the door shutting behind her.

Graeme simply stared at him, then gave a half smile. 'I'm going to pay for that later...Anyway, that's my problem. What's yours?'

'Not a problem, as such… Mark Manning—'

'The police tech guy?'

'Yeah, that's him. He's been looking at Jamie's last session on the computer at the internet cafe. He used binary code to send us a message, says Mark.'

'Tell me that in English. What message?'

'There's a kind of code table we use. Basically, every letter and punctuation has its own set of numbers – quite a long series of numbers. It's not so easy to spot because you wouldn't normally expect to find it. But Jamie seems to have wanted to give us important info – just before he was killed, too… '

'And he did it this way because…?'

Adrian smiled. 'Presumably he was pretty sure someone like Gonzales wouldn't spot it, but nerdy geeks like Mark and myself would… Anyway, it reads a bit like a telegram… *Gonz knows. Warned me. Told Beavis.*'

Adrian paused, hoping his boss wouldn't shoot the messenger when he heard the next bit.

'Is that it?'

'No, there's another line. One you definitely need to hear… Jamie ends his message by writing: *Beavis knows Hargreaves.*'

'What? No I bloody don't!'

'Apparently, Jamie sent a note to his mother as well, saying we have to follow the trail to Beavis: the man supplying the hard porn through Gonzales.'

'And I'm supposed to know this guy?' Adrian nodded. 'Bollocks. Never heard of him.'

'Could it be someone from way back? Someone with a grudge? We'll need to think it through. Mark's boss will be following up on it. They've got some blurry CCTV images which Mark said might help jog your memory. They're being pretty good, sharing the info with us.'

'Ok, ok… It is good to be in the loop. But I might have

known this would bounce back at me. Christ, am I going to have any business or credibility left after this?'

Adrian nodded with a confidence he didn't feel. 'Definitely, especially if we can help the police crack this case. I'm happy to do some digging around. The police are working their way through Beavises who live in the area. Maybe if you just thought back, just in case the name comes back to you?'

'I will, but it's a waste of time. I'd be happier if you could do some work on it. Shouldn't be too hard to track the little pervert down, should it? What about all these paedo networks we keep hearing about? Chances are he's one of them. And keep that guy Mark onside, whatever you do.'

He stood and checked his gold Bulgari watch, then sighed. 'Get yourself home, while I work out how to persuade Sue to forgive me for being such a shite.'

Adrian decided to give the tram a miss, and clear his head with a three mile walk back to his apartment in Salford Quays.

Something in Graeme's eyes when he mentioned the name Beavis, had troubled him, but he couldn't work out why. Walking helped him think, and Adrian had always wanted to resolve niggles before they blossomed into big problems.

The light rain felt refreshing. Lengthening his stride, he turned left off Regent Road onto Ordsall Lane.

He knew Graeme was good at projecting an image that got the right result, whatever the audience. Most employees of the company thought well of him: they said he always had time for them, and 'he seems a decent bloke.'

Adrian had no complaints about the way he'd been treated since he'd been headhunted, but he'd seen Graeme's temper, his unpredictability, and been only too aware of how his eyes would bore into your soul, searching for your motives; the meaning behind the cliches everyone uses in business meetings.

But when Adrian mentioned Beavis again tonight, Graeme had averted his gaze for once.

Turning right onto West Park Street, Adrian was walking quickly now, feeling the energy returning. And at six two and weighing in at fourteen stone of muscle, he was used to the fact that pedestrians tended to clear a path for him. He smiled an acknowledgement as an old boy in a flat hat stepped into a shop doorway with elaborate nimbleness.

The rain was clearing now, but he couldn't let go of the feeling that Graeme was holding something back. He'd been so quick to dismiss the idea that Beavis knew him, and had then thrown in that line about checking paedophile networks. Where had that come from? They'd never talked about it before.

By the time he'd picked up a wire basket at the entrance to the M&S food hall, Adrian had made his mind up to do the digging around Graeme wanted him to do.

He'd be looking for Beavis, of course. But he would also be discreetly digging into Graeme's past.

As expected, Jane was furious.

Allan jumped as she flung her knife and fork onto her plate and turned on him.

'I told you, keep away from it! And you go for a cosy chat with her the very next day? For crying out loud, Allan…'

He held his hands up in supplication. 'I know, I know, but I'd promised I would see her. And, I am entitled to interview whoever I want.'

'Oh, so now you're going to run a story, are you? I thought we'd agreed… ' Jane stared. 'You've been so supportive. I thought you'd understand why I didn't want you to get involved.'

'I did. And I'm not involved, I promise. I just listened. And…' Allan paused, wondering if now was a good time for the revelation, and deciding to go for it. '…she said she used to work for someone called Beavis.'

Jane nearly choked on her Malbec. 'What? When?'

'A long time ago. She said he owned a betting shop where she did casual work.'

'Did she say anything else?'

'No, but I felt there was a change in her; like she was keeping something back. She didn't seem quite as vulnerable as the first time I met her.' Allan shrugged. 'Just made me wonder, so I thought I'd tell you.'

Jane gave him a knowing look, and – to Allan's relief – a half smile. 'So now I'm not meant to be angry; I'm meant to be grateful… Nice one, Allan.' She stared into her empty glass, then looked up again. 'So are you running a story on her?'

'Not yet. I need a new angle but I don't want to exploit her, and I don't want to make things harder for the investigation. I did wonder about doing a piece about her having a pile of money she couldn't spend, but even that might make life difficult for her.'

'Yes, I suspect it would.'

'Sarcasm is the lowest form of wit, you know.'

'And the most rewarding… Interesting…'

'What?'

'What you said about Irene not being as vulnerable. She's had a tough life and I bet she's very streetwise. I wonder why it's taken her so long to remember the name Beavis…'

'She only saw Jamie's note a couple of days ago.'

'Yes, but the note also told her about a trail we should follow. You'd think she'd be obsessed with that, looking back, looking for any clues.'

'She probably thinks that's your job.'

'What were you saying about sarcasm…?'

'Fair point. You OK with me now?'

Jane smiled and held his hand. 'Just about. Sorry. It was quite a good day, but it ended with me suspending a beat bobby who didn't notice someone going into a hospital room, even though he was on guard duty right outside. Anyway, are you OK with me?'

'Yeah. I'm sorry I upset you. I know how difficult this Beavis thing is...'

'You've been my rock. I just don't want us to be tainted by this... mess. But I'll tell you what: this isn't half as difficult as something I have to do tomorrow.'

She saw the anxiety in his eyes, and loved him for it. 'What is it?'

Jane did her best impression of a sulky child. 'I've got to go and see my mum.'

Allan leaned back with mock horror on his face. 'Oh my God! Make sure you've got a police escort.'

A catch up with Phil and George next morning established that, yes, Gonzales died of the same lethal infusion as Jamie; Sutton was still in custody, at his own request, and hoping for a deal, pending a review by the Crown Prosecution Service; Jag wasn't having much luck beefing up the CCTV images but Lorry had volunteered Mark's help; and the team had narrowed down the list of possible Beavises to ten.

George said the rest of them were, in his words, 'too old or too bloody perfect, with nowt hidden in the cupboard.'

Phil commented half jokingly about ageism, then announced that his attitude to hospital doctors had mellowed slightly. He told Jane: 'I can't really blame them. That stuff is so hard to detect.'

An email came through from Mark while they were in their meeting, confirming his translation of Jamie's coded message. So Jane instructed George to track down a Beavis who once managed or owned a local betting shop, and reminded him to go back to all the others to see if any of them had any connection to Graeme Hargreaves.

'We're closing in,' she told them. 'But I've got a funny feeling that Irene is holding something back.'

George nodded thoughtfully. 'Hmmm. Now you mention it, we've just taken her word for it that Jamie never told her anything—'

'—but her first reaction when I went to see her was that she knew he'd been up to something.'

'Mother's intuition?' said Phil.

'That's how we've explained it away, but I wonder if she knows more than she's telling us.'

'Ross reckons she should be a suspect, ma'am.'

'Yes, George, I know. Instinct told me he couldn't be right, and it still does...But... I do need to talk to her again. On my own, this time.'

'Might be useful to have Shirley French with you, ma'am? She and Irene seem to get on well.'

'Not this time, George. Someone out there has killed two people. Getting on well with Irene is not my first priority.'

TWENTY

'Oh, it's you.'

Not the friendliest of greetings, but Jane smiled as Irene opened the front door cautiously. 'Morning, Irene. Can I come in?'

Irene silently stepped to one side to let her in, by way of an answer. Jane was undeterred. 'Through to the kitchen?'

Irene nodded, and led the way down the hall. They sat at the little formica-topped table, just as they'd done the first time. Irene's reaction had been enigmatic then, to say the least, but now the atmosphere was icy.

'I thought it was time we talked again, Irene.'

'Oh yes? I was talking to your... partner?... yesterday. I was half expecting to see you again.'

Jane thought for a moment... she thinks I put Allan up to it, and resents me for it. Now she's expecting the follow-up. But why would she worry about that? 'Yes, Allan told me you knew someone called Beavis. Is that right?'

'Like I said, it was a long time ago.'

'Have you heard from him since?'

'It must have been 10 years ago.'

'Since you heard from him?'

'Since I saw him.'

Jane ploughed on. 'Can you describe him? What did he look like?'

'Plump, creepy, oily hair, stank of aftershave.'

Jane hid a smile. That was a good pen picture…'What was his first name, Irene?'

'Stan, I think. You don't think he's the one, do you?'

'We've got to follow up on everything, Irene. As you know, the name Beavis is specially significant. As soon as Allan told me what you'd said, I wanted to see you again.'

She leaned forward. 'You see, Irene, whoever killed Jamie has killed again, we think.'

Irene held a hand up to her mouth. 'I'm sorry – I know it's painful – but I think you know something important; something that would help us. Maybe it was something Jamie said, or something you found, or saw. I need you to think hard, Irene. Help us, please?'

Irene looked down, and nodded, as if an internal voice had given her permission. 'There is something. I told your… Allan… I was scared. And I am.'

'What is it, Irene? Tell me, and I can make sure you are looked after.'

Irene began picking at the skin round her nails, and Jane could see they were red raw. Then she started talking, very softly and slowly…

'I followed Jamie once. I told you, I was worried what he was doing. He went into town, into one of those cafes what have computers…'

'Internet cafes?'

'If you say so. I saw him go in, and I was going to give up, but I thought I would see if I could see in through the window. It was just him, talking to this fat foreign looking bloke. I didn't like the look of him. He looked like he was having a right go at Jamie. And there was another bloke there, looking out at them from the back room. There was a door, but it was open a bit. I don't think Jamie could see him from where he was, but I could.'

'Who was it? Did you recognise him? Think Irene, this could be vital.'

'I didn't recognise him. But—'

'But what?'

'He scared me.'

'Why? What do you mean?'

'It was… I don't know… the look on his face. He looked so mean.'

Jane did her best to hide the frustration from her voice. 'Why didn't you tell us this before, Irene?'

The words poured out now. 'I just – didn't want to believe that anyone would want to do Jamie harm… I knew he was up to something, but it was like I didn't want it to be true. That he might have been killed… I don't know who those men were, but I just wanted to shut it all out. I'm sorry.'

Jane walked round the table and knelt down, looking up at her. 'It's ok, Irene. We've all got things we keep inside us, and it hurts, and we know we should talk about it, but something stops us. There's no sense to it, is there? But we convince ourselves it's the right thing to do…'

Irene nodded and dabbed her eyes, visibly pulling herself together. She looked older, and Jane remembered she'd soon be having a similar conversation about how she'd shut things away from her mum. She sat down again and waited, as Irene blew her nose.

‘Ok now?’

‘Yes, thank you. Sorry.’

‘No need to be sorry. You’ve been honest with me, that’s the main thing. Can you do one more thing for me? I need you to describe the man you saw looking out through the door.’

‘I’ll do my best. The thing is, I was sure I’d seen him somewhere before…’

Jane phoned through the description, then began the slow drive to her mum’s house in the suburbs that helped soften the edges of Manchester’s expansion towards the Pennines.

It seemed that the concept of rush hour had expanded, too. It was only just after 4pm, but the roads were clogged with mums and after school kids; older couples on their way back home after a carvery; delivery vans driving up everyone’s arse to try and get their round over as quickly as possible.

Jane switched off from the stress that seemed to spread by magic on busy roads, keeping her distance, and being rewarded by lane shifters cutting her up.

She had the feeling the investigation was at a turning point. If they could just make a positive ID combining Irene’s description and the CCTV images… Could they then find Beavis from the shortlist George and team had come up with? It wouldn’t be proof, but it would certainly be their best hope.

The nagging doubt in Jane’s mind was whether, if Beavis was the main man behind the hard porn business, he would be the one to get his hands dirty by taking out people who threatened his security. Would he really risk it, or was he more likely to get a henchman to do it?

She suspected the latter, particularly as Irene’s description suggested a different nationality. She had described eyes that seemed wider apart, a close shaven head with a swarthy complexion, and full lips.

Jane jerked back to the driving as she saw a sign politely welcoming her to Didsbury. She'd be at her mum's house in less than ten minutes.

Graeme Hargreaves put the phone down after yet another attempt to soothe a disgruntled shareholder.

The polite ones wanted to know when it would be business as usual, but the majority – like this one – were looking at their paper losses and wondering what the hell Greaves was playing at.

Graeme stuck to his soothing assurances that the online betting hack had only a minor impact, and that the site would soon be re-opened with fail-safe security. One or two mates in the business press had done him a favour by following that line, too, but, understandably, a lot of loyal investors were very twitchy.

He was a popular choice on the motivational conference circuit, and one of his mantras was that the only way to rise to the top was to confront problems rather than use them as excuses.

'There's no point putting pretty posters on your office wall,' he'd say. 'Strength comes from inside, not some recycled Facebook cliche about embracing change.'

Now, though, as he faced the prospect of Greaves being dragged into the glare of publicity over a hard porn business run from the company's premises, Graeme wondered if he had the strength to get through it. How many problems could a company overcome?

He'd made peace with Sue last night with the considerable help of a Michelin-starred chef he'd persuaded – at considerable cost – to prepare a meal for the two of them in their own kitchen.

Afterwards, they'd sat sipping cognac, and as he felt the adrenaline slowly seeping away, he'd told her everything.

Sue had recoiled when he told her about the porn, but then she'd frowned as she thought it through. Her first question was: 'Do you think this man Beavis is deliberately targeting you?'

The idea had soon got lost in the comfortable fog of fine food, alcohol, and – later – Sue's beautiful soft body, as they fell into bed. But it was back again now, and Graeme couldn't shake off the feeling she was right.

But how could she be? He'd raided his memories, and couldn't recall anyone called Beavis. Of course, he'd made enemies – lots of them – but Graeme prided himself on knowing who they were. There again, this Beavis may not be known to him: he could be doing someone else a favour – someone who really did have a grudge against him.

Graeme strode to his office window and stared out, willing himself to follow his own advice, and confront the problem. All he had to do was identify one person. He was out there, somewhere. And if he was setting himself up to destroy the company he'd built up, he couldn't rely on the police. He had to be found; and quickly.

Walking back to his desk, he opened the top drawer and took out the mobile phone he saved for special occasions. He paced impatiently as it started up, then hit a speed dial number.

It was answered straight away. 'Morning Mr Hargreaves. What can I do for you?'

'I need to find a guy called Beavis. He's running a bloody disgusting porn video business. We're talking under-age children here. And what's more, I reckon he's been running it on my premises.'

'Very naughty. So it's personal?'

'I think so. Can you find him?'

'Behave. Leave it with me.'

Graeme shut down the phone and put it back in the drawer. If anyone could help, it was Charlie. He'd made a mint buying rundown houses, using pals to modernise them, then selling for a tidy profit, more often than not to people who worked on the shady side of the street. He knew people. He knew their secrets. And that made him powerful, and pretty much untouchable.

They'd been pals ever since they teamed up at school, selling sweets they'd got wholesale through Charlie's dad, at twice the price—

Graeme stopped and stared into space. Something Charlie said had taken him right back. That was it… 'Behave…'

Behave… Why was that ringing a very loud alarm bell right now? Another kid at school… that was his nickname, wasn't it? Behave…

Graeme screwed his eyes shut, trying to remember. He could picture the boy. Spotty red face, fat legs, smelly, always in trouble, hence the nickname… Always first in the queue for sweets, even though everyone bullied him.

That was it! Brian Avis! B. Avis… He'd always been a target. They'd yelled at him, pushed him around; even some of the teachers said it: 'Behave, B. Avis!'

Graeme thumped the desk. Right or wrong, it was the best lead he'd got.

He took out the phone again and punched speed dial.

TWENTY-ONE

JANE CLOSED HER EYES as she hugged her mum.

It had been so long since they'd been this close, and she felt so frail, as if one squeeze would shatter her bones. She smelled of soap and coffee, and Jane caught a hint of the Estee Lauder she'd used her whole life: probably still using the same bottle.

She'd looked shocked, disbelieving, when Jane told her about Harrison. 'That English teacher? No!'

Jane said she'd found it hard to believe, too, but mum hadn't been angry that Jane kept it to herself. After all the angst as Jane told her story, she'd simply said; 'I can see why. I think I would have done the same. It would have killed your father.'

And so, it was done. The truth had been told, and it was almost a disappointment for Jane that it was over without any histrionics; as her mum always described any display of emotion.

But then, her mum had stood and held her arms out, inviting Jane in. And she felt the years slip away so that she was that anxious teenager again. Would mum's hugs have made any difference at the time? Made the trauma somehow more bearable? She thought not.

But now, it felt they'd reconnected, and Jane was finding it hard to hold back the tears.

Her mum squeezed a little harder as she felt Jane shaking, but she said nothing and Jane eventually pulled away.

'Don't tell me; you've got to go.'

Jane nodded. 'Can I have a cup of tea first?'

Mum smiled. 'I'll put the kettle on.'

Jane sat and waited, shaking her head at her mum's lack of emotion, but then marvelling at her toughness, and realising that's where her own resilience came from. It explained why Jane had kept the secret locked away. Neither of them were what you'd call demonstrative. She looked round the room – not a family photo in sight – and reminded herself that we can't choose our family, and we can't help who we are. And that goes for mum, too. We can maybe chip away at the edges, but we are essentially children burdened with the adult experiences that take us further away from ourselves.

So they sipped tea and the old clock on the mantlepiece ticked loudly as they talked about Allan, and work. Jane asked why she didn't go back to church: 'Because I don't like many of them, and the vicar smells of cigarettes.' They laughed. Jane couldn't remember the last time she'd seen mum laugh. What a day this was proving to be: a mummy hug and laughs, too...

Yet there was still an edge of politeness in the atmosphere, which meant Jane put off the big question till last. She reached across the table to hold mum's thin hand. 'Mum... will you come and have a meal with us soon? Meet Allan? We'd love to have you, and we'd come and pick you up...'

Driving back to work, Jane grinned happily as she pictured Allan's forced smile when she told him mum had actually said yes this time.

George was in a strop. The search for Beavis was going nowhere fast, and he had indigestion from eating a jumbo sausage roll too quickly.

He couldn't fault the time and effort they were all putting in, but his stomach was making strange noises, and they'd gone through the whole list of bloody Beavises and not one of them matched Irene's description.

Now the boss was on her way back, and all the optimism he'd felt was vanishing fast.

George knew his grumbling was his way of motivating himself, but he didn't want the young 'uns to follow his example. Their heads were certainly dropping now after hours of phone calls and visits.

Back from another trip to the toilet, he tapped his coffee mug on his desk to get attention, and cleared his throat to make sure. 'Right, you lot. The boss is on her way in, and she's hoping we can come up with something. So, let's have another think. What are we missing? Where the hell has this Beavis got to?'

Ross lounged in his chair and ran a hand through his hair. 'It's proving even tougher than Where's Wally, George…'

'Well, thank you for that contribution, Ross. If you want to redeem yourself, the kettle's over there.'

Lorry and Jag laughed as Ross sighed and headed off to brew up. Lorry said: 'Maybe it's time to widen the search. We've pretty much covered Greater Manchester, but who's to say he's not based in London, or anywhere else?'

George scraped a hand over his stubble. 'It's possible, Lorry. But we have to start somewhere, and we do have that connection with Irene, who says she used to work with someone of that name. Plus the bloke she saw when she followed Jamie, so…'

'And we've got those CCTV pictures, George, though I can't match them up with Irene's description yet.'

'Ok, Jag, keep trying, will you? Maybe we can get something by comparing their physiques. Irene said her guy looked tall and well-built. Look, I know we're struggling, but let's not give up.'

Ross started handing round the drinks, then stopped as he put a mug on Jag's desk. 'Maybe we should look at it differently, George?'

'That's good. Go for it, son.'

'Well, we're assuming there's a connection between Jamie and Irene, and Beavis, but we also have Jamie's message saying that Beavis knows Graeme Hargreaves. Hargreaves says he doesn't know anyone of that name, but why don't I call that guy Adrian Cheshire at Greaves and ask him on the quiet if they've turned anything up? I can't believe they're not looking, too.'

Lorry slurped her tea hastily. 'Be careful, Ross. Mark's working on this with Adrian and says he's being very co-operative. We don't wanna risk upsetting that, going behind people's backs.'

George looked thoughtful, then winked. 'That guy Adrian is a big bloke, too… wouldn't want to upset him, would we, Lorry…? Ok, Ross, call him up and have a cosy chat. See if you get anything out of him. I'm willing to bet that our Mr Hargreaves has got an interesting past… But be careful, all right?' He drank his coffee in one go and grimaced. 'Bloody hell, Ross, that's the last time I trust you to make me a drink.'

Ross smiled innocently. 'I was hoping you'd say that, George.'

'Cheeky bugger. Now come on, you lot. Work to do. Ross – make that call now. Lorry – collate everything we've done today on Beavis so I can show the boss. And Jag – contact Mark and tell him you're still waiting for his help on those CCTV images. We're going to nail this if it's the last thing we—' He broke off as Mark walked in. 'Speak of the devil… right Mark, sit down with Jag and get us a decent set of images, and dimensions.'

Mark winked at Lorry. 'Good afternoon to you too… I'll do my best.'

'Bloody right, you will. I'm going to see the boss in exactly one hour. Your job, all of you, is to give me some good news to pass on…'

Jane put her elbows on the desk and steepled her hands.

'Got any good news for me, George?'

'Yes and no, ma'am.'

'Let's have the negatives first then.'

'We can't match Irene's description with any Beavis on our list, and we're struggling to manipulate the CCTV image, so no joy there yet, either.'

'Ok. And the positives?'

'Ross has spoken to Adrian Cheshire…'

'Hargreaves' tech guy?'

'That's him. Ross's idea was to see if he could weedle anything out of him about Hargreaves' past that would help identify this Beavis.'

'And?'

'A new line of enquiry, ma'am. Cheshire remembers Hargreaves laughing about some of his layabout schoolmates – his words – who applied for jobs with his company years ago. Turns out he rejected most of them out of hand. Cheshire told Ross it was like he had a real axe to grind, so…'

'… We need to get into his school records and find some names. You're keeping in touch with Child Exploitation and Online Protection, too, aren't you?'

'Yeah, they're helping, but they've got nothing for us yet. Nobody called Beavis on their radar. And we're already on the school names, ma'am. Ross has done well today.'

'Good, thanks George.' Jane sat back and sipped sparkling water. 'I don't know about you, but I've got the feeling that there's something personal here; something new. Maybe that's why CEOP haven't come across any activity round here lately. I'm just not sure whether it's about Jamie and Irene, or Hargreaves and his company. So that school angle could be interesting…'

'They always say look at the people closest to the victim, don't they?'

'True. Though you could say the real victims are the poor children in those videos, not Jamie and Gonzales.'

'Perhaps we should think of Hargreaves as a victim, too, ma'am.'

'Hmmm. Has anyone spoken to him lately?'

'No, ma'am.'

'Ok George, leave that with me. Time I visited that office of his again; see how the other half lives.'

'Mark's a big fan. He couldn't shut up about it yesterday – especially the shortbread biscuits.'

'That settles it. Let's see if I can get myself invited round for elevenses, eh?'

'One other thing…'

'Yes George?'

'Ross tells me that Hargreaves wanted Cheshire to make his own enquiries about Beavis; to see if he could turn anything up.'

'Fair enough…'

'But Hargreaves has now told him to back off.'

'Which suggests either he's being public spirited and wants to leave it to us; or, he's got something to hide…'

'Maybe he knows who it is.'

'Now that would be interesting… Or there's something else in his past he doesn't want Cheshire to find.' Jane pressed the power button to start up her desktop. 'Ok George, thanks. And give Ross a pat on the back will you?'

'I'd prefer to give him a kick up the arse, ma'am.'

'You have my permission to do that if he fails to put a note on the case log by the time I get into the system. Oh, and George?'

He stopped at the door. 'Ma'am?'

'Thanks. You're doing a great job. Do you think we need an extra pair of hands in there? It feels like we're getting nearer.'

George smiled. 'You can be sure I'd be hammering on your door if we did, ma'am. But, to be honest, those young 'uns have surprised me. They're doing more than their share, and doing it well. Plus we're getting some good support from region.'

'I should think we are. Speaking of which, we're going to have to brief the media, probably later tomorrow. The Chief Constable wants us to be more 'visible'. He says we need to get the media and the public onside.'

George was unimpressed. 'Better than being offside, I suppose.'

'Well, let's hope we get a result soon… that's the surest way of getting people onside. By the way, would you be ok if I took Jag with me to see Hargreaves tomorrow? He must be square eyed looking at CCTV for days on end, and I could do with his unfettered opinion of the guy – as well as his note taking skills.'

'No problem.'

'And George – Lorry was going to trawl ebay and facebay type sites to see if anyone is selling a laptop like Jamie's. Any news on that?'

'No, ma'am. Plenty of similar model laptops on sale, but no matches yet.'

'Not surprising, but worth a try. Whoever did take it has probably trashed it… Anyway, George, how about you get an early night tonight for once?'

'Can we settle on me leaving at around 8pm?'

Jane looked up. 'Yes, of course. Catching up on beauty sleep, are we?'

'No; I don't want to get home too early. My wife'll be watching Emmerdale, and I can't stand it.'

Jane sent an email to Graeme Hargreaves, asking if he was free for a meeting tomorrow morning. He'd suggested a one hour slot from 9.30am, because he had to host a meeting about the relaunch of Greaves online betting site later. He added: 'Although we need to think of a better name for it. Greaves Online Betting will lead to the wrong kind of acronym, don't you think?'

Jane resisted the temptation to reply that GOB Site sounded about right, but she said yes to the appointment, then found herself momentarily thrown by the humour. Was he for real? The company is in all kinds of trouble; his own reputation is on the line; and he has been linked to Beavis, the prime suspect in a double murder investigation.

Was she being over sensitive because the case had become more of a personal crusade? Or was Hargreaves showing the over-confidence of someone who has grown used to playing the odds and winning – and not caring too much?

The more she thought about it, the more she was inclined to think the unthinkable. Beavis may be a prime suspect, but Beavis wouldn't be working alone, as CEOP had reminded her. Porn and child exploitation was big global business. Hargreaves ran a big business. Could he be part of it; using the pretence of close working to disguise his own involvement? Had Jamie inadvertently stumbled upon a highly influential business group, whose members were indulging their own foul perversions while making a fortune from sick people who got their kicks from this disgraceful exploitation?

The more she allowed herself to drift down this route, the more motivated she became. She recoiled at the video images she had not yet seen but could imagine, and the revulsion swelled inside her, just as it had all those years ago at Harrison's house.

Then she caught her breath and realised this was about far more than her and Harrison; more than Beavis, and Hargreaves, and Sutton, and whoever else. It was about fighting to protect children and smash the empire that was destroying them.

It was also about Jamie, who must have feared for his young life after discovering this filth, and yet was brave enough to lay a trail; one that she vowed she would follow to the ends of the earth.

Jane swivelled in her chair and looked at the picture she'd pinned to her corkboard. She whispered a promise: 'I'll finish the job you started, Jamie. Whatever it takes.'

The rain was falling steadily onto glistening black empty roads as Jane drove home.

The rhythmic swish of the wipers was soothing, and she had to work to stay alert, blinking her eyes, sitting up straighter, and sipping from her water bottle.

She thought about how quickly things change…

Only a few days ago, she'd been convinced her relationship with Allan was coming to an end; that she'd never reconnect with mum; that Phil was going to retire; that she'd be completely lost without Charles. And that this murder inquiry was all about online betting.

She'd also thought she could trust Graeme Hargreaves.

Now everything was turned on its head, and as if to underline it, when she got home, her hair glistening with drizzle, Allan was being Mister Perfect, welcoming her with a lingering kiss and her favourite comfort food: soft boiled eggs and buttery toast.

She listened as Allan talked about his day. He was having a good spell, too, with new advertisers coming in, and circulation figures improving. He told her he'd decided not to write about Irene, and Jane said his reward would be an invite to a news conference in the next day or two. Afterwards, they almost fell onto the sofa – her with a glass of wine box red, Allan with the remains of a can of Guinness.

They were both too tired to talk. Jane leaned back on his chest and felt her eyes drooping. Allan gently eased the glass away as it began to tilt out of her hand.

Next thing she knew, Allan was nudging her and the clock showed 1.15am.

He whispered in her ear. 'Last one upstairs is a cissy.'

One minute later, Jane was looking smug as she sat on the bed. 'What kept you, cissy?'

Allan was not amused. 'I wasn't expecting to be rugby tackled at the bottom of the stairs…'

Jane laughed as he belly-flopped into bed.

He was asleep within a few seconds. Jane lay awake for a while, telling herself to save any worry about Hargreaves tomorrow; to take it one day at a time.

A George Harrison song came into her head. It was before her time, but he was her favourite Beatle; the one who was brave enough to walk away once. When he came back, they chose not to use this composition. Some people said it was the best song the Beatles never recorded. She'd loved the mystical, almost religious, influence behind it. Its message to her had always been not to get upset if things go badly, or too over the moon if things go well. It had been on her playlist for years, and she was singing it in her head as she drifted off… *'All things must pass… none of life's strings can last… so I must be on my way… and face another day… All things must pass… all things must pass away…'*

'What's the game, Adrian?'

With ten minutes to go before Jane Birchfield arrived, Graeme's voice was relaxed, but his posture was anything but. He stood facing him, hands on hips. Adrian stepped slightly towards him; a clear sign he was not going to be intimidated.

'What do you mean, game?'

'Well, let's see...' Graeme counted off on his fingers. 'Taking my file from HR; interviewing the people I knew from school who I offered jobs; retrieving job interview notes to find out who didn't get a job... Quite the detective, aren't we?'

Adrian decided aggression was his best defence. 'Look, you asked me to look into this Beavis character—'

This time, Graeme made no attempt to conceal the venom in his voice. 'You're right, I did. But I didn't ask you to snoop into my past life, which is why I told you to back off. So, I repeat, what's the game?'

Adrian sighed and held his hands out, palms facing Graeme. 'OK...when I joined the company, I remembered you were having a laugh about all your layabout school mates – your words – who applied for jobs here, and how you'd rejected almost all of them out of hand. So I thought there might be a Beavis in amongst them. That's it. That's all there was to it.'

'Interesting you didn't see fit to tell me what you were doing... Makes me wonder if you're getting a bit cozy with your mate Mark. Is that it? Working with the police now?' Adrian hesitated for a split second, and it was enough to convince Graeme. 'That's it, isn't it? You're in with them now, right? The note said Beavis knows me, so all your loyalty goes out of the window and you're doing your best to deliver me on a bloody plate.'

Adrian towered over him, but Graeme showed no trace of fear as he moved in even closer, looking up into his eyes.

'Well you picked the wrong side, son. Did you think you could score some points today when the lovely Jane sits down with us?'

'Boss, I—'

'What? You're not going to say sorry, surely? A big lad like you. You must be thinking you could flatten me easily… Or maybe that's what this is all about? My reputation at rock bottom. So let's cripple him completely, eh. Maybe you can see an opportunity for yourself?'

He was almost shouting now. 'You are a stupid twat. You've undermined me with my own staff, set lots of tongues wagging. So well done. But don't worry, I've survived far worse than this, and I've beaten tougher opponents than you.'

Adrian felt his own temper rising and couldn't resist any longer. Now he was shouting.

'I am not your opponent, for Christ's sake! I know how tough this is, for you and the company. I'm just trying to find a way through it. Get a result. That's what you always say, isn't it? Don't give me explanations and excuses: give me a result!'

Graeme's desk phone rang, and he turned away. His smile carried no warmth. 'That'll be Jane. You're staying here for this. Let's see what you make of the result I've got, all right?'

He snatched up the phone. 'Yes, yes, give me two minutes, then show them in, and organise coffee for four, will you? Thanks, my love.'

He pointed to a leather chair, and spoke formally. 'Take a seat, Adrian. Whichever way you look at this, you should have told me what you were doing. The fact that you didn't worries me, makes me a tad suspicious. But let's put that to one side and welcome our guests. Oh, and I'll do the talking, if you would take notes.'

He turned as Jane and Jag walked in, followed by one of the temps in his outer office, carrying a tray.

'Come in, come in, and sit down. Thanks for the coffee, Jen, we're fine now.'

The introductions done, Graeme played it cool, sitting

back as if waiting for Jane to take the initiative. Jag sensed tension between the two Greaves guys, and made a note for himself during what felt like a prolonged silence.

Graeme laughed. 'Well, we are quiet, aren't we? Shall I kick off then? Jane – you wanted a catch up. Was there anything specific on your mind?'

Jane bought herself a few more seconds as she slowly sipped her coffee. It felt like being an unwelcome guest at a party, where the host was making a determined effort to make everyone feel uncomfortable. The atmosphere didn't sit well with Hargreaves's apparently relaxed pose, but she guessed from Cheshire's face that something was going on between the two of them.

It made her feel that her re-appraisal of Hargreaves last night may have been justified. She put her cup and saucer down on the coffee table and sat back with her most relaxed smile.

'We'd been thinking about Jamie's note, in which he said that Beavis knew you.'

Graeme looked at her blandly, offering no reaction. 'Oh yes?'

'And the more we thought about it, the more we came round to the idea that maybe there is something personal behind this: something between you and him.'

'I see.' He turned his attention to Adrian, who was looking steadfastly at his notebook. 'Adrian… anything you want to share with Jane at this point? I know you've been doing some digging of your own.'

Adrian thought wryly that if Graeme had wanted to make him squirm, he couldn't have planned it better. He had realised as soon as Jane sat down that he was up to something. But all he could do was play the game and hope he could see where it was leading before it got there. He sat up a little straighter.

'Yes, boss. You asked me to do some background checks, and I started looking into former schoolmates of yours. It turned out quite a few had applied for jobs here and been turned down.'

Jane watched as Jag's note taking speeded up. 'That's interesting, Adrian. Did you learn anything that would help us? Anyone called Beavis in there?'

Graeme breathed heavily through his nose. It was somewhere between laughter and disapproval. 'Drew a blank, Adrian, didn't you?'

'That's right.'

Graeme leaned forward and took a thick chocolate biscuit, breaking it neatly in half. 'So, Jane... As you know, we – I – have been co-operating fully with your inquiries. I'm just wondering if my reward for that is your, shall we call it unwarranted suspicion... You see, I don't like the implication that somehow I am personally involved in something as abhorrent as the use of children in porn videos.'

He put a piece of the biscuit in his mouth and chewed; his eyes fixed on Jane.

Jane knew he was pushing her, but how much of it was bravado, and how much gamesmanship. She had the strong feeling he was building up to something. She kept her voice and her body language neutral.

'I – sorry, we – are paid to be suspicious, Graeme. We are investigating two murders, possibly by the same person. It's a high profile case, and not just because of your involvement. I'd argue that no suspicion is unwarranted, when it comes to solving a despicable crime, and trying to protect other children from the same fate.'

Graeme smiled, and nodded. 'I completely understand. So let me see if I can help you.'

He picked up a brown envelope from the seat next to him, and took out some papers. Glancing at Adrian pointedly, he said: 'I've been doing some research of my own, using an old school chum I don't think Adrian has come across – though your people might have, Jane.'

He selected a sheet of paper and slid it across to Jane. Jag leaned forward, and started to speak, then stopped himself.

Graeme caught his eye. 'You recognise him, don't you Jag?'

'Yes, sir, I do.' He looked at Jane for permission, and she nodded. 'That's Charlie. Charlie Pearson.'

'That's him. He and I were at school together in Ashbridge – primary through to secondary. I stayed on the right side of the law. He moved to the other side when he was a lot younger. But he's seen the error of his ways. Done very well for himself in property, and knows a lot of people, on both sides of the street. I asked him if he might know who was behind these porn videos, and he promised to have a scout round for me.

'But then, I remembered someone. The typical fat lad at school who gets pushed around. I couldn't remember his name, but then Charlie said something that triggered it.'

He looked at each of them, and realised he'd got them on the end of his line now – especially Adrian.

'His name isn't Beavis, though.'

He was gratified to see the deflating effect of his words. He allowed them to sink in, before he delivered his punchline.

'He was called Brian Avis.'

Jag was first to catch on. 'B. Avis… Beavis said differently.'

'Spot on, Jag.'

Jane sat forward, wanting to read the papers. 'So you're saying Jamie got it wrong. We're not looking for Beavis. This Mr Avis is behind the operation? How do you know he is, Mr Hargreaves?'

'Woah! Hold on! Give me some space, will you, Jane? I'm trying to help, remember? I don't *know* anything. But Brian Avis and I were sworn enemies at school. And—' He looked at

Adrian with a smile . '—he applied here for an IT development job around 10 to 15 years ago, but he never made it to interview because I spiked his application. I'm sure Adrian could dig that out of the records for you. Charlie says the word in Manchester is that our Mr Avis has a thing for little girls.'

He smiled at Jane. 'So you were right, Jane; it does look like it's personal. Brian Avis deliberately targeted my company as a base from which to sell this filth, because he knew it would destroy me if it ever came out.'

'Why should it ever come out? That wouldn't be in his interest, surely?'

'Think about it. He wants to hurt me. He could sell this stuff anywhere in the world. I reckon he's trying it out here, seeing how much cash he can make, establishing it as a business. Then, why not make it public, bringing me and my company down, with him disappearing to some bloody safe haven anywhere in the world, ready to start up again. Win, win…'

Jane stared at the papers on the coffee table. 'Are you offering this to us as evidence now?'

Graeme's acting was over. He'd had his moment, and now he was ready to move on to his next meeting. He held Jane's gaze confidently.

'It's all yours, Jane. I'm sure Adrian will help you dig him out, if needed, but you'll find his last known address in the file here. Now, I'm sorry, we have to go and sort out the relaunch of our new betting site.'

Jane held out her hand. 'I don't want to thank you yet. It sounds plausible, but I'll need time to make sure this stacks up. If it does, I'll come back and say it. Apart from anything else, I'm wondering why Jamie would get the name wrong…'

Jag cleared his throat. 'Perhaps he heard the name from Mr Gonzales. He had a Mexican accent, ma'am.'

Graeme smiled: 'There you go. You're a smart guy, Jag.' He

shook Jane's hand. 'That's one reason I respect you, Jane. I've no idea what you really think of me. But you keep the personal feelings to one side. It's strictly business. You're like me: the result's the thing, right?'

Jane smiled but her eyes were sharp. 'Exactly. We'll be in touch; if and when we feel we do have a result.'

Jag drove back to the station. Jane sat in the back. Graeme Hargreaves obviously enjoyed manipulating meetings, and today was another example. But it all rang true, too. They had to follow up on it, but a news conference was scheduled in two hours time, so there was no chance of using any of it now.

But what could she say without looking a prat in front of the media, and Chief Constable Simon Hopkirk? Was now the time to go with the child protection angle, or would that just, understandably, stir up the fear and paedophile hate that led to extreme anti-social behaviour? Jane wondered whether it would help or hinder the investigation.

Should she suggest naming Beavis as a person of interest, even though that may well now be out of date? It would certainly make Brian Avis feel smug and secure, which could be helpful…

The Chief had a reputation for being media friendly, and that made Jane feel even more nervy. He'd want to offer something today, but Jane instinctively preferred giving nothing away. She decided the blurry CCTV image might be the best compromise: it gave the media something to get excited about, without revealing too much about the latest lines of enquiry.

Filing that thought away, Jane reflected on the fact that they now had a name and an identity. Someone specific to focus on. But at the back of her mind was the question she'd still couldn't categorically answer: could she trust Graeme Hargreaves?

She looked up and saw Jag's eyes in his rear view mirror. 'So Jag, what did you make of Hargreaves?'

'I didn't trust him at first, ma'am. There seemed to be something going on between him and Mr Cheshire.'

'Yes. They'd clearly had a disagreement just before we turned up.'

'Yes, ma'am. And he knew we had that feeling, and it was like it didn't bother him. But when he told us about Mr Avis being Beavis, I believed him.'

'That's interesting. Why, Jag?'

'The way he was behaving: he was showing off, ma'am. And I thought that, well, he is that kind of person, so…'

'So, the way he told us, the attention-seeking… that's in his character?'

'Yes, ma'am. I have never met him but I thought his story was true because of the way he said it. Sorry, ma'am; I'm not explaining this very well.'

'Yes, you are, actually Jag. I know what you mean. He was being true to himself, however strange his behaviour seemed to us… You studied psychology, didn't you?'

'A long time ago, yes, ma'am.'

'Anything else strike you?'

'I was just thinking that I would be very angry if I was Adrian Cheshire, ma'am.'

'Why?'

'Mark told me how helpful he has been to us, but Mr Hargreaves didn't include him in the meeting at all.'

'Well, Jag… I suspect Adrian has been just a bit too helpful, and Graeme wanted us to know that he is the one in charge. I think it's one of those macho arm wrestling contests. Adrian is a big guy, must be quite intimidating if you're a fella. Graeme just wants to remind him who is actually in charge.'

Jag pulled up at a zebra crossing, and smiled as he turned to look at her. 'I think perhaps you studied psychology, too, ma'am.'

TWENTY-TWO

SIMON HOPKIRK, CHIEF CONSTABLE of Greater Manchester, adjusted his peaked cap with its black and white chequered band, and, as was his habit, gently tapped the Queen's Medal he wore on his uniform jacket.

He'd been awarded it for tackling a terrorist on London Bridge during his time at the Met, and he'd tapped it for luck ever since his interview for the Manchester job three years ago. He'd felt its reassuring heaviness against his heart as he walked in to face the panel.

His glasses made him appear bookish, but he was anything but. He liked to lead from the front in major incidents, and he was well liked, and known for supporting and encouraging female and ethnic minority representation at higher levels of command.

His support for Liverpool FC was tolerated by Manchester colleagues only because he was born there.

Turning away from the mirror, he smiled at Jane. 'How do I look?'

He was over six foot tall, even without the cap. Jane looked up from her position eight inches below. 'Formidable, sir.'

He laughed. 'You're too kind. But flattery always works, so you've obviously done your homework.' Then the joke was over and the smile was gone as he reached for the folder on his desk. 'So, we've got five minutes; how do you want to play it today?'

'I'd like to open up to the media about the CCTV image we have of a suspect, sir, if that's ok with you. We do have one or two leads – one of them we're hopeful about, but I don't want to give too much away on those—'

'—because it might show our hand too soon? Yes, agreed. I'd normally want to give the media more, but… I like the way you're handling it, Jane. You should know I have been in contact with the Met and they will help with identification of those who are… performing… in the videos: see if there are any known offenders and so on.'

'And the children, sir.'

'Indeed. We've taken your suggestion, and extended the search to identify vulnerable children and known groomers so that we cover the region. There's every chance that many of them have been smuggled in, of course. We will spread the net wider if needs be. But all of that is between us. The last thing we want now is to spread alarm among parents, and violence among paedophile watchers.'

He offered Jane a glass of water. As she sipped it, he gazed out of the window, and spoke more conversationally. 'I was sorry to hear about Charles. He was a good man; a good copper. You must miss him.'

Jane hadn't expected this, and the instant lump in her throat made her pause before answering. 'Yes sir. He was a great boss, and a good support to me personally.'

He turned and smiled. 'He would be proud of you now. You're running the division, and leading only your second murder investigation. If he was here, he'd be on the phone telling me how well you're doing. I just wanted you to know it's not gone unnoticed, all right?'

He gave her no time to reply, or even to register any emotion; he just walked to his office door, checked his watch, then held the door open. 'Shall we?'

Jane nodded, wondering if she'd been on the end of a throwaway platitude, or a hint of greater things to come. But then she felt her heart thud as she heard the hum of conversation from the journalists waiting in the conference room. It grew louder as she followed the Chief down the carpeted corridor. Allan would probably be there, so at least there was one friendly face.

She hoped.

Adrian stretched out on the sofa in his office, and pressed the remote.

Mark leaned back in the armchair, relishing the comfort, and the seemingly endless supply of coffee and biscuits brought in by Adrian's PA, Chloe.

This was definitely the life. He told Lorry last night that working with Adrian had turned his head. 'I can't believe the working conditions, never mind the pay.' She'd tutted and warned him not to overreact.

'Yeah, you might get a comfy chair and a few extra quid, but will you get the same job satisfaction?'

To which Mark had replied, after no consideration at all: 'Yes.'

His daydream of managing an IT budget and being able to get the best kit was pushed to one side as the tv burst into life to reveal a close up of Chief Constable Hopkirk and Jane Birchfield. Jane was talking as the picture switched to CCTV footage Mark was very familiar with.

'We would very much like to speak to this man, who was seen on CCTV going into the Pretty Cool Cafe at around or just before the time Jamie Castleton died. As you can see, he is wearing a cap, but also what we think are the kind of trousers often worn by medical staff. If anyone knows, or recognises, this man, we'd very much like to hear from you...'

Adrian sipped his coffee. 'That guy looks like he works out.'

'What, like a bodybuilder, you mean?'

'Maybe, or even a boxer. He has that physique, and that way of walking. Reminds me of me when I was a lot younger and full of myself.'

Mark laughed and reached for another custard cream. 'Yeah, well, I wouldn't know about that. I'm usually just full of biscuits.'

Adrian snorted and turned up the volume as a journalist asked a question. 'Are you suggesting that we could be looking at the man who killed two people?'

The Chief Constable paused as he considered his answer, then spoke firmly. He was obviously keen to wrap things up.

'We could be, yes. But, equally, we could be looking at an innocent man who just happened to be on the scene when Jamie died. We are keeping an open mind, so at the moment, as Jane said, we just want to talk to him.

'Let me remind you we are investigating two murders, and the production of offensive pornographic material. We are working on the basis that these separate offences are linked, and we will not rest until we have brought those involved to justice.

'If anyone knows anything, or anyone, I would say it is your duty to come forward.'

Adrian turned it off as the tv switched to the perfectly smooth face of a newsreader, and turned to Mark.

'Still no joy improving that image, then?'

'Well we can zoom in, but he's wearing a pretty good disguise: the cap, the collar up on his coat, and his head down.'

'Not really the behaviour of an innocent man... Might be worth checking out a few gyms, or boxing clubs, you know.'

'Yeah, thanks, I'll be sure to pass that on.' Mark looked at the clock and reluctantly heaved himself out of the chair. 'I must be away. No more luck identifying this Avis guy?'

Chloe walked in and stopped to listen. 'That rings a bell.'

Adrian looked up as he put his coffee cup back on the tray. 'Sorry?'

'Avis. I heard people talking about Brian Avis earlier, and I've been wracking my brain to recall him. I know it from somewhere.'

Mark moved to stand next to her. 'Chloe, it would be helpful if you could remember, and that's an understatement. We've tried to track him down from personnel records, but they're years out of date and he's not known at the address he gave when he came for an interview.'

Chloe frowned, staring at the tray for a moment, then began to clear away. 'I'll certainly try. It'll probably come back to me as soon as I stop thinking about it.'

Adrian smiled. 'Time to get home anyway. Thanks Chloe. Just call me if it does come back to you, ok, otherwise I shall see you in the morning.'

'Yes, goodnight, Adrian; Mark.'

They waited till she'd gone out, then Adrian shook Mark's hand. 'I'm willing to bet she'll phone me tonight.'

'And if she comes up with a positive ID, and an address, I will buy you both a meal in Chinatown.'

'Fair enough...and if she doesn't, I'll buy you and Lorry a meal in Chinatown.'

'That would be amazing. She'd love to meet you. Yeah, you're on. Hey, if we're lucky, we might find his name and address in a fortune cookie.'

'That would be lucky. Tell you what, though, can you send me the CCTV file so I can take a proper look. I'd like to see how that guy moves. There's something about him that's nagging away at the back of my mind.'

Mark phoned through to Jag on his way out and asked him to send Adrian a link to the CCTV video straight away.

Adrian watched it as he stuffed that night's paperwork into his rucksack, ready for his power walk to Salford Quays, which had now become a daily event. Then he sat down and replayed it, and that's when it clicked into place.

He could swear he'd seen that guy on one of his evening walks home.

Allan stared at the computer screen again as the cursor blinked patiently, waiting for him to commit his thoughts to pixels.

But he was struggling to come up with something original to say about the murder inquiry, and it was getting frustrating. He kept telling himself he was living with the head of Ashbridge police so he should be the one coming up with the exclusive angle. But it was actually a massive disadvantage, because he couldn't betray the trust Jane showed him. And he couldn't risk exposing the fragile Irene to what could prove to be relentless media attention by printing her story.

After the news conference, every other paper would be using the time-honoured 'have you seen this man' story. And that meant it would be old hat by the time his paper came out.

Or would it?

Allan remembered something Jane said about the possibility of that guy on CCTV working in the medical profession. There weren't that many hospitals and clinics in the area, and Jane said they'd already checked them out, as you'd expect. But she'd never mentioned care homes or the private companies that were providing services to the NHS, including ambulances and paramedics. How closely were they vetted? How easy would it be for a crook from one of those companies to steal drugs, while everyone automatically assumed it had to be linked to the NHS itself?

It could be a long night. Allan texted Jane… '*I'm going to be late, so don't hurry home! U were brilliant on tv. C u whenever xx*' Then he made himself another coffee and began compiling a list of major private health and care providers, starting with those operating hospital services in and around Ashbridge.

He quickly narrowed it down to six companies, all of which were offering the full range of treatments and surgeries. They were all based locally, but they had outlets throughout the North West.

There was just the chance that someone might know who Mister CCTV is. Allan felt the familiar adrenaline rush that only a lifetime as a newshound could give, as he picked up the phone and began ringing round.

There was an optimistic feel about the place tonight, and Jane's instincts told her she needed to remind everyone there was a long way to go yet.

On the other hand, she couldn't help feeling that the end was in sight.

Mark passed on Adrian's hunch that the guy on CCTV may be a bodybuilder or a boxer, and she immediately flashed back to Sutton's arrest at the gym. Was that pure coincidence, or is there a connection?

She put a note on the log for George to ask Sutton if he recognised the image, and to put someone on a trawl of local gyms and boxing clubs, then smiled with something approaching relief as Allan's text came through and she realised she wouldn't need to do any clock watching tonight.

A phone call to Irene revealed she hadn't yet remembered where else she may have seen the menacing looking guy at the PC Cafe that time she followed Jamie. It was unlikely Irene was going to come up with anything.

So everything hinged on finding Brian Avis...

She took a bite out of the cheese and pickle sandwich Jag had brought her, and was still chewing when Mark walked in. He was looking very pleased with himself, until he realised he'd marched into the boss's office without knocking.

'Oh, sorry ma'am...'

Jane held a hand over her mouth as she carried on eating. 'Ok Mark, I'll forgive you, if you've got good news for me.'

'I think I have, ma'am. I've just had Adrian Cheshire on the phone. His PA Chloe thought she knew the name Brian Avis, and promised to think about it.'

'And...?'

'She's just called him at home. There's a Brian Avis who's a member at her tennis club, and she remembers him saying he used to know Graeme Hargreaves. She reckons he's worth a few quid himself now. Not sure why he joined because he never plays tennis. Apparently, he's the size of a beach hut and about as mobile. Likes the ladies, too, she says.'

Jane put the remains of her sandwich back in its wrapper, then stood and held her door open. 'Come on Mark. Let's give the guys in CID a little job, shall we?'

It took ten minutes for Lorry to breathlessly announce she'd got a phone number for the tennis club secretary, and ten seconds for Jane to ask her why she wasn't on the phone already.

Jane stood looking over her shoulder as Lorry made the call. The secretary was clearly not eager to co-operate, but Lorry frostily reminded her that murder investigations tended not to adhere to office hours and were rarely convenient.

Mark looked on, too, as the seconds ticked by. Lorry held a hand over the receiver.

'She's gone to get the membership books.'

Jane looked at her watch. 'Where the hell does she keep them? Wimbledon?'

Lorry cut short her laughter. 'Yes, yes, I'm here... You've found him? Can you give me his address and phone number please, and any other contact information...'

She wrote it all down and finished the call, holding up the note for Jane, who grabbed it and called the desk sergeant.

'Alex? I need a response team outside ready to go in five minutes. We're going to pay a social call on a murder suspect, and we need to assume he won't come quietly. Target lives at Ashbridge Lodge on Park Road. Usual procedure... and we'll need a few uniforms to keep the neighbours at a safe distance... We'll need blocks at both ends of the street. I'll be with you in the lead car. No sirens, ok? Brief you on the way. Oh, and Alex, put Sykes on the team if he's on duty, will you? He needs to know he's got a future, despite the cock-up at the hospital, all right? Ok, good, thanks.'

Jane turned to see Lorry and Mark's expectant faces. 'Lorry, you're coming with us. Sorry, Mark, can you stay here and man the phones? Thanks you two – great job.'

Lorry hurried beside her as Jane walked back to her office, and watched as she put on a protective vest under her uniform jacket.

'Ready for this Lorry?'

'I think so, ma'am.'

'A bit nervous?'

'Yes ma'am. Mark's gutted he's not coming.'

'Well, it happens. He'll get over it. Now come on. Let's see if we can persuade Mr Avis to come and spend the evening with us.'

TWENTY-THREE

SERGEANT ALEX GLEDHILL PARKED the Vauxhall Insignia a few yards east of the driveway to Ashbridge Lodge, and turned to Jane.

'We're in position and all set, ma'am. I estimate the drive to be around 15/20 yards long, and it bends on the approach to the house, so we can't be seen until we are a few steps away. I've got six officers in two cars in position at each end of the road, and another two to link up with us as we access the property.'

'Good, thanks Alex. I want you and the uniforms in front. Lorry and I will follow behind. No noise, no drama. We just ring the door bell and take it from there, all right?'

'Understood, ma'am.'

'OK, let them know we're making a move.' Jane peered into the distance as something caught her eye. 'And tell them to turn the bloody blue lights off.'

Alex cursed under his breath and passed on the orders. He was a tactical response veteran, with 20 years on the clock, loved his job, and expected perfection. Someone was going to get a bollocking later tonight, for sure.

They closed the car doors quietly, and walked slowly onto the gravel drive. This was a quiet area, and their footsteps sounded unnaturally loud. The air was cool and loaded with fine drizzle. A faint smell of grass clippings and wood smoke floated in on a gentle breeze.

Jane and Lorry were dwarfed by the uniforms in front of them. One of them was PC Sykes. He had smiled and saluted Jane when they met in the car park. Jane was impressed: he'd been quick to own up to his mistake on guard duty outside Gonzales' room, and had taken the ear bashing – and the official verbal warning – Jane gave him, without flinching.

Since then, he'd been a model PC, and Jane wanted him to know that she'd noticed.

Now, he was walking confidently in front, alongside Alex, as they neared the front door.

It looked like solid oak, and there was a stainless steel light fitting to one side, above a large slate slab with Ashbridge Lodge etched in white. To the right of the door, a large bay window was showing lights behind vertical slats.

Jane took a breath as Alex talked quietly into his radio, then turned to her. 'When you give the word, ma'am.'

'Ring the bell, please Alex, then let me do the talking.'

The bell rang out like church chimes, so loud that Jane felt Lorry jump beside her.

There was a low hum of chatter coming through Alex's radio. It was taking too long.

Someone should be opening the door by now, unless the lights were just a deterrent, and the Avis's were out.

Jane was just about to order Alex to break the door down, when they heard a bolt being pulled back. The door opened slowly, and a seriously overweight man appeared, wearing a red dressing gown hanging open to reveal a hairy chest and stomach, and blue and white striped pyjama bottoms. He was breathing heavily. and smelled of whisky. Jane stepped forward.

'Mr Avis? Brian Avis?'

He seemed totally unfazed by the sight that greeted him. It was almost as if it was a social call. 'That's me. What can I do you for?'

Jane did the formal introductions as politely as she could manage. 'Would you get dressed Mr Avis, please? We'd like you to come to Ashbridge police station for questioning in connection with the murders of Jamie Castleton and Paolo Gonzales.'

'Who?' His accent was a mix of Manchester and Home Counties, and though his expression was a combination of surprise and innocence, Jane noted his eyes remained locked onto hers. He paused, then shrugged and opened the door wider.

'Why don't you come in? I'll come with you if you really want me to, but I don't see how I can be of help.'

Hia oily self confidence was already getting under Jane's skin, but she held his gaze without blinking. 'That's very kind. We'll wait just here while you get changed.'

'As you wish.' He walked slowly towards a wide carpeted staircase, calling out casually over his shoulder. 'Shan't be long.' He stopped on the stairs and turned, smiling. 'You can come upstairs and keep an eye on me, if you like. Just in case, you know?'

'Is there anyone else here with you, Mr Avis?'

'Oh, no. I'm all alone in the world, I'm afraid. I do apologise for my attire. I find the less I wear, the more relaxed I feel.'

Jane glanced at Alex as Avis carried on up the stairs, and he nodded, following a corridor at one side of the staircase that led towards the back of the house, and nudging Sykes to follow Avis.

Jane turned as she heard Lorry's sharp intake of breath. 'God, he's disgusting.'

'Don't let him get under your skin. It's an old trick. He wants to wind us up so we make mistakes. This is going to be difficult enough, so we need to go by the book, ok?'

Lorry nodded. 'Thanks, ma'am. I'm learning…'

'It never stops, Lorry.'

Jane's radio crackled as Alex gave the signal to confirm all exits were covered and all was quiet out on the street.

Lorry looked round the hall, taking in the paintings in matching gilt frames. Contemporary sculptural pieces were positioned beside each interior door, each with their own display stand. 'He must be made of money, ma'am.'

Jane merely nodded, counting the seconds till they could get Avis into the car, and she could breathe a little easier.

She heard a door clicking shut from upstairs, then Avis appeared, with Sykes a few paces behind.

He'd changed into red trousers, a bright yellow v neck sweater, and a blue shirt. His shoes were tan leather brogues and he carried a navy jacket over one arm.

'I take it I'm not under arrest?'

'No, sir. We simply want to talk to you as part of our inquiries. We appreciate your co-operation.'

'I can't think of a better way to spend an evening, than in your company.'

Jane wanted to throw up, but turned to open the front door instead, as Alex marched through from the back to join them, and stood next to Avis. 'Shall we get in the car, sir?'

'By all means.' Avis smiled at Jane provocatively. 'Oh, by the way, I have friends coming round tomorrow morning for a business meeting, so don't wear me out tonight, will you? Right, lead on…'

They drove back to the police station in silence. Avis sat in the back, squeezed between Lorry and Sykes, and alternated between staring ahead and closing his eyes.

Everything about him suggested to Jane that he wasn't going to make it easy for them. He maintained an annoying level of calm politeness, and had the commonsense to use the drive to the station as the chance to relax, and, no doubt, to plan his strategy. The irony was that his behaviour ramped up Jane's belief that he was the one.

He carried on playing the part of the perfect guest when they got to the interview room, accepting the offer of a cup of tea and smiling as he asked Lorry for a biscuit. 'I'm addicted to sweet things, you see.'

Jane drank coffee in her office, in the vain hope that delaying might disturb his composure; but she wasn't holding her breath. When she walked in with Lorry, he was leaning back in his chair, sipping tea, and humming a tune.

Sykes was on the door, observing, just in case.

Jane nodded at Lorry to start the tape, and run through the formalities. 'Well, thanks for your co-operation, Mr Avis. As I said we want to talk to you about the murders of two people in Ashbridge last week. If I remember correctly, you implied you didn't know either of them. Is that right?'

'Yes, I've never heard of them, so I'm not sure I'll be much help to you. But, please, fire away.'

'What do you do for a living?'

'Oh, I dabble in shares, property, and businesses.'

'What kind of businesses?'

'Ones that I think will make me some money, in return for an investment of my time and money.'

'Such as...?'

'Oh, let's see... My portfolio extends across many sectors, but I do have stakes in an estate agency, a fashion house, games software... Their names wouldn't mean anything to you, yet.'

'What about films and videos?'

'What about them?'

'Do you have film and video businesses in your... portfolio, Mr Avis?'

Avis looked sulky, but it was clearly part of the act. 'Your tone of voice suggests you think I do, which in turn suggests it has something to do with these murders. But, as it happens, no; I can assure you I don't do movies or videos, apart from video games.'

Jane decided to up the pressure and asked where he was on the nights Jamie and Gonzales were killed. Avis dealt with it serenely, setting out apparently perfect alibis and giving the names of people he was with. 'I was having dinner with friends on the first occasion, and I had an early night – with a very good lady friend of mine when your Mr Gonzales sadly passed away.'

Jane nodded at Lorry, who produced the CCTV image taken outside the PC Cafe.

'Do you recognise this man, Mr Avis?'

He laughed. 'I'm not sure anyone would recognise him, are you, dear? No, not a chance. No idea who he is, sorry.'

Jane smiled. 'By the way, Mr Avis, how do you get on with Graeme Hargreaves?'

If Avis was thrown, he hid it very well. But not quite well enough. For the first time, he needed thinking time, and he picked at a fingernail briefly. Then he looked up.

'Graeme? Haven't seen him for years. Done very well for himself, of course, but I won't hold that against him.'

'No? How about when he turned you down for an IT development job at Greaves – what? ten or so years ago? Must have been very annoying: you, with all your experience, being rejected by a former school pal...Do you hold that against him?'

Avis settled back in his chair and held Jane's gaze confidently. 'Oh dear, we are getting worked up now, aren't we…? I'm not sure what this has got to do with anything, but… yes, I did feel annoyed, momentarily. I had the qualifications and the experience, so I can only assume that either he'd interviewed a superstar who was better than me; or it was purely personal.'

'Why would it be personal?'

'Well, we didn't actually get on that well at school—'

'He bullied you, didn't he?'

'Yes, he did. But I survived, and I've done quite well for myself since then.'

'But you still bear a grudge, don't you?'

Avis looked shocked. 'A grudge? Dear me, no. I have moved on; isn't that the expression? Graeme did me a favour. His rejection motivated me to show what I could do.'

'Let's talk about Charlie Pearson, shall we?'

Once again, Jane got the reaction she wanted. Avis got interested in his fingernail again, and said he didn't know the name.

'He knows you, Mr Avis.'

'A lot of people do, Jane.'

'My name is DCI Birchfield, Mr Avis.'

Avis winked. 'Ah, sorry… DCI Birchfield. Anyway, who is this Pearson chap?'

'Funnily enough, he dabbles in things too – like property. Just about stays on the right side of the law.'

'Very wise.'

Jane knew she was guessing, though she preferred to call it exploring. 'So, you've had no dealings with him?'

'No I haven't.' Avis looked at his watch. 'Is this going to take much longer? It's obvious I'm not being much help, and I do have a full day tomorrow…'

It was Jane's turn to smile. 'You'll need to bear with us,

Mr Avis. Before we go any further, we need to check the alibis you have given us, which may take us a little while. I'm sure you understand we have to follow procedure to the letter, especially in a murder investigation. Can we get you another cup of tea?'

Avis scowled and shook his head. His good humour was evaporating, and Jane notched that up as a small victory in what could turn out to be a long siege.

She scraped her chair back and stood, nodding at Lorry, who spoke for the tape. 'Interview suspended at 9.45pm. DCI Birchfield and DC Irons leaving the room; PC Sykes remaining along with Mr Brian Avis.'

Jane let him go just after 11pm. Avis's contacts had verified the alibis, and she asked Sykes to drive him back home.

Logging her notes as the clock ticked towards midnight, Jane was even more certain of Avis's involvement. If she was right, the only way forward was to break the alibis, which seemed unlikely, or prove that Avis ordered the killings.

But she knew what the Chief Constable would say… all she had was a feeling; a hunch. And if Avis had perfect alibis, and had proved himself more than able to handle police interview techniques, how was she going to get evidence, let alone a confession?

Jane stabbed the power button on the base unit under her desk and stood to stretch.

She felt the frustration build inside and drove home more aggressively than usual.

Allan was already in bed, but she knew she wouldn't sleep – not yet. She poured a glass of Malbec and sat at the dining table, in the faint glow of the streetlamp.

Everything she knew told her Avis was the man. But it was clear it would take everything she knew and every ounce of commitment to bring him to justice.

She hated the sight of him. He disgusted her. For the first time in her career, and despite all her training and mentoring and experience, Jane was driven by a desire to avenge Jamie's death and those exploited children's wrecked innocence.

And Avis was guilty as hell.

Jane tipped the glass back, drank the last dregs and thumped her glass on the table.

TWENTY-FOUR

NEXT MORNING, JANE CLUTCHED the mug of tea Allan had made for her with both hands, like it was a long lost friend.

He sat beside her at the small kitchen table, and yawned hugely. 'So how's it going, boss?'

'Don't ask.'

Allan grinned, then got up again, heading towards the toaster. 'OK. I won't. Are you eating this morning?'

'Toast and honey would be perfect, thanks Aga.'

'Blimey, you haven't called me that for ages.'

'Must be something about us being in the kitchen together.'

He dropped two slices in and sat down again. 'What?'

'Aga… kitchen?'

'Oh, right. Anyway, what's new, or can't you tell me?'

'Well, I can't prove anything, but I think we've got our main man.'

'Beavis? Wow! That's amazing.'

Jane explained the slight twist to the name, and the tennis club link to Brian Avis.

Allan frowned, wondering about the wisdom of owning up to his internet searching, but his thought process was interrupted by the loud tinny slam of the toast slices bouncing up. He put two more in and started spreading marmalade on his.

'Is there some connection I'm missing?'

Jane squeezed honey onto her toast. 'What do you mean?'

'There just seems to be this health and fitness link, doesn't there? Sutton at the gym; Avis at the tennis club; and that guy's comment at Greaves… you know, the one who said the CCTV image looked like a bloke who worked out, or was a boxer.'

Jane felt the tea and the sugary kick of the honey doing their best to kick her into life. 'I never made that connection, but you're right. It's worth a look. Plus, there's the medical profession bit, too.'

'Eh?'

'The guy on CCTV was wearing what we think was hospital gear.'

'Oh yeah, and that guy Gonzales died in hospital.'

'One big problem, though – Avis is too fat to move, let alone play tennis, though he might make a good punchbag.'

They chatted, and ate more toast, and washed the pots, and cleaned their teeth and kissed goodbye on the doorstep, closely observed by Nora Nosey in the house opposite. Jane smiled as she drove to work, and gave thanks for the precious moments she could just be herself.

As she parked her car, she wondered if Allan had hit on something with his comments on the health and fitness connection. He'd been a massive help during the Fiona Worsley case, and showed every sign of becoming indispensable again.

It didn't take Ross long to discover that Avis had connections with a fitness company. Bridge Health was formed two years ago by a couple of local lads who'd built muscle and now wanted to build an empire. With Avis's cash and connections, they'd opened two gyms which had been converted from old properties near shops and offices, each with a membership of around 300 paying an annual fee of around £500.

Ross told Jane they also ran fitness classes and personal training which were generating extra income.

'Might be worth me paying a visit, boss?'

'Oh yes, I think so, Ross. Make it very official, will you? We need to spread the message that we are very much on this case.'

'So, no Mister Laid Back Nice Guy?'

'Certainly not. Be more Mr Cold As Ice.'

Ross smiled, then froze it. 'Like this, ma'am?'

'Seriously, Ross, you should be on the stage. Now go on, get outta here. And remember we really need to find our CCTV guy.'

'The Incredible Hulk? If he's that big, he should be an easy target.'

Jane frowned as Ross closed the door behind him. '*An easy target…*' If her theory was correct, Avis would use people to do his dirty work, just as he used them to make profits on his investments: up to and including murder.

She tapped her thoughts into the log as she worked things out.

And where would he naturally go to find his *easy targets…* answer: the contacts he'd made through acquiring businesses; the people who owed him. Avis revolted her and Lorry, but she could imagine him convincing others – particularly men – to do him a little favour in return for all the support he'd given.

She copied her notes into an email and sent it to George with a message: '*We need to pay a visit to each of Avis's businesses. See if we can find our CCTV guy. And ask around about the way Avis operates. How hands on is he? He must also have lots of property, some of it could be officially empty, so let's see if anyone can point us in the direction of porn video production from one of those empty properties, and where those children came from, and where they are being kept.'*

George replied to say he'd added a few more visits to what he called Ross's royal tour, and that Jag would be dispatched to research and check out empty properties.

Next, Jane grabbed George for a quick catch up with Sutton, who was happy enough to remain in custody for now. But the time limit for holding him was approaching, and Jane wanted to see if the prospect of being allowed out, to face the low-lifes who had nobbled him, had increased his desire to communicate.

He'd clearly kept himself in shape during his few days in custody, though he was losing weight.

Jane sat down on the bed next to him, with George's bulk blocking the door. 'How are you doing Martin?'

'Yeah, fine.' His attempt to look indifferent wasn't working. Obviously hadn't got any training from Avis.

Jane spoke quietly, as if inviting him into her confidence. 'It'll soon be over. We know who's behind it all...'

Sutton clasped his hands together tightly. 'You found Beavis?'

'Yes, Martin. We have already interviewed him. He's got lots of connections; has shares in lots of businesses – including gyms.' She let that sink in, then added. 'Is that where you met him? In one of the gyms?'

Sutton nodded, and George moved in closer. 'Sorry, mate, was that a yes?'

'Yes.'

Jane nodded and George carried on. 'Can you describe him for us?'

'I only saw him once.'

'But you must be able to remember something. Come on, Martin… remember, the more you help us, the better it is for you.'

He sighed. 'Ok… he was pretty fat, black hair greased down, about 5 foot 9.'

'How old?'

'Middle aged – about 40?'

'So, you'd recognise him if we showed you a picture of him, no trouble…'

'Well, yeah.'

Jane leaned forward. 'Martin, this is really important. Did he tell you his name, or did you hear it from someone else?'

Sutton paused, remembering. 'I think he just said his name was Brian.'

'Ok, good. What about his last name?'

'He didn't tell me. Gonzales said he was called Beavis, so…'

'You're doing really well. If we are to bring this to court, we're going to need confirmation of his identity. That means we need to get you to walk through an identity parade and pick out the man you know as Beavis, ok?'

Sutton put his head in his hands, breathing heavily. 'Jesus! He'll kill me, I told you!'

George sat next to him. 'No he won't. He won't be getting anywhere near you. All you have to do is help us put him away. You'll get some time for what you did, but you won't be anywhere near him. And you'll be out before you know it. So come on, Martin, do the right thing or you'll regret it for the rest of your life.'

An hour later, Jane gave the order for Avis to be brought in again. Ross had drawn up a list of half a dozen people who could potentially be a match for the guy on CCTV, and was now chasing them up, helped by Lorry.

Simon Hopkirk had been as good as his word and sent porn video files to the Serious Crimes Squad, who were now looking at background shots, in case there were any clues about the locations.

Mark Manning was working with Adrian Cheshire, tracking down people who'd paid for access using digital currency in the mistaken belief they were untraceable payments.

But, as Jane said to Hopkirk during one of their daily phone calls: 'We're slowly catching the easy targets, but we can't pin anything on the man at the top.'

'What about the guy on CCTV? Any leads from the public?'

'We've had a couple of dozen calls, and we'll follow them up, but nothing to get us excited yet. Have your people got anything at all on Avis?'

'One of my deputies knows of him. Word is he's a first class creep who works hard at buttering the right people up, but no-one is fooled. He's not liked, but there's nothing we can pin on him. I've sent the details off to the Met to see if he comes up on their systems. So you never know...'

'He's the one, sir. I'm convinced of it.'

'Well, then, you have my permission to prove it, then it's up to the CPS. You're going to need to act quickly, too. He probably knows you're digging around into his background and his businesses, so I guess it won't be long before he starts making waves. The clock is counting down, Jane.'

Jane didn't admit that she spent most of her day checking the time now, conscious that she needed to nail Avis. But what hurt the most was the realisation that every second must feel like an hour to the children Avis was exploiting, and abusing.

The thought of snooping around deserted offices and business units in back streets didn't exactly fill Jag with joy.

In fact, it was probably the first moment in his time at Ashbridge when he'd felt disgruntled. He saw himself as more of a thinker, a planner, an organiser, and – though he'd faced some pretty squalid situations as a beat officer – he'd assumed that rising to the heights of detective would give him more scope to use his brain power.

And that was why he felt gloomy now, as he sat in his car on a drizzly afternoon, staring at the shoddy, badly painted door of yet another vacant property that was part of Avis's empire.

George had winked as he told him to use his discretion about getting inside to have a look round. And that went against the grain, too. In Jag's ordered, logical universe, there were rules to be followed. So where did discretion come into it, he wondered.

George had sighed. 'We're looking for a killer, and a pervert who is exploiting children in disgusting ways. I don't particularly care how you get in. Just bloody well check them out, whatever it takes. Just make sure no-one's looking when you break in, ok? My orders, Jag… not your call; not your problem if it goes pear-shaped.'

Jag'd use of discretion had already cost him a tear in his trousers where he'd climbed in through a sash window, and he'd shelled out on a new box of wet wipes so he could clean his hands and shoes before getting back in the car.

At least this was the last one of the day. It was listed as a former storage depot that supplied some of the small shops Avis had bought.

Either the shops had gone bust, or he'd found a better way to keep them supplied, because it certainly looked empty now.

Jag locked the car and patrolled the street, checking for signs of life, but finding none; which was a bit unusual for late afternoon on a working day. It was as if the disease of dereliction had spread: the storage place shuts down, so the greasy spoon and the mobile phone repair shop on either side get no passing trade.

Jag concluded it was safe to look more closely at his target, and peered in through the grubby window.

All he could see was lines of shelving, but he noticed some of them still had boxes on them. That stirred a thought in his mind: maybe it is still being used, but not officially.

Jag felt the first spark of curiosity he'd had all day, and decided he needed to get in there.

The door was locked with a padlock the size of a cabin bag. The windows looked like they had been painted up, and he didn't want to break glass, unless he had to.

He walked slowly down a narrow passageway that divided the depot from the cafe next door. The rain was coming down heavier now, and he felt cold drops hitting his head and running down his neck.

He wrinkled his nose as he caught the stench of rotten food, no doubt left behind when the cafe shut its doors for the last time. Stepping carefully to avoid puddles of what he hoped were just rainwater, Jag turned right at the end and saw a gate, which he pushed open carefully.

It led him into a small backyard almost completely taken up by dustbins, most of which were overflowing. Jag was offended to see that the rubbish was mainly paper and cardboard; the sort of stuff that should be recycled, but clearly the council had abandoned its waste collection service here.

The back door was solid enough, but Jag could see the nearest window hadn't been latched properly. He dragged a dustbin over, and climbed up. There was just enough decayed wood to allow him to slide his penknife in and force the catch up.

A couple of minutes later, he was in.

He'd expected cobwebs, but he was immediately on the alert because there weren't any. It looked tidy, too. There were six rows of shelving units of standard steel construction, still in good condition, and every row housed at least a dozen cardboard boxes. They too looked clean, as if they had only recently been put here.

Jag took pictures on his mobile phone, then switched to video mode and walked through the whole ground floor.

He cursed when he'd finished recording, because his phone battery was now showing critical at 2 per cent.

A voice inside was telling him he needed to phone this in. He knew this didn't qualify as an empty building any more, but he didn't dare risk making a call that wasn't an emergency.

The light was fading as the rain clouds darkened, and he had planned to use the torch on his phone. Annoyed with himself for forgetting to charge it in the car, he switched to '*do not disturb*' and put the phone in his inside jacket pocket.

Then he tensed up. There was an internal door in the far corner that he was pretty sure wasn't on the floor plan he'd studied in the car. It looked new.

Jag moved slowly towards the door. It was painted white and had a modern chrome handle, which looked totally out of place here.

As he got closer, he stopped, convinced he'd heard something. Slowly and silently, he crouched down so he could look under one of the lower shelves next to him. He twisted on his toes to widen his sphere of vision. There was nothing there.

Jag relaxed and tutted to himself. 'Jag, it's a rat. You should know. Your house used to be full of them.'

He walked to the white door and pushed it open.

It was like a bedroom showroom at the local furniture store… with a double bed, a large wall mirror, a dining chair, and a small sofa.

Jag struggled at first to process the image in front of him.

Then he realised he was probably looking at a film set.

Now was definitely the time to call it in.

He reached for his phone, then stopped. There was that noise again, sounding closer this time; they were footsteps and they were getting louder.

Jag turned so he could watch the door, but it happened too quickly for him.

He just had time to register that the guy was big, and wearing a buff to hide his face.

Then everything went dark.

TWENTY-FIVE

JANE LOOKED OUT OF her office window, watching the lines of rain slanting down, lit up like grey steel as they sliced through the car park's floodlighting.

The sky was stereotypical Manchester, dark and heavy, as if the clouds were doing their best to land.

Try as she might, she couldn't obliterate the image in her head of innocent children, kidnapped and locked up; many of them smuggled in after being 'bought' for pennies from hoodwinked parents desperate for money. The promise of a new life had instead dragged them into imprisonment, ill treatment, and degradation.

Jane turned away, massaging her forehead, and took a sip from her water bottle.

The cold clean taste jolted her out of the aggression and the loathing that she knew was guaranteed to impair her judgement.

She sat at her desk, and went through the log, again,

searching for clues, inspiration… anything that might open the case up.

A lot depended on Sutton being able to ID Avis, but going through the formality of an identity parade now, was too risky. She had asked George and Lorry to show Sutton a series of photos, with one shot of Avis shuffled in the pack. If he picked him out, that would be a breakthrough; enough to get him back in.

Ross had come up with a couple of leads on his calls at some of the Avis-owned businesses. Staff at a wholesale outlet recalled regular visits from Avis, who was on several occasions in the company of a guy who looked like a club bouncer; and a girl behind the counter of a camera shop gave a similar description, with the extra detail that he looked Eastern European and had, in her words, 'a weird flat face with his eyes wide apart.'

Ross's log note wrily noted: 'Mark needs to work miracles on that CCTV image. Otherwise,we might as well say it's Boris Johnson so we can all go home!'

It wasn't going to be easy, but the more she went over it, the more Jane felt it was coming together. But they needed hard evidence – ideally forensic evidence – if they were to make it stick.

Without it, Avis could simply repeat his 'perfect alibi', shrug his shoulders, and innocently wish the police every success in the future.

Jane checked her watch. George and Lorry should be back by now. She walked through to CID, to find Mark on the phone, looking concerned.

He put the receiver down straight away. 'What is it, Mark?'

'I can't get an answer from Jag, ma'am. He was looking at some empty buildings, but he should be back by now. George asked me to check in with him.'

'Where is Jag likely to be now?'

'His last call was at a former storage unit just off Adelaide Street, ma'am.'

'When was the last time we heard from him?'

'Mid-afternoon. He rang in to say he was having no luck.'

'Worrying. It's not like him to go AWOL.' Jane put a reassuring hand on Mark's shoulder, though she felt anything but relaxed. 'Let's play safe. Get onto Alex, see if he can get a couple of uniforms down to that storage unit straight away. Tell him it's from me, and tell him we're worried about Jag, so no delays.'

She turned, heading back to her office, then stopped. 'Oh, and ask George to come and see me the minute he gets back, will you?'

Mark shouted after her, just as she made it back to her office door. His voice was a mix of panic and disbelief.

'Jag's just called in, ma'am. He's been attacked...'

They found him slumped against the steering wheel of his car. His clothes were soaking wet, there was blood on his head and neck, and a nasty swelling on his cheekbone.

The paramedics refused to let him move until they'd checked him over. After five minutes, one of them walked over to where Jane and George were waiting.

'Looks as if he got punched in the face, very hard, and very accurately.'

'Accurately?'

'Yes, erm...'

'DCI Birchfield... Jane.'

'Ah, right. Yes, well, whoever did this picked the right spot, if all they wanted to do was knock him out. It's one of those pressure points. If you get it right, it makes the head spin round, and that's what causes the loss of consciousness. The only question is whether the force of the punch had any other effect, so we'll need to get some scans done straight away. We're done here, so...'

'OK if I have a quick word with him?'

'Just for a minute, but he's very dazed.'

Jane climbed into the back of the ambulance. Jag 's complexion looked grey and his eyes were swollen and bloody.

'I found it, ma'am.' His voice was so hoarse, she had to put her face right next to his.

'Found what, Jag?'

'The filming. Studio, in that building. Not empty inside...'

Jane put a hand on his chest. 'Ok, Jag, we'll take a look. Good work. Just relax now... I'll come and see you later.'

The paramedic jumped in beside her. 'We're ready to go.'

Jag pulled weakly at the sleeve of her jacket, as she was about to stand.

'It was him.'

'Who, Jag?'

'CCTV. It was him.'

Jane sat down and leaned across to the paramedic, so she could see his name tag.

'Sorry, Stephen, I need a minute to hear this...'

She smiled at Jag. 'Try to remember. Tell me what he looked like.'

'Very tall,... six foot plus... heavy... coloured buff or scarf round his face... bushy eyebrows...foreign accent...'

'What kind of accent?'

'Not sure. He'd hit me. Was on the floor, Heard him talking...'

The paramedic pointedly looked at his watch and began checking Jag's pulse, then wrapped a blood pressure strap round his arm. 'We need to get him checked, now, please.'

'Ok, yes, sorry.'

She stepped down and watched as the door slammed shut and the ambulance moved slowly away down the cobbled street.

She saw it turn left onto the main road, and heard the siren.

George moved quietly to stand next to her. 'We'll get the bastard who did this, ma'am.'

'Yes, we will George. And God help them all if there's any permanent damage.'

She turned and walked towards the storage unit, talking quickly as George struggled to keep up with her. 'Jag is sure he was attacked by the CCTV guy. That gives us a probable link to Jamie's death, and the fact it happened on a film set on Avis's property leads directly to him.'

'And – I didn't get chance to tell you – we have Sutton's positive ID of Avis.'

Jane didn't break stride; her eyes fixed on the unit Jag had investigated. 'Even better… Right. Get Phil down here, now. I don't want these uniforms standing around looking smart; I want them knocking on doors, finding out who saw what. I want CCTV footage so we can get a clearer shot of the thug who did this to Jag. Avis will wriggle and run if he can, so we have to make this watertight, and I'm not going to rest till it's done. This has gone too far. It ends here.'

She looked at George as they reached the back door of the unit. 'Whatever it takes, ok? Now, come on, break this bloody door down.'

Irene burst into tears straight away, and Shirley didn't blame her. Graeme Hargreaves had a reputation as a hard faced bastard, so this had come right out of the blue. In fact, she'd almost cried herself when George had given her the job of passing the info to Irene.

The word was that the new online betting site was doing well, and Hargreaves wanted – in his words – 'to start to put things right'.

He'd sent word through Mark Manning that he didn't hold a grudge against Jamie for what he'd done.

Shirley told Irene over their cup of tea that Hargreaves said he admired Jamie's skill and would have signed him up for the company if he could. And he was impressed that he'd hacked the website to make money to give his mum a comfortable life, knowing that his life was in danger for exposing the porn video business.

Shirley had held Irene's hand and looked into her eyes as she delivered the punchline.

'He was very moved by what Jamie had done, Irene. And he realised that, after all that, you wouldn't be able to touch that money because it came through illegal activity. So… he wanted us to give you this.'

She handed Irene a blank white envelope. 'What is it?'

Shirley smiled. 'Open it, Irene, and find out!'

She tentatively pulled out the flap and took out a sheet of paper. A cheque floated neatly onto the formica table, but Irene just looked at the letter Graeme had written.

'What does it say?'

Irene put on her glasses and read, her voice breaking more and more with each sentence. *'I know we've never met, but you are a remarkable lady, Mrs Castleton. You must be, to have such a remarkable son. I'm sorry I'll never get the chance to meet him and shake his hand, but you must be very proud of him, and you should be. He used his skill, did what he had to do, to give you a decent amount of money, knowing that he wouldn't be around to look after you financially.*

'I know the police are unlikely to let you have that money, which they rightly say belongs to my company.'

Irene handed the letter to Shirley, unable to continue. Shirley read out the rest for her. *'But Jamie was a hero in my book, and I couldn't let his bravery be for nothing. So I am enclosing a cheque, with my very best wishes, for an amount of money that will give you the financial security Jamie wanted. And if there's anything else you need, just let me know. Yours, Graeme Hargreaves.'*

Feeling a bit like the host of a tv game show, Shirley picked up the cheque and handed it to Irene, who turned it over and stared, shaking her head.

Eventually, she forced the words out. 'This can't be right.'

'Why, how much is it, Irene?'

Irene roughly wiped her eyes on the sleeve of her cardigan, and whispered, as she was afraid if she said it out loud, the cheque would disappear.

'It's a cheque for £100,000!'

Shirley managed to stay poker-faced, and she later admitted to her boyfriend it was the first time that had happened. But then she moved next to Irene to see for herself, made her stand up and gave her a bear hug.

'Oh my God, Irene! That's incredible! We all thought he might give you the £40,000 and that would have been generous enough, but this… Wow!'

Irene laughed and hugged Shirley fiercely. Then, she sat down again and went quiet.

Shirley understood. She stood behind her and put her arms round her neck, whispering into her ear.

'You deserve this, Irene. And the thing is, Jamie would be so happy for you – to know that you don't have to worry about money any more…'

'I know. He would. But I'm frightened to spend any of it. I should just frame it and keep it on the mantelpiece.'

'No you can't do that… Jamie would want you to use it. He'll be up there, smiling, watching you – happy knowing you're having a better life.'

Irene reached for her tissues again, dabbing the tears away.

'I know. I just wish he was here. I've never had much money, but I always had Jamie…'

Shirley sat quietly, holding her hand, waiting for the sobs to subside.

After a few minutes, Irene looked up. 'You must think I'm mad, crying about being rich.'

Shirley laughed. 'Don't be daft, Irene. You've had a lot of shocks and surprises, you must be feeling all over the place.'

'That's true, love. But you've been an angel and I'll never forget that.'

Later, as Shirley stood up to leave, Irene reached out a hand and touched her cheek.

'What's that for?'

'For caring about me.'

'Awww, thank you. Now you need to be a bit selfish and care for yourself a bit more. Spoil yourself, just a little bit.'

'I wouldn't know how to.'

'I bet you would, and, be honest, it would be fun learning.'

Irene laughed again.

'Are you going to be ok now? Don't forget we're still keeping an eye on you, and you've got my number if you need a flying visit, or a chat on the phone.'

'I think I'll be ok, love. There can't be any more surprises, can there?

Shirley hugged her, and as she waved goodbye from the pavement, she had the feeling that, this time, Irene really was going to be ok.

Whoever attacked Jag had done their best to leave no traces.

The furniture was gone, and the only boxes left on the shelves were open, and empty.

Jane and George were checking them when Phil arrived with a couple of technicians and the photographer.

He smiled and gave them the thumbs up. 'Glad to see you're wearing your shoe covers.'

George grimaced. 'We have done this kind of thing before, Phil.'

'I know. Sorry… Right, what have we got and what are we looking for?'

Jane pointed to the door in the corner. 'Jag was assaulted in there, which he said looked like it was a film studio. We want any traces you can find, priority – anything that will help us identify who attacked him, and who else has been in here recently. You'll need to do the same in here, but… the room first, please, Phil. They've had to move quickly to get this place cleared, but they haven't had time to do a deep clean, so let's hope we get something.'

Phil puffed out his cheeks. 'OK, this is going to take a while, so best get down to it. How is Jag, any news?'

'He was talking, but he was very groggy. I'll go to the hospital in a bit; leave you to it.'

'All right. Say hello from me, will you? And if you don't mind, I'll call in a couple of reinforcements – get this done quicker.'

'Fine. And George will make sure there's someone on both doors, just in case.'

She wasn't certain Phil had even heard her, he'd moved across to the white door so quickly.

On her way out, Jane told George to start rounding people up for an identity parade. 'By the book, George, ok? Let's not leave any loopholes, because if we do, Avis has got the money and the influence to make the most of it.'

'Understood, boss.' George sighed. 'I just thought… I would have been asking Jag to help me with that.'

Jane unlocked her car door and climbed in. 'I know. But this is a chance for Lorry to step up. I'll see you later,

George. Shout if you need anything, but I want Avis in for the identification tonight, without fail.'

'Will do, ma'am. And tell Jag I need him back at the ranch, will you? He's the only one who knows how to make me a proper brew.'

Jag was propped up in bed with his eyes closed, and Jane got a flashback to the first time she saw Charles Aston in hospital. He'd woken the instant she walked in, and he was smiling and chatting like there was nothing wrong. Two weeks later, he was moved to the hospice.

Jane had never found religion, but looking at Jag's young face, with his hair sticking out in a black tuft above the bright white bandages, she wished she could pray, and believe her prayer would be answered. Truth was, she was as scathing about religion as she was about IT. In her mind, they both belonged in 'the Cloud' – that virtual space that was beyond most people's understanding.

A nurse walked in briskly, nodded at Jane, and checked the clipboard at the bottom of Jag's bed.

'Is he going to be ok?'

He looked up briefly, then jotted something on the notes. 'Sorry, I can't say, other than he's comfortable. You'll need to ask the doctor. I think he's on his rounds now, but sister might know.' He put the clipboard back and hurried off. 'Sorry.'

Jane walked down the corridor to find the ward reception area, where four nurses in different colour uniforms were deep in conversation.

'Excuse me, can I speak to the sister, please?'

A small chubby woman emerged from the group chat. 'How can I help?'

When Jane introduced herself, she took her by the arm and walked into the rest area, where two old boys with vacant expressions were staring into space. 'Jag is a tough young man, but he's taken a hell of a blow to the head.'

Jane tensed up. The tone of voice suggested there was a punchline. 'Is he all right?'

'There's no brain damage that we can see, and his vital signs are good, but... I'm sorry... the doctor thinks he may lose sight in one eye, and have impaired vision in the other.'

'Oh God...' Jane couldn't think of anything else to say. Her first thought was that this would destroy Jag. 'Does he know?'

'No. His wife is coming in to see him later. She's had to wait for child care to be arranged.'

Jane cursed herself. She should have thought of that and arranged something. But no, she'd been too obsessed with nailing Avis to think about one of her most loyal and hard working officers and his family.

The nurse looked at her intently. 'Are you OK, may I ask? This must come as a shock to you...'

'Yes, it is a shock. I'm finding it hard to take in. Hard to take at all, actually.'

'We do need to do more tests, and there is some hope we can save his sight in one eye, but obviously we'd need to operate and we can't do that until he has regained some strength, and we are sure he's stable. I'm so sorry...'

'Thanks. I know you'll do everything you can. I think maybe I should leave, let him see – have his family with him. I'll come back tomorrow.'

Jane walked out of the ward quickly, unable to turn her head to look at Jag as she went past.

She wanted to believe that Jag would be ok. She would do whatever it took to keep him on the team.

But there was no time to dwell on that now. As her uncle was always telling her: 'Pigeon holes are there for a reason. Use them.' Sometimes she wished she could forget her uncle Bob. The more she remembered, the more he seemed like a walking motivational poster. But his advice had helped her through some tough times – and this was certainly one of those.

So, for better or worse, Jag was in a pigeon hole now – her phone rang as soon as she got outside.

'Yes, Phil.'

She listened as he ran through what the team had found so far, then zapped the car remote and climbed in.

She could feel the adrenaline zinging as she drove away.

Everything was set for a showdown with Avis.

TWENTY-SIX

George and Ross had managed to drag in eight mainly willing volunteers to stand in line for the identification parade.

George had joked that it was an easy one. 'Shouldn't be too hard to find eight overweight middle aged blokes in Ashbridge, should it?' Though he wasn't too amused when Ross suggested he should join the line up himself.

Sykes had gone with Lorry to bring Avis in, and they were five minutes away by the time Jane had arrived.

She used the time to brief George. 'Phil's found traces of DNA all over the place at the storage property, so we can run that through the database when he gets back. Plus, we've got finger and footprints, and fibres… quite a haul.'

'Good news, boss.'

'We're getting closer every minute, George. I need you to keep an eye on me when we get to interview Avis after the ID parade…'

'Why's that, ma'am?'

'One of his henchmen has probably left Jag blind in one eye, and with limited vision in the other. I may very well lose it, if Avis plays his usual smarmy innocence routine, so be warned.'

'Jesus… that poor lad. Ok, ma'am. but as you know, I'm not known for restraint.'

'I know George. But this is too important. We both need to play it cool, so let's do our jobs, and help each other.'

Sykes put his head round the door. 'Suspect is in the waiting area, ready for the parade, ma'am… sir. And his solicitor has arrived.'

'Thanks, Sykes. OK George, off you go. You and I are going to have to stay away from the parade, as you know, so take a break and I'll see you in the interview room when it's over.'

Identification was over in minutes. Sutton walked the line slowly, twice, and hid his nerves really well. At the end, he pointed to Avis and said his number clearly, for the video recording.

Avis was impassive throughout, and was now in a huddle with his solicitor in the interview room.

Jane went down to the cells to thank Sutton first.

'Well done, Martin, you've been a great help. It's going to help a lot when your case comes to trial. In the meantime, I'm recommending that you either go home, or we can put you somewhere safe for a few weeks until we get this sorted.'

Sutton shook his head. 'No way am I going home. They'll find me. What's the safe place?'

'I've got someone waiting outside who can explain all that to you. I think you've met before.' Jane stood and opened the door, and Shirley French walked in. 'Good evening, Martin.'

Sutton recoiled, embarrassment all over his face.

Jane smiled. 'I'll leave you two together, then. Don't worry, Martin, Shirley will keep you safe.'

Sutton scowled as she closed the door, then hunched forward, elbows on knees, and refused to look as Shirley sat down next to him.

'Come on Martin. I thought you'd be pleased to see me again.'

'Very funny. Just get me out of here will you?'

George was already in position: notebook on the table, one hand hovering near the recorder, a half empty mug of coffee in front of him.

Avis looked up with a bland expression as Jane walked in, closing the door deliberately loudly behind her and scraping her chair back. She was gratified to see Avis wincing.

'Right, Mr Avis…'

'What am I doing here, exactly?'

'All in good time, Mr Avis. The procedure here is that we ask questions, and you answer them, all right?'

Avis sighed dramatically and leaned back. 'Do fire away then.'

'So, the ID parade tells us that you knew Mr Gonzales and had visited him at the Pretty Cool Cafe, from where he was running a lucrative little side business; selling access to obscene porn videos featuring under age children to the cafe's customers, in fact.'

'And…?'

'And – Mr Avis – we now also suspect that one of your allegedly empty premises in Ashbridge was being used as a film studio… And that when one of our officers went to investigate, he was viciously assaulted, and the studio set miraculously cleared away in double quick time.'

Avis smiled, as Jane knew he would. But this time, she remained unmoved. 'What can you tell us, Mr Avis?'

'Well… Ms Birchfield… perhaps you could enlighten me, and my solicitor, what any of this has to do with me?'

'Do you deny knowing Mr Gonzales?'

'Of course not. I know a lot of business people, and I do make social visits on some of them now and again.'

'How many times had you visited Mr Gonzales at the cafe?'

'No more than a couple of times, possibly three, I suppose.'

'Yet we have CCTV coverage going back around two months – which is strangely when the porn video business began – showing you popping through that door… oh, let me see… yes, 11 times.'

'Really? How awkward. Well, I never was very good at maths. But, what on earth does any of this prove? That I knew him? OK then, guilty as charged. Now, if there's nothing else I can help you with…'

'So your original answer was that you had maybe seen him a couple of times. Now you are admitting that you went to see him on many different occasions. A rather different story… which makes me wonder how we're going to know if or when you are telling us the truth.'

Avis winked at his impassive solicitor. 'You'll just have to trust me, Inspector. After all, as you know, I was otherwise engaged when both those people were so tragically killed.'

Jane smiled, unmoved. 'When did you begin using under age children to make pornographic videos, Mr Avis?'

'I don't know what you're talking about.'

'Sure about that? We have a forensic team at the studio you were using. Your people didn't have much time to clear the evidence away after they assaulted one of my officers, and we already have fingerprints, DNA, traces of fibre from clothing…'

'Really? How—'

Jane cut in sharply, raising her voice. 'Your clients seem to enjoy watching children perform obscene acts on your videos, Mr Avis. Where do you get your children from? Where do you keep them locked away before you abuse and exploit them?

You see, Mr Avis, we have plenty to talk about tonight, so I don't expect you'll be getting an early night. Your best policy now is to start telling us the truth.'

Avis stonewalled through the rest of the session. His solicitor looked like he wished he was somewhere else. Jane suspended the interview and asked George to send out for coffee and flapjacks. 'I need to find energy from somewhere.'

'Wine gums do it for me, ma'am. But he's a real smoothie, isn't he? I'd love it if we could nail him.'

'The more I see of him, the more convinced I am that he's guilty. He paid for two killings, and he's behind the porn videos.'

'But we can't prove it, and he knows it.'

'Yeah, there is that... We're missing something, George. Trouble is, I have no idea what it is..'

'Let's hope Phil comes up with something.'

'Yes, let's. But first, we should leave Avis to stew for a while. I want him to feel as tired as I do. Phil's running his samples through the database, and of course we'll need to take a few samples from Mr Avis...'

'Oh, he won't like that, ma'am.'

It seemed to George that she was staring right through him. It was a look he remembered from the Fiona Worsley investigation, when it seemed they were never going to crack it. She'd looked every member of the team in the eye and left them in no doubt that she was going to get a result, whatever it took.

Jane spoke quietly, as if to herself. 'We'll get him, George. It's too late for Jamie, but we have to find those children... We have to.'

A picture of his grandchildren flashed into George's mind. They were eight and 12 years old. 'We'll find them, ma'm, and we'll lock Avis up. And God help him when his jail mates find out what he's done.'

An hour later, Phil almost fell through Jane's door: 'We've got a match!'

Jane hastily signed off her text to Allan... '*Won't be back till early hours. All happening. Hope ok. C u jx*'

'OK Phil, tell me...'

Phil's attempt at a Polish accent didn't quite come off. 'Szymon Mazur.'

'Come again?'

'He's from Poland. We had to ask the Met to run the print for us. He's part of a group they've been watching in connection with smuggling.'

'As in people smuggling?'

'As in anything smuggling. They're like fixers... whatever you want, wherever you want it, in Europe that is.'

Phil, still breathing heavily from his dash down the corridor, handed over a photograph. 'It's off the copier, so not great, but they're sending me everything they've got right now.'

'What about Avis? Any traces?'

Phil shook his head. 'Sorry Jane. Nothing. We got samples from him not long ago, and there is nothing we can use to say he was ever at those premises.'

'Shit.'

'But...' Phil had a glint in his eye, and Jane's hopes lifted.

'But what Phil? Come on...'

'The good news is, having seen his picture, we're certain this guy is the one on CCTV, and there's enough trace evidence to show that he was the one who attacked Jag. So...'

'...all we have to do is find him, and get him to talk; point us to Avis...'

Jane sat down and wrote quickly on a sheet of paper, then handed it to Phil. 'Give this to George for me. Tell him Avis will have to wait. We have to find this guy.'

Jane's hunch proved correct.

George read her note, followed orders, and went straight round to see Sutton, and showed him Mazur's photograph, mixed in with a dozen others. He picked him out straight away. 'That's the guy who came in that afternoon, when Jamie copped it.'

Ross was on his way home after a 14 hour shift when George called.

'Ross, mate, you're going home the long way round, all right?'

Ross opened George's message with Mazur's picture as an attachment, and started a tour of hospitals and health centres. Lorry was glued to the phone, trying to persuade gym and fitness clubs to go through their membership records.

Jane was briefing Simon Hopkirk over the phone – or rather, he was talking at her.

'Yes, you keep telling me you are close, but we still have nothing to tie Avis to these murders. You're not dealing with any old crook here. He's a respected businessman with an unblemished record who has – your words – a perfect alibi for both crimes. Now you tell me you have someone known to the police, who was known to be at the scene where the first victim died. So tell me – why are you clinging to the idea that Avis did it?'

Jane fought to control her temper. 'Sir, I understand all that. I'm asking you to trust my judgement. Avis is behind it. These are contract killings, and Avis is the client. He's giving off all the signals I need to be certain of it, and—'

'—signals? What, you mean he looks guilty? Come on, Jane – this isn't enough and you know it.'

'I just need a few more hours to track Mazur down. Then we need to get him talking. Once he knows the game's over, he'll have nothing to lose. He'll implicate Avis, confirm he's acting under orders—'

'—or he won't, and you're back to square one.' She heard his heavy sigh blowing like a gale down the phone line. '...Ok, I'll give you 12 hours, but he goes home by midday tomorrow unless you've got this nailed down tight.' He paused, his tone softening slightly. 'And Jane... let me know if you need any resources, ok?'

'Thanks for that, sir – much appreciated. I expect we will once we get a sense of where those children are being held.'

Jane replaced the receiver slowly and drank the last of her coffee.

She tried to remember a famous phrase... what was it? 'A week is a long time in politics'.

She thought about the children. A week is a lifetime for them. Jane wondered what might be happening to them right now. She knew she couldn't dwell on it or she would totally lose focus. She looked at her watch... 10.30pm.

Hopkirk had given her until midday tomorrow. It would be a miracle if they pulled it off.

But miracles do happen.

Mark Manning had given up hope of Jamie's laptop turning up.

He'd thought it might have been stashed at the storage place Jag had checked out, but no such luck.

It wasn't as if he expected it to unearth anything he didn't already know. Jamie was a smart guy: he must have thought that using the internet cafe computer would make it more likely that someone who knew code would be able to follow his trail to the porn business.

But now they were following a different trail, that the boss was convinced led to Avis.

At times like these, Mark felt pretty helpless. Lorry and the other guys had been assigned tasks they could concentrate on as part of the team. But now the tech stuff was more or less done, he was feeling left out. While they were following up leads, he was lying on a sofa watching 'Would I Lie To You' on catch up.

Lorry had messaged to say she'd be working all night, and not to wait up. But he didn't feel like sleeping.

He topped up his glass with the remains of his can of Guinness and did what he always did when he couldn't switch off; he switched on his laptop.

The dark eyes of Mazur seemed to be staring right at him as he opened the file. Mark stared back. He thought how weird it was that you could get waves off someone, just by looking at a photo. But he looked like a real piece of work: heavy eyebrows, dark stubble and hair the same length; his eyes set wide either side of a flat and slightly kinked nose. Almost like an artist's impression of a villain. Above all, it was the look in his eyes – blank, like he didn't actually care.

He thought about Greaves; how they looked after their staff; the facilities; and the biscuits… Then he remembered what Adrian had said about the bloke on CCTV; that he had the look and the body language of someone who boxed, or at the very least, did weights.

10.45pm… chances were Adrian would still be up and about…

Mark quickly attached the image to an email and keyed in a message, and marked it confidential: '*Hi Adrian. We think this is the guy we saw on CCTV. Name is Szymon Mazur. He's Polish and known to the Met for people smuggling activity. We need to talk to him urgently. Bit of a long shot, but just wondered if the name or the face rang any bells. Let me know, ok?! Cheers, Mark.*'

He pressed send, then pulled up Mazur's info. He'd hardly had time to browse through when Adrian's reply came through.

'Now I know why I was so sure about him. I'm 99 per cent certain he lives in the block of flats next to mine at the Quays. I've seen him in the convenience store, and at the gym. Must be 40 flats in the block. No idea which one he lives in, or whether he's just a regular visitor. But worth checking out. Let me know if you're coming over, and I'd be very happy to help. He's a tough looking guy… Best, Adrian.'

Mark's heart was racing. He didn't even think of replying. He just slammed the laptop lid down, stuffed it into his bag, and drove off.

Allan poured one more glass of Malbec and sat looking at the laptop.

He was trying to catch up on copywriting, but couldn't concentrate; couldn't rid himself of that familiar restlessness that comes with waiting for Jane to come home, expecting her any minute, sighing as the time ticked by, unable to settle…

To be fair, she did say she wouldn't be back till the early hours, but Allan was back in his dark zone, wondering how many more nights he would be expected to sit, waiting, trying to stay occupied, while Jane was doing the job she loved, and too busy on important stuff to even think about him.

He walked over to the fridge, and grabbed a bar of chocolate… He'd already eaten a ready meal for two out of its foil container, followed by half a family size apple pie, and the Malbec he'd bought on the way home was nearly gone.

He'd watched Celebrity Masterchef and an episode of Poirot. And edited an inbox full of submissions from some of the paper's village correspondents; most of them so dire they needed complete rewrites. He didn't have the energy or the inclination to do any more.

He slumped on the sofa. He idly wondered where they could go on holiday when this was over, then rephrased the thought in his head… maybe it was a case of *if* this was ever over.

That was the point: when would it actually end? Whichever way he looked at it, he knew he couldn't go on like this.

TWENTY-SEVEN

JANE WAS WAITING ON the quayside with George and Alex when Mark arrived.

They rang the bell for Adrian's apartment and were buzzed in. He was on the second floor, overlooking the canal, with a distant view of the Manchester United stadium.

He came to the door in white T shirt and grey tracksuit trousers, and had the healthy glow of someone who'd been working out. He showed them into his living room, which was dominated by an exercise bike facing a large flat screen tv, and drew back full length curtains from a side window.

'That guy lives in the next block, but no idea which flat.'

Jane moved next to him to take a look, and immediately felt small. 'Same design as this block, I take it?'

'Yes, identical. You can see better in daytime, of course, but I do have the plans I was given when I was looking the place over.'

'You say he lives there, but we checked on the way over, and he's not down as a buyer or a tenant…'

'No, well, in that case, he's either a regular visitor or he's living with someone. I see him around a lot.'

'No idea which floor?'

Adrian shook his head.

Jane turned to Alex: 'We can't go blundering in, obviously. We're going to need to do some very discreet door knocking, which means averting the entry system. Can you get onto the agent?'

As Alex moved to one side and started talking into his radio, Jane remembered her manners.

'Sorry, Adrian, I haven't even said hello or thank you for your help. It's very much appreciated.'

He laughed and they were so close Jane caught the musky scent of his shower gel. 'No problem. I understand completely. I thought I worked under pressure, but… nothing like this.'

Jane smiled. 'This job does have its moments…'

Alex interrupted. 'Agent will be here in five, ma'am.'

'Ok, let's wait outside, but stay out of line of sight of the flats. Alex, wait here until I know we have access. Keep the van where it is until we've located Mazur. George, let's go.'

Adrian walked to the door with them. 'I'm happy to help, if you need it.'

'That's good of you, but—'

George butted in. 'Adrian looks nothing like a copper, ma'am. Might be very useful when we find Mazur, to have someone the guy may have seen before knocking at his door. Might just look like a social call… distract him long enough for us to get him secured.'

Mark nodded. 'I agree with George, ma'am. It might just throw him off his guard for a second…'

Jane stopped. 'Ok, Mark, thanks. George, you're right. Adrian – get your coat.'

They got lucky at the seventh attempt. A young, intellectual type with thick black hair flopping over his thick black glasses, recognised the photo.

Mazur lived directly above him, he told them in a stage whisper. 'They're very quiet when they're in there, but they're always going out or coming in, and – well I don't like to tell tales, but... it's all hours of the night. Most people here are like, you know, second homers, and there's lots still for sale so it's pretty quiet – apart from them. Just my luck.'

'You said, they. How many people live there, Mr...?

'McIntosh... Just the two, I think. The other one is a girl. She's got lovely long dark hair. But, like I say, I wonder if they ever sleep, the amount of comings and goings. Luckily, I'm a bit of a night bird myself. I'd love to know what they're up to.'

'And when did you last see – or hear – them?'

'Oh very good!...Or hear... Yes, well I definitely haven't heard any noises tonight, so I guess they're in there now. Anyway, come on, what's occurring?'

George gave him one of his frostier smiles. 'Best if you stay inside, sir, stay quiet, and lock your door. We just want a word with them about something. All right?'

'Ok, I get the message. Say no more.'

Jane put a hand out to stop the door slamming. 'Try not to slam the door, Mr McIntosh...'

He giggled from the other side of the door. 'Oh yes, that would be ironic, wouldn't it?'

It clicked gently shut. Jane rolled her eyes, and they moved to the end of the corridor, where a fire door led to the concrete stairs. George radioed Alex to get the unit into position in and around the building, and they waited until Alex had jogged up the stairs to join them, wearing his full protective gear and firearm.

'All set, ma'am. Ready for your signal.'

'Ok Sergeant. Let's move up to the next floor. Check with the agent, find out who the occupier is. I guess it's rented...' She turned to Adrian. 'You still ok to do this?'

'Very happy, yes. Glad to be of help.'

Alex grimaced. 'No heroics, please.'

Adrian nodded cheerfully. 'No problem, Sergeant.'

They waited as Alex moved down the stairs to talk to the agent. He gave them the thumbs up when he'd finished. 'That flat is rented out to a Mr Kowalsky. And the guy downstairs was right; they confirmed they currently have only 5 per cent occupancy at the moment.'

Jane nodded. 'Ok, even more reason for them to use it as a base. Let's move in.'

Once at the door, Alex threaded a wire into the keyhole and peered through what looked to Adrian like a pocket telescope that was attached to the other end. 'No visual, door area clear.'

Jane signed them to back off. 'When we're set, Adrian, I want you to knock on the door and be ready with your story, which is...?'

'I work at the fitness centre and wondered if you'd – oh sorry! I must have got the wrong flat, etc etc... Like that?'

George smiled. 'An IT genius, and a good actor... not bad, mate.'

'Thanks George. Seriously, though, if he tries anything, I'll just flatten him, if that's ok.'

Alex sighed. 'No, sir, you won't. I'll be to one side and one of my men on the other. Do not assault this man.'

Jane nodded. 'Otherwise, you could jeopardise the whole arrest process.'

'Of course, sorry.'

They heard the muffled sound of rubber soles on concrete coming up the stairs, and Alex gestured them into position, with Jane and George standing well back.

He nodded to Adrian, who rang the doorbell. They heard the door chain being pulled back, then the door inched open, then stopped. A voice said: 'Who is this?'

Adrian put on his friendliest voice. 'Hello, I'm a neighbour. I just wanted to say hello…'

A man opened the door. It was Mazur and he was almost as intimidating as Adrian. He was also instantly hostile.

'I don't know you.'

'Well, I go to the fitness centre, and I've seen you around, so I wondered—'

Mazur tried to close the door, but Adrian put out a hand. He stepped out of the way as Alex and the other officer moved in yelling 'Police. Down on the ground! Now!'

Jane heard the thud of internal doors, then some shouting, then silence.

Next, Alex's calm voice… 'All clear, ma'am.'

'Stay here, please Adrian. Come on, George.'

Mazur was flat on his face, hands cable wired behind his back, cursing into the carpet.

The officer kneeling on his back nodded. 'Alex is in the next room, ma'am.'

'Well done, Sykes.'

Jane left George and moved to the adjoining room. It was as big as the living room, but looked more like a dormitory, with bunk beds lined up against three of the walls, and wooden slats nailed across the window. Alex was kneeling on the floor trying to comfort four young girls who were crying.

Jane's heart skipped a beat. She could see tears streaking their makeup. They were wearing mini skirts and sleeveless tops. Yet they looked like they'd barely reached teenage.

There were other children on three of the beds – two boys and another girl, all similar age. They were just staring, emotionless..

The girls were hugging Alex, babbling words none of them could understand, but sounded Eastern European.

Jane found it hard to believe. Seven children locked away in a modern apartment block, and no-one any the wiser: proof if it was needed that sometimes it's easier to hide in the obvious places.

It was her mission to find and save these children. But there was no sense of triumph now. She told Sykes to radio in, requesting emergency social services support.

She suddenly felt the adrenaline draining from her system, but there was no time to be tired.

This was just the beginning. Would Mazur talk and incriminate Avis? If not, could any of the children identify him? Where was the girl who McIntosh said was living here, and who was she? Were these all the children they were using for their foul videos, or did they have more locked up somewhere else?

She wanted to scoop up the children, hug them, and tell them everything was all right.

But that would have to wait.

Everything was not alright. Yet.

TWENTY-EIGHT

Ross was on his way back from checking out hospitals and clinics, having got one positive result. He phoned George to say that Ashbridge General had found discrepancies in a supplies audit, with some drugs missing.

Ross pulled over into a lay by to phone in. 'No-one could ID Mazur though. But this might be a lead. Phil would have to talk to them, find out which drugs, I reckon.'

He'd bitten back a remark about being overworked and underpaid when George told him to get down to the address in Salford Quays. 'We've got Mazur, but he was apparently living there with a woman. Link up with Sykes on arrival, stay out of the way, and bring her in when she turns up.'

Ross replied but the phone had already gone dead. 'Thanks Ross. You're doing a great job... Oh, cheers, George, no problem...'

He took a long swig of energy drink, yawned, and set off for the Quays.

They didn't have to wait long.

An hour later, they were signing the girl in at the station. She'd refused to talk when they arrested her at the apartment, and in the car.

But Ross knew her straight away, and knew she'd recognised him from his visit to the Deansgate internet cafe. She'd identified Sutton's photo and confirmed to him that Sutton had been there before.

Ross smiled at her as Sykes put the cuffs on. 'Small world, isn't it? Have you missed me?'

Jane opted to set up three interview rooms: one each for Avis, Mazur and the girl, who had so far refused even to give a name. Herself, George and Lorry would be asking the questions.

She got them together for a briefing, in her words, 'before the fun begins.'

'They each need to know we have the others in for questioning at the same time. We want them to get the idea that one of the others is giving info that incriminates them; saving their own skin. We'll start by making sure they see each other in the corridor. Keep a note of the questions you ask, so we keep track. We'll change places after about half an hour. Let's work them hard. I know you're tired, but this could be the breakthrough, and I can only hold onto Avis till midday tomorrow.

'Mark's been out for sandwiches and knowing him there'll be a mountain of them, so fill up, get a drink, relax for a few minutes.'

Lorry was first out of the door. George chuckled. 'The way that girl eats, I'll be left with a plate of crumbs by the time I get there.'

Jane laughed. 'That's if Mark hasn't eaten them already. Go on George, go and get stuck in.'

'Don't worry about me. I'll throw my weight around, ma'am.'

Jane's smile quickly froze as she was left alone. This is it, she thought. I cannot mess this up.

She spent the next ten minutes working out her attack, as she chewed on yet another flapjack and sipped water.

She phoned through and asked them to bring the suspects upstairs, so they could see each other in the corridor before entering their separate rooms.

Jane walked through to the room nearest her office. She'd decided to interview Mazur first – the thug who had assaulted one of the finest officers she had ever met, and quite possibly ended his hopes of a career as a detective.

She was looking forward to making him pay.

The first round of interviews was over.

It was rewarding to see Avis so obviously thrown when he saw Mazur and the girl before his session with George, but he'd still stuck doggedly to his mantra that he couldn't have done it because he wasn't there.

The girl had become more talkative, thanks to Lorry, and had finally given her name – Brygita Kaminski. Mark was now checking the name through the system but without success, so far.

Jane had a tough time with Mazur, who had simply stared her out when she told him he would be charged with assaulting a police officer causing grievous bodily harm. But, she told George and Lorry, she hadn't pushed on because she wanted him to have time to think. She was going to stick with him for the second session, but wanted George and Lorry to swap over.

It was 1am when they resumed. All of them were now living off caffeine and energy bars, but, as Lorry told Mark: 'This is why we joined up, isn't it?'

George made the first breakthrough with Kaminski. She

now believed she'd be facing serious charges, and her first line of defence was that she'd been intimidated into acting as chaperone for the children by Mazur.

'I didn't know what they were doing with them; I was just the driver and the nanny, you know?'

It was a small step forwards, and it seemed to loosen her tongue. He told Jane that Brygita claims she was physically abused by Mazur, and that he also threatened her family if she didn't co-operate.

George slurped another mug of coffee and stretched. 'She was born and brought up in Manchester, but she says one of her uncles used to be involved with the gangs in Eastern Europe, and one of the gang leaders kept in touch with the family when they moved to Britain.'

'Whatever the background, we've got something to hit Mazur with. Are you ok to tackle him next?'

'It would be a pleasure, ma'am.'

By the time most people were in their cars heading for work, Ashbridge CID were celebrating the breakthrough, and Jane was on the phone to the Chief Constable.

'Sir, the children are safe, and we have enough to charge all three of them.'

Hopkirk sounded surprised. 'Including Avis? How did you swing that?'

'By the tried and trusted method of convincing him that his own people had told us everything we needed to know.'

'And he fell for that?'

'He did, sir, for the simple reason that it was true... Mazur confessed to both contract killings, and made a statement confirming he was acting under orders from Avis. He also admits assaulting Jag, and procuring children for Avis's porn production business.'

Hopkirk now sounded suspicious. 'Don't tell me, Mazur made a deal…'

'The only deal we made with him was to guarantee we would go easy on Brygita.'

'What? Who's she?'

'His little helper. She claimed Mazur forced her to help. Her role was limited to being a chaperone to the children, and I decided that it was a small price to pay to unlock the case to offer her a lesser charge in return for a full statement.'

'Something tells me Avis will find a way out of this, Jane.'

'Well we're putting the whole lot together now for the CPS, sir, so I guess it's up to them now, as always.'

Hopkirk sighed. 'Yes, and they haven't done us many favours lately. Tell you what, I'll have a word, exert what little influence I still have. You've done well Jane – very well. I think you and I need to meet up soon, have a chat about the future…'

Now it was Jane's turn to be surprised. 'Yes, thank you, sir!'

'Don't sound so surprised. You're an asset to the force. I believe in rewarding people who show not just talent, but total commitment. Right, got to go, keep me posted.'

Jane replaced the receiver and sank back into her chair. She should have been punching the air at the thought of what could be a big promotion.

But all she wanted to do now was summon up the energy to get home and climb the stairs to bed. She wasn't confident.

TWENTY-NINE

'ANOTHER SLICE OF CAKE, Mother?'

Jane smiled as Allan cut a wedge of 'home made' Victoria Sponge and passed it across. He had clearly won mum over. She couldn't quite believe how well she and Allan were getting on. She may as well have gone off to work and left them to it.

Allan's sulks were never far from the surface these days, but at least they were over the worst now.

It had been a tense few days. Allan had come home from work the day after she'd been up all night on the Avis case, and found her flaked out in bed. She'd crashed out at around 4pm and didn't emerge until after 7 the next morning, woken by Allan slamming the door as he left for work.

She'd resisted the temptation to phone him up and call him names, and had spent a day at work, feeling like a zombie until she got the call to say she could visit the children, who were in care while social services tried to trace their families across Poland, Hungary, and Slovenia.

Jane had insisted on taking the whole team, and they'd stopped off at the shop en route to stock up on treats.

One or two of the girls were still traumatised and stayed on the sidelines, until George started pulling funny faces and doing crummy magic tricks. Lorry sat with a girl on either side, reading a book in English with a completely unnecessary Eastern European kind of accent; and Ross played cars with fierce determination.

Jane just watched and marvelled at the recovery the children were making.

Hopkirk had phoned to confirm that Mazur's activities had been passed on to Europol's trafficking unit, and region had taken on the job of tracking down Avis's customers. 'We'll nail the lot of them, including Avis, don't worry.'

They called in to see Jag on the way back, and he was much brighter – sitting up and holding his own in conversation, despite George's insistence that he should get out of bed and make coffee.

Jag told them, without a trace of self pity, that he had lost the sight of one eye. But there was a glimmer of hope that he may have some vision in the other.

Jane chatted with him as the others headed off.

'Whatever happens, Jag, you're coming back to work – assuming you want to, of course.'

Jag smiled. 'Definitely, ma'am. Try and stop me. But—'

'What is it, Jag?'

'Maybe you should ask someone else to go through CCTV footage next time?'

Jane filled him in on the latest. Phil had followed up Ross's lead at the hospital. A small quantity of Sux – the drug used to kill Jamie and Gonzales – had been stolen, and Brygita had been a part time clinical assistant until a few months ago. Jane said that meant her hopes of a lenient sentence had vanished.

Sutton was fairly certain to get a suspended sentence because of his co-operation.

'Oh, and I nearly forgot… Phil's decided not to retire just yet.'

'Champagne for everyone, then, ma'am?'

'Only when you come back, Jag…'

By the time Allan had come home from work that night, the Big Freeze had begun to thaw.

Jane was laying the table for three, when Allan walked in, smiling happily.

'What are you looking so cheerful about?'

'Hello to you too, darling… Ask me who has finally got an exclusive about a certain murder investigation..' He grinned as he saw Jane's immediate discomfort. 'No, don't worry, it's ok. I bumped into Irene, who is now a regular at Betty's—'

'—I bet she is.'

'—and she told me she is going to give half the money Hargreaves gave her to the women's refuge in Ashbridge.'

'Oh my God, that's wonderful!'

'Yeah, I thought so too. You know she was abused by her husband? Well, she said she wanted to do something to help others. So that's my front page sorted. I bet the nationals will take it, so that'll be a few quid in the coffers. Hargreaves will be chuffed. He comes out of this looking like a saint… You got any news for me?'

'How about Lorry and Mark deciding to get engaged?'

Allan shook his head. 'That's not even surprising.'

'Ok… Well, they went out for a Chinese with Adrian Cheshire and he proposed, and insisted Adrian should be best man. That's romantic, isn't it?'

'What? Proposing over a chow mein? Come off it.'

'Suit yourself. Anyway… you haven't forgotten mum's coming round…?'

Allan walked into the kitchen and came back carrying a white box. 'No, I haven't. I even got us a sponge cake.'

'Betty's?'

'Where else? We'll have a deliriously happy time overdosing on cake with your mum, then we can pack for our romantic trip tomorrow.'

Jane looked puzzled. 'Romantic trip? What? Where?'

'What do you mean where? You have got time off, haven't you? Tell me, you haven't forgotten...'

It was her turn to look annoying. 'Only kidding... I can't wait.'

Fortunately for Jane, her mum rang the doorbell just as Allan was about to throw a cushion.

Jane leaned back in the passenger seat as Allan kept to a soothing 60 on the inside lane of the M5. They'd be in Lyme Regis in time for a seafood lunch. He'd got it all planned.

Closing her eyes, she felt herself drifting away, the rush of passing cars as soothing as the sound of the sea...

She was sitting cross legged on the floor in school assembly; bare knees, pleated green skirt; Mr Harrison was saying prayers, but looking at her and licking his lips, and walking towards her... she looked round and saw the children that Avis had used for his videos, watching and waiting...

Then Harrison morphed into Charles Aston. Jane ran to him, and buried her head in his chest. Her hot tears turned cold as they soaked into his white shirt. He smiled and held her at arm's length and told her to let go. Her heart was pounding as he backed away. 'Don't go, don't go'... she pleaded with him, as the children joined in, chanting it, louder and louder—

She came out of it, disorientated, and turned to see Allan's anxious face switching rapidly between her and the road ahead.

'Are you ok, love?'

Jane smiled and put her hand on his leg.

'I'm fine. Just getting that case out of my system.'

'That's good.' He paused, and tried to sound casual. 'Did you hear any more from the Chief Constable?'

'He just said he'd see me when I got back from our trip.'

'Sounds like you're being lined up for a promotion.'

'Or just a pat on the back for being a good girl.'

'And are you a good girl? Remember, this interview is on the record.'

'Of course I am. Almost all the time.'

'And do you promise to behave on our dirty weekend?'

'Certainly not.'

Allan laughed. 'Good.'

Jane tried to relax again as the road uncoiled before them. God knows, she needed a break. Covering Charles's post while running a complex and distressing murder investigation had taken its toll, and three days in Lyme Regis wasn't going to get it out of her system.

She thought about her career, and the price she – and Allan – was paying for it. She wondered: was she fated to follow a road that led to promotion after promotion, whatever it takes?

She remembered Charles's words when she visited him for the last time: *'Don't let work take over your life, Jane… Not worth it… Look at me. I was counting the days… retirement, golf, rugby on the box… meals for two offers at Marks and Sparks… Things don't always go according to plan..'*

She thought about Irene's regret about the distance that opened up between her and Jamie. It was all too easy to drift apart. She and Allan had come pretty close to doing exactly that.

The question would soon have to be answered: what would she do if Hopkirk offered her a big step up? Which would win? Career or relationship?

She knew it was all about making a call, calculating if a decision is a price worth paying. Uncle Bob seemed always to be a point of reference in Jane's life. He used to tell her that we know the decision we should make: we only think about it as a way of putting it off, or sparing someone's feelings.

Jane filed the thoughts away and sat up straight. Allan was pointing ahead: their exit was coming up. 'Come on, love, I'm relying on you to navigate from here. The sat nav's buggered, remember…'

'Bloody computers.'

'I don't mind, your voice is nicer than hers.'

Her heart lurched as a patrol car raced past them, siren blaring.

'Just as well we're turning off. Looks like there may be trouble ahead.'

Allan grinned as he slowed for the exit. 'Reminds me of a song. Shall we?'

Jane laughed. 'Try and stop me. I actually know the words to this one.'

'Yeah but can you sing in tune and navigate at the same time?'

'But of course.'

'Such talent: a whole new career beckons.'

Jane sensed the edge in his voice. 'Well, if you say so.'

Matador